LIVING TOGETHER

LIVING TOGETHER

SHORT STORIES AND

A NOVELLA BY

GLORIA WHELAN

WAYNE STATE

UNIVERSITY PRESS

DETROIT

© 2013 by Wayne State University Press, Detroit, Michigan 48201.
All rights reserved. No part of this book may be reproduced without
formal permission. Manufactured in the United States of America.

17 16 15 14 13   5 4 3 2 1

Library of Congress Cataloging-in-Publication Data

Whelan, Gloria.
[Works. Selections]
Living Together : Short Stories and a Novella / by Gloria Whelan.
pages cm. — (Made in Michigan Writers Series)
ISBN 978-0-8143-3896-4 (pbk. : alk. paper) — ISBN 978-0-8143-3897-1 (e-book)
I. Title.
PS3573.H442L58 2013
813'.54—dc23
2012040551

Publication of this book was made possible
by a generous gift from The Meijer Foundation

Designed by Quemadura
Typeset by Maya Whelan
Composed in Bodoni, Electra, Garage, and Modula

TO JANE AND GEORGE BORNSTEIN

LIVING TOGETHER

KEEPING ORDER

The day before Mrs. Brady's annual tea for the residents of the Martha Mary Home for Working and Retired Women, Esther Birdwell, a retired teacher of domestic science, was praying earnestly for something she did not want. She was praying that the five harlots stay on at Martha Mary so that they might be redeemed. Esther could not bring herself to refer to them as prostitutes, or sex workers, which sounded like something to be considered on high-school career day. She preferred the biblical word as a reminder of what the Lord expected of her: charity, forgiveness, and love—one thing more impossible than the next.

Esther rose from her knees. She knew she must go to Sister Agnes and tell her of the sinful scheme she and some of the other residents had hatched. Still, she hesitated, looking about her room for some pretext to postpone facing Sister Agnes's disappointment and censure. Esther's room was small and ugly with walls the soiled tan of potato skins. Her single window faced north and even on this bright June day was stingy with light.

It was a room much like the one assigned to her when she had first moved into Martha Mary years before as the residence's first black woman. Esther, always insisting upon her seniority, progressed to larger and larger rooms until she had achieved the luxury of two windows and enough space for a comfortable chair.

There were things at Martha Mary that made you feel warehoused: the rows of mailboxes and shower stalls, the piles of trays and bins of silverware. Against all of that Esther had her room. When the sun came flooding in through the south-facing windows, touching her pale yellow walls and gilding everything she loved, the room had buoyed her up like a sea filled with good salt.

Then Martha Mary's board of directors, chaired by Mrs. Brady, had decided to bring harlots into the home. Mrs. Brady called a meeting of the residents. Sitting next to Mrs. Brady was the director of Martha Mary, Sister Agnes, one of those charged women whose energy consumes flesh, leaving her thin but glowing. Sister Agnes told the residents that the Lord was bestowing upon them a great opportunity and privilege.

Theresa Sullivan had whispered hopefully to Esther, "I'll bet they're going to let us have booze in our rooms." Esther knew better. Sister Agnes's idea of privilege ran to world hunger fasts when all the residents were urged to eat nothing for dinner but a bowl of rice. The endearing thing about Sister Agnes was that she was no saint. That is, she didn't have the courage of her convictions. The night of the fast she invited all the residents down for a late snack of cocoa and peanut butter sandwiches.

On this day Sister Agnes's privilege had turned out to be the harlots. She referred to them as Five Troubled Girls but everyone knew what she meant. The Protestant residence hall down the street was taking in girls who were involved with drugs. Esther could imagine how gratifying it would be for Sister Agnes to announce to the director of the Protestant home, "We're going to have prostitutes."

Lee Simon, who worked as a receptionist in a podiatrist's office and was considered the resident expert in medical matters, raised her hand to ask, "Will we be sharing bathrooms?"

Sister Agnes was no prude and knew what Lee was asking. "The girls will all have thorough physicals before they arrive here. If we can just find it in our hearts to give them love and acceptance, I'm sure they won't return to their old ways. We must keep in mind that living at Martha Mary is a condition of their parole. They will have every reason to cooperate with us."

Theresa, who like Esther had achieved spacious quarters, asked in a nervous voice, "What rooms are they moving into?"

Sister Agnes looked distressed. "Well, I'm not sure." She hesitated. "I know some of you are very attached to your rooms…" The implication was that their possessiveness was regrettable, perhaps even a sin.

Mrs. Brady, a little apprehensive, like someone giving a gift that might be the wrong size, interrupted Sister Agnes. "I'm going to be perfectly frank with you," she said. "The board felt it would defeat our purpose to put the girls in the smallest and least desirable rooms. Their self-image is already poor. We want them to know they have our respect as well as our love." She smiled at the residents to let them know they were a part of a charming little conspiracy.

Each year on the first Saturday afternoon in June the residents of Martha Mary were bused to Colonial Heights to visit the Brady home, where fruit punch and little sandwiches were served to them and they were encouraged to stroll through the spacious rooms and gardens, admiring outdoors the Bradys' iris collection and indoors their collection of French paperweights.

The residents were allowed the use of the Brady powder room where paper towels with the Brady initials in gold were set out on the marble sink for their use. Occasionally one of the residents dried her hands on a piece of Kleenex and took home a paper towel in her purse as a memento. The sweeping stairway that led to the second floor and the more intimate Brady quarters was cordoned off with a pink ribbon. The residents never minded; it gave them something to speculate about on their way home.

Mrs. Brady, after making her announcement about the harlots, was surprised by the looks of dismay and anger on the faces of the residents. Hurriedly she said, "I want all of my good friends here to know the board doesn't want to do anything behind your backs. That's why we're having this meeting with you today. We want all of you to share in our decisions, and we're certain you will welcome the opportunity to take these troubled girls to your hearts. Remember we have the example of Our Lord who opened his arms to sinners. And who among us would not admit to being a sinner? I hope you will look on these girls as a real challenge."

Mary Magdalene was mentioned as Sister Agnes ended the meeting with a final plea.

"I don't know that Our Lord ever *lived* with people like that," Theresa whispered.

"He certainly didn't share a bathroom with them." Lee looked at Esther, who usually made up their minds for them.

"I don't suppose it will hurt us to do what we can to help," Esther said. You didn't teach school for forty years, as Esther had, without believing in amendment.

When the rooms were reapportioned Esther's had been among

those awarded to one of the troubled girls. Had she been able to afford an apartment in a decent and safe part of the city, Esther would have considered moving. The residence hall was not all that desirable, located as it was in a deteriorating section of the city where many of the stores were boarded up and older women were preyed upon by muggers. The food at the residence was dismal — spaghetti with meatballs the size and density of marbles, weeks of fruit cocktail.

All the residents were required to take one meal a day in the cafeteria. Esther chose lunch. She prepared her own dinners, making do with the snack kitchen's electric frying pan and the combination microwave and toaster oven. From time to time she invited a friend to join her, perhaps for an omelet *fines herbes* with a nice salad. She would have loved to serve a little wine with her dinners, but it was strictly forbidden to have spirits on the premises and Esther had survived her seventy-two years, not all of them pleasant, by cleaving to firm principles and orderly ways. With laxness came clutter, wavering, despondency, and death.

She had learned cleanliness from her mother, who fought the disorder of their neighborhood with soap and scrub brush. There had been plastic covers on the couch and the lampshades. Had it been practical, Esther's mother would have wrapped her in plastic to protect her from the contamination of the streets. This insistence on cleanliness had swept Esther's lax father from the home, but her mother had never regretted her priorities, and Esther was on her side.

In her years of teaching domestic science in an inner-city school, Esther had brought order into the disorganized lives of her students. Before her girls—and in recent years a few boys—were allowed to pick up so much as a measuring spoon, they had to produce in their notebooks a letter-perfect copy of their recipe. The same notebooks held diagrams indicating the exact placement in the cupboards of every pot, pan, and mixing bowl. For many of the students these notebooks were their first hint of an alternative to havoc. Some of the students learned to read while puzzling over directions for fettuccini Alfredo—Esther had taught order, but it was not a graceless order. She was sure none of *her* girls ended up on the street.

With this in mind, she approached Sister Agnes shortly after the troubled girls arrived, offering to teach them cooking. She saw them, pencils at the ready, faces turned toward her, eager to be initiated into a world of rules. She would instruct them on the mysteries of keeping house, and then they would find a house and keep it. Although Esther herself had never married, adopting her mother's rule that men by the time they came of marriageable age were irremediable, these girls, she felt, could do worse.

An enthusiastic Sister Agnes put a notice in the girls' mailboxes. When the hour came for the class, Esther was waiting in the residence kitchen with five notebooks she had bought with her own money, and before her were the ingredients for a soufflé (she believed the girls would appreciate the dramatic). No one came. Finally Sister Agnes, looking in to see how things were going, expressed a polite interest in taking the class herself. She surprised Esther by turning out to be a competent cook. "My dad owned a bar and grill," Sister Agnes told her. "We all helped out."

The girls had been at Martha Mary for three weeks when Lee

Simon and Theresa Sullivan crowded into Esther's small room for tea. Theresa, who worked as a receptionist in a funeral home, brought a rescued arrangement of orange lilies for Esther, but their grandeur made Esther's dark room shabbier than ever.

"Did you hear those tramps coming in at all hours last night?" Theresa asked. "They were running up and down the halls at four in the morning, laughing and screaming. Why doesn't Sister Agnes get after them?"

"She's tried, but it doesn't do any good," Esther said. "Haven't you noticed how much time she's spending in the chapel?" Some of the shine had gone out of Sister Agnes.

Lee said, "I haven't been able to have the children here since they came." Lee had a number of nieces and nephews who enjoyed pounding on the piano in the lounge and playing Ping-Pong in the recreation room. "I don't care what Mrs. Brady told us. I'm afraid to let them use the bathrooms."

"I don't blame you. I hate to use them myself." Esther passed the macaroons she had made earlier in the day. "They leave hair all over everything. The sinks are filthy and," she lowered her voice, "they don't flush."

"We saw your sign," Lee told Esther. Esther's "Please Keep Things Clean" sign had been covered with lipsticked vulgarities. "I heard someone found a hypodermic syringe in one of the waste baskets."

"You can't tell me that isn't pot they're smoking. I can smell it." Esther had patrolled the school lavatories regularly and more than once had charged the boys' room in pursuit of an offender.

"That gold ring Mary Butler got when her mother died was

stolen," Theresa said. "Eleanor Wright's wallet disappeared out of her room, too."

"Who are those men in the big cars that come by for them? I saw the blonde getting into a Mercedes with a …" Lee was about to say "a black man," but she remembered Esther in time and changed it to "a man in a leather jacket."

Esther never let things like that pass. "The *black* man was a pimp." The pimps made themselves at home in the visitors' lounge. Tall, thin, elegant men in bright colors with long claw-like nails, they flocked in the lounge like exotic birds, directing indecent remarks to the residents and hustling girls out to waiting cars with proprietary fanny pats.

"Did you ever hear such language?" There was caterwauling among the girls late at night, and Lee had lain with her hands over her ears blocking out the graphic obscenities. "Why don't we tell the board?"

Esther said, "Some of us wrote Mrs. Brady, but she just said we weren't doing enough to make them feel wanted." Esther had drafted the letter to the board herself. "I wish Mrs. Brady could have seen them in the cafeteria this noon." There was a strict prohibition against appearing in the dining room unless you were fully dressed, but Del, a bony, horse-faced creature with hair the color of lemon marmalade, had wandered down for lunch in a filthy terrycloth robe. Behind her had come Bobby, the only black woman among the girls. Bobby was at least six feet tall and looked in her red satin robe like a spreading conflagration. Holding Bobby's hand was Dannette, a pale, puffy girl with hair upholstered in pink foam curlers. She was wearing cowboy boots and a white lab coat over baby-doll pajamas. They paused, a bizarre tableau, at the entrance of the cafeteria. Bobby grinned. "Look at all these little ladies eatin' their lunch already. They goin' to bed *real* early at night. They *good* girls, not like us."

In a fit of giggling, the top of Dannette's flimsy pajamas ditched its responsibility.

Bobby turned to her, "Cover yourself up, girl," she said sternly. "We gotta behave like *ladies* here."

To protest this aberration, Esther had marched out of the dining room leaving her lunch half-finished, no hardship since they were having Spanish rice for the second time that week. Esther had been particularly furious at Bobby. Black women in the residence lived up to Esther's standards or received a visit from her, which they never forgot.

And in fact after lunch Esther went to Bobby's room, the room, as it happened, that had once been hers. She knocked sharply. When Bobby opened the door, Esther gasped—disorder everywhere: shoes strewn on the unmade bed, black net stockings draped over the lamp, dresser drawers leaking their embarrassing contents, and under the bed...

"Honey, you be the cutest thing I ever seen," Bobby had greeted her. "I noticed you right away when you was going into the shower with those little white rubber shoes on your feet. I got a auntie jus' like you. She say, 'Roberta, you gonna come to no good.' I give her a microwave oven last Christmas and she wouldn't have it in her house. 'Where that money come from?' she ask me. She hurt my feeling sometimes, but she be one wonderful person."

Esther interrupted her. "There are wine bottles under your

bed." Esther was appalled that such a thing could happen in what she still considered to be her own room. "Drinking is strictly forbidden at Martha Mary."

"Don't you worry about us, honey. We know you sweet little ladies don't want us here. We be as anxious to get loose of this tight-ass place as you be to get us out. The probation officers, they *sentenced* us to this place. But you *know* we gonna find a way to get out jus' as quick as we can."

What shocked Esther the most was the discovery that Bobby did not consider living at Martha Mary a privilege.

Esther reported the visit to Theresa and Lee at breakfast. "You should have seen my room," she moaned. "It was a pigsty."

"Wait until they turn up in Mrs. Brady's living room next week," Lee said with relish.

The invitations to the annual tea had appeared that morning in their mailboxes: "Mrs. Walter Brady requests the pleasure of the company of the Martha Mary residents on Thursday, June 10th, at half after three."

"You don't think Elizabeth Brady would allow those sluts in her *own* home? They didn't *get* an invitation," Theresa told her.

"How do you know?" Esther was deeply disappointed. Like Lee, she had been consoling herself with agreeable fantasies. If Mrs. Brady could just see those girls, Esther was sure she'd have them out of Martha Mary in no time.

"Sister Agnes told me," Theresa said. "I got there just after she put the invitations in the mailboxes, and I noticed there weren't any in those creatures' boxes. She said Mrs. Brady called her twice to explain the invitations were just for the 'regular residents' and not the 'new girls.' I could tell Sister didn't think that was right."

The three women fell into a rich silence. After a while Esther asked, "What time do they pick up their mail?"

"On their way down to lunch—breakfast, for them," Theresa answered.

"And Sister Agnes is down in the cafeteria then."

The two women nodded.

"There are five of them," Esther said. "Between us we've got three invitations. Where can we get two more?"

"Mary Butler because of her gold ring," Lee said. "And Evelyn Palumbo. One of them tried to pick up her brother in the visitors' lounge."

"That's enough," Esther nibbled thoughtfully on a piece of burnt toast.

The morning of the tea Esther opened her Bible, as she did every morning of her life. Right there in Matthew was the passage about the tax collectors and the prostitutes entering the kingdom of heaven before anyone else. Was the Lord trying to tell her something? Guilt overwhelmed her and she got down on her knees and, adhering to the biblical language, prayed that the harlots be allowed to remain at Martha Mary.

The change in Esther had come gradually. A few days after Esther's visit to Bobby's room, Bobby had knocked on her door. "I heard they turned you out of your room an' put me there. I tried to get you your room back, but that Sister Agnes, she set on killin' us with kindness. But don't you care; we're lookin' to get out first chance we see. Here's somethin' for you." Almost shyly Bobby handed Esther a bottle of expensive perfume. "It be delicate as shit, jus' like you."

Esther was going to refuse the perfume, but she recalled the story of Bobby's aunt and the microwave. Holding the perfume between two fingers, she thanked Bobby and, when she was alone, hid the gift in the back of her closet.

Then Dannette had appeared in the dining room with a black eye and a reddish-purple bruise on her cheek. Esther, who never allowed herself to dwell on what the girls actually *did*, found herself having to admit that there must be times when it was not pleasant for them.

It was not unlike teaching, where you tried to remain objective, to keep a little distance between yourself and your students, but as the term progressed, and in spite of yourself, you began to care first about one student then another, and in no time you were lost.

Esther sought out Sister Agnes and confessed to having given the girls invitations to the tea. "How are we going to keep them from coming with us?" she asked expecting Sister Agnes's anger and worse her disapproval.

Instead, Sister Agnes looked pained. "Something has happened. Dannette had a man in her room last night."

They exchanged looks. For different reasons Esther and Sister Agnes had kept out of the way of men. Now, after all, it was possible that even here at Martha Mary a man might appear in one's bedroom.

"I believe you were quite right," Sister Agnes said, appearing more luminescent than she had in a long time. "Surely Mrs. Brady just made a mistake by overlooking the girls. It was generous of you to share your invitations. I think the outing to the Brady's home will do us all good."

Esther saw there was to be war and that it was to be a holy war.

As the women gathered in front of Martha Mary waiting to board the bus that would take them to Colonial Heights, their noses twitched in the soft spring air. June had breached the city. The smell of automobile exhaust was rich as roses. They stood in light spring suits and dresses, happy as schoolchildren that have taken off their winter coats. As they boarded the bus, Esther looked nervously around, wondering where the girls were; perhaps Sister Agnes had second thoughts.

The bus door was closing with a hydraulic whoosh when a mélange of black leather, gold boots, sequins, frizzled hair, short skirts, and see-through blouses emerged and ran toward the bus.

"They've put on their working clothes," Lee said, encouraged.

The girls lined up on the back seat giggling and nudging one another like children on an outing. The bus moved through the streets of boarded-up stores. Where once there had been homes, field daises and Queen Anne's lace had sprung up like second thoughts. Then they were on the expressway and the city was behind them.

When at last the bus reached Colonial Heights, the troubled girls began to whisper among themselves. At the sight of the Brady's large home and expanse of green lawn, the whispering intensified. They were the last to leave the bus and by the time they strutted up the geranium-lined path, most of the residents were already in the Brady home. Esther saw that Mrs. Brady was paralyzed by the sight of the girls and would not have the presence of mind to shut the door in their faces. When she was able to move, she looked around for Sister Agnes and some explanation, but Sister

Agnes had hurried into the Brady living room and hidden herself among the residents.

"Why don't we all go out into the garden?" Mrs. Brady managed. "It's such a lovely afternoon."

Once outside the troubled girls ran around the garden exclaiming over the irises, which were at their peak. "Look here," Del giggled, "each flower's got its own name on a little stick. I gotta have some for my room." She began breaking off blooms the colors of port wine and green grapes.

"No!" Mrs. Brady's voice was shrill. "Please, it's taken years. We have to have the blooms to hybridize. Wait!"

But the girls were sweeping through the garden snatching at every flower they could get their hands on, from the palest skim-milk blue to the darkest mahogany.

The residents stayed where they were.

Like beauty queens or presidents' wives, the girls with their arms full of flowers wandered back through the French doors, Mrs. Brady at their heels. Bobby reached a long arm up to one of the lighted glass shelves where the paperweights were displayed. "These pretty glass rocks must cost you plenty." But Mrs. Brady was in search of Sister Agnes. The girls crowded around the paperweights and gazed wonderingly down into the kaleidoscope of colors. When the huddle broke up Dannette hoisted her purse strap farther up her shoulder to accommodate increased weight.

Mary Butler thought of her mother's gold ring lost to her forever. Eleanor Wright thought of her wallet with the one picture she had of the only man who had ever proposed to her. No one said a word.

"You all come and see this pretty pink ribbon they got wrapped 'round out here," Bobby called from the hallway. "Just like we getting the whole damn upstairs for a present."

Dannette yanked at the ribbon stretched across the stairway from the newel post to the wainscoting, draping it around her hips and tying it in a bow. She did a few bumps and grinds and then ran up the stairs, the other girls skittering up behind her.

Mrs. Brady followed them calling, "I'm sorry, I'm afraid you can't go up there." But the girls had disappeared into the bedrooms. Mrs. Brady cried wildly down to the residents, "I could use some help up here!"

Sister Agnes's ascension of the stairway was slow. The residents sat on their chairs sipping punch and nibbling little cream cheese and chutney sandwiches. Esther thought the combination interesting, but she gave poor marks to the cucumber sandwiches, which were soggy. "Should have buttered them first," she said to Lee. Overhead she could hear pleasurable cries of discovery.

July was always a quiet month at Martha Mary. Those who could escape the heat of the city did so. Esther didn't know anyone with a cottage on a lake or a place in the country, but this year she didn't mind; she was back in her old room. The dirty fingerprints were scrubbed from the yellow walls. The floor was waxed. A freshly laundered and starched scarf covered the nail polish stains on the dresser. A cloud of Lysol hung reassuringly over the room. Streaming though the polished windows, the summer sun clung like a warm shawl to Esther's shoulders. She was pouring sherry for Lee and Theresa. With the sherry Esther served a perfectly relaxed wedge of Brie.

Theresa had brought a bouquet of yellow sweetheart roses garnished with tendrils of ivy. "The minute I saw it come in, I knew it would be perfect in your room," she told Esther. "I changed the water each day myself and kept the roses in the cooler with the bodies at night—things spoil so fast there. She enjoyed bringing the flowers from the funeral home. Once she got them outside they seemed to take on new life.

"Doesn't it feel funny having liquor in your room?" Lee asked.

"It's not liquor," Esther corrected her. "It's only fortified wine." Still, Esther had to admit Lee was right—it *was* against the rules. But Sister Agnes had been transferred, and the new director, Sister Elizabeth, was away part of each day working in a real-estate office. Although the girls were gone, the residents no longer bothered to keep the bathrooms tidy. Some of them even appeared for breakfast in their bathrobes. Right this minute, Esther thought, feeling a chill in spite of the sun, she was breaking the Martha Mary rule about having spirits in your room. For a moment it was as if the girls had never left, as if the liquor bottles were still under her bed.

INCOMER

In all of his imaginings Luke Klein had not imagined himself in jail. As in most things in his Detroit suburb, his cell, scrubbed clean, was upscale. There were even a few thumbed copies of *Vanity Fair*. Some preppy with time on his hands and no little talent had painted a pink-and-green crocodile on one of the cell walls. After a drunken teenager had been returned, penitent and tearful to his parents, Luke was the jail's only resident. His wife, Miranda, was with her father, who was posting bail and who was furious with Luke. Luke's foolishness would reflect on his father-in-law and his father-in-law's business. Luke's own partners would not be happy. What was a doctor doing with a gun? He wondered if his rifle would be returned to him or confiscated. It was his dad's and he wanted it back.

Luke and Miranda had argued because Luke put out food at night for the coyote. Articles in the local paper said not to do that. A couple of little dogs had been attacked, and Luke and Miranda had a Bichon named Sip. The Bichon had belonged to Miranda before they were married, and it snarled and nipped at Luke when he got close to Miranda. It wasn't a breed Luke would have chosen. When he was growing up in Michigan's upper peninsula, his family had a series of German Shepherds with names like Blitz and Rebel.

Most of the homes in the suburb were comfortable three- and four-bedroom colonials with a few Tudors left over from the twenties. Their own place was located on one of a handful of streets of small spruced-up cottages. Mansions had once lined the suburb's lakeshore, and the cottages had been homes for the servants who worked in the mansions. Living in the suburb was Miranda's idea. It was where she had always lived and where all of her friends had settled. Luke disliked living in a servant's cottage. He had grown up in one. But he was just finishing his oncology residency and it had been all they could afford.

He was as much an alien in the suburb as the coyote. When he went for a walk he found handprints on everything, a landscape of plan and order instead of chance and scatter. Only the suburb's trees appeared transcendent, their height and breadth making them too formidable to tamper with. The nearby lake was placid and no substitute for his boyhood Lake Superior, whose storms swallowed freighters. He had to make do with rabbits and squirrels instead of wolves and moose. He ignored the tame world around him and walked with the images of the wilder world in which he had grown up. Somewhere he had read that you could imagine only what was absent.

Luke and Miranda met because Miranda's parents came each summer to a private club, Arcadia, in Michigan's Upper Peninsula. Luke's father, Ed, was the club's caretaker, and Luke and his parents lived in a cabin on the club grounds. Luke would trail around after his dad as he repaired screens or primed a well. When he was little he had the idea the whole club would fall apart were it not for his father. The club members were polite to Luke, calling him by name and teasing him about his skill as a fisherman. That was a double-edged compliment because the brookie he had caught when he was just twelve, one for the record books, had been caught in a stream that ran through the club and was for members only. Luke shouldn't have been fishing there.

He hadn't had much to do with Miranda in those years. She was three years younger than he was, practically a baby. All the children of the club's members had to have Minders. The Minders were full-time baby sitters, taking the kids on hikes, supervising their swimming in the club pool, and doing whatever it took to keep them out of their parents' way. Luke's mother hadn't thought much of the arrangement. "What's the point of having children if you're not the one to bring them up? It isn't as if those ladies had something else to do." A couple of local women did the housework in the cabins of club members. Dinners were taken in the big lodge.

His dad didn't like to hear criticism of the club. "As long as I'm living on their land and taking their money, I owe them some respect." Although a couple of times he had nearly resigned, like the time the club acquired several hundred acres of land that years ago had been lumbered and then abandoned for taxes. Locals had always hunted there, but the club told Luke's dad to put up "No Hunting" signs. His dad complained to Luke, "I'm not going to do it. I've got to live here in this township and I won't be able to look my friends in the eye."

Ed Klein simmered for a day or two and then marched over to tell the club president, who happened to be Douglas Raynart, Miranda's father, "Either you let the locals hunt there or you'll have to look for a new caretaker."

Raynart had laughed. "I had no idea. Not a problem."

Ed took the whole thing seriously and hadn't liked being laughed at.

Luke received an academic scholarship to University of Michigan. After his graduation he entered the university's medical school. When the members at Arcadia heard, they quietly took up a collection. Every year of the four years they handed over an envelope in the fall. His dad always checked to be sure Luke had written a thank-you note. Luke didn't need prompting. Without the help of the club, he would have ended up with a lifetime of loans.

Luke stayed on to intern at the university hospital. His medical fraternity gave a party, and Miranda had been there with a date. He wouldn't have recognized her but when he heard the familiar last name, he asked. He was always looking for a way to bring his northern home into his life. She ditched her date, and the two of them headed out to walk in the nearby university arboretum. Luke ran there in the mornings, and even with no moon the paths were familiar to him. A couple of student beer parties were going on, but they were in the distance. It was early September. The nights were still warm. Cicadas sung in the trees. The grass was damp, and Miranda held on to his arm as she took off her shoes. She was so slight he hardly felt her weight. Once in Florida on a spring break he had smelled real orange blossoms, and that was what she smelled like.

"These woods are so dark and mysterious," she said.

"Not very mysterious. In the daytime you'd be able to see signs identifying every bush and tree."

"When I was little I was terrified of going on those hikes in the woods with our Minders. I was sure we'd run into a tiger or a lion.

Do you get back often?"

"No. I haven't had the time or the money. Dad died a couple of years ago and Mom's living in Florida with her sister. I dream about it a lot." He hadn't meant to tell her about the dreams. "How about you?"

"The family goes back each summer, but I usually stay in town."

That should have been a warning, but Luke was lost in the wonder of being with someone who had spent her childhood summers where he had. They talked about how nearly impossible it was to swim in the freezing waters of Lake Superior; how deer browsed on the flowers the club members planted; the summer the bears, driven away by a new fence around the town dump, had begun scrounging the club's garbage cans. She even knew the bog where there were sundews and pitcher plants that digested flies. He believed she had discovered it as he had, wandering in the woods, only learning later that she had been on an "ecology walk" the club put on for the kids.

They began dating, and Luke survived the awkwardness of meeting her parents. "Of course," Mr. Raynart said, "Ed's son. I remember when you were a little fellow giving your dad a hand. I was sorry to hear you lost him. We had a little dust-up once over some hunting rights, but Ed was the best caretaker we ever had. Well, we have a lot to talk about. I hope we see more of you. All the members were proud when you went off to medical school."

The transition had been made from caretaker's son to Miranda's young man about to be a doctor. When he traveled to spend a week with Miranda and her parents at Arcadia, the club welcomed him. Because of his knowledge of the best fishing spots, he was much in demand among the club's fly fishermen. Miranda complained she never got to see him. The truth was, he spent every minute he could steal revisiting his favorite trails or hiking the shore of Superior, scrambling over logs and boulders. At first he tried to take Miranda with him, but she said, "You're behaving like one of the Minders." She worked on her tan and played bridge with her mother's friends.

In the evenings he sat with the family on the Raynarts' big porch sipping drinks, waiting for the moment when the sun slipped down behind the trees and the cool breeze that had been waiting swept in from the big lake. There was talk about past events at the club and a special effort was made to bring Luke into the talk. He was ecstatic about being back. He imagined his summer vacations there with Miranda, bringing their children to all the places he loved. Sometimes, if he didn't push it quickly from his mind, he wondered if it wasn't Miranda's gift of Arcadia, rather than Miranda herself, that attracted him.

They were married at the beginning of the second year of his residency. He had hoped Miranda would want a wedding at Arcadia. He saw them exchanging vows on the shore of Superior. His relationship with the wild lake was religious, and the marriage needed its blessing.

Miranda protested, "You mean a destination wedding? Arcadia isn't the Bahamas. It's not an attraction. Where would everyone stay? In one of those Upper Peninsula motels? They probably have bedbugs. And who would we get to cater it? The cooks at the club aren't up to much more than fried chicken and apple pie. Anyhow, months ago when she saw where we were headed Mom snagged a Saturday afternoon date at our church and at the country club."

He didn't object, but he hadn't appreciated being anticipated.

The wedding was a big affair. The Raynarts had so many friends no one noticed that, apart from Luke's fellow residents and their dates, his mother and aunt were his only guests. He was afraid all the airs and graces might overwhelm his mother, but to her the Raynarts and their friends were still the people who rented out their kids all summer and were too lazy to cook their own meals. She was polite but contained. His aunt Mary, though, could hardly get enough. Her digital camera kept winking as if it had something it its eye.

When his residency was ending and it was time to consider his future, Luke asked Miranda, "What would you think about my practicing up north? There's a large hospital only a couple of hours from Arcadia. We could live in town, and summer weekends we'd stay at the club."

"I could never live there. I don't know a soul. What would I do? I was bored up there even in the summer, and it snows from September to June."

"That's an exaggeration." Though he knew it wasn't, having seen snow in both of those months. "Anyhow, it's a college town, not the end of the world. You'd make friends, and in the winter we could snowshoe and cross-country ski in the woods." He was thinking of his own silent journeys when he had scared up a fox or sent a grouse exploding out of its snow bank cover. Once in a snowstorm he had come upon a rare white-coated moose. He could close his eyes and see it still, the great white moose walking through white snow, its appearance a convergence with another world.

When he brought up practicing in the Upper Peninsula for the second time, Miranda went to her father, and Mr. Raynart introduced Luke to a friend of his, the head of a local internal medicine group looking for an oncologist. Luke was offered a position. He took it, and Miranda and her mother began working with a realtor to find a larger home in the suburb.

Around that time, the local paper published the first picture of a coyote. "Spotted on Lake View Drive," the headline said. That was only two blocks from their home. The coyote had wandered from the country club's golf course, thought to be its home ground. Luke studied the grainy picture of the coyote in the newspaper, happy to see a bit of wilderness in all that tamed landscape. Miranda, seeing the picture, stopped letting Sip out in the back yard. When she took the little Bichon for a walk on its leash, in addition to the usual plastic bag, she carried a can of pepper spray.

The coyote entered Luke's dreams, an elusive shape slinking into shadows and loping down darkened pathways. Luke considered writing a letter to the editor of the paper in support of the coyote. "We should be pleased," he wanted to write, "that a wild creature has chosen to live among us. We should welcome the coyote." Or perhaps less compassionately, "If you're worried, get a *big* dog." When he ran in the mornings he headed for the trails on the golf course where the Raynarts were members. It was early November and the course was deserted, the ghosts of summer's players implicit in the occasional golf ball. The bare branches of the trees cut into gray skies. There were a few blue jays and some undecided robins, and once he had seen a red-shouldered hawk, but no coyote, and then on a Saturday morning he found tracks at the edge of a water hazard.

That night he left some of Sip's dog food out on their patio. Later when he turned on the porch light he found the dish was empty, the coyote's tracks still visible in the snow. Luke was thrilled. After that, without saying anything to Miranda, he put out food every night and then got up early in the mornings to remove the dish. Sometimes the coyote had been there; sometimes he hadn't. Luke was surprised at how happy the coyote's appearance made him, how it transformed his day. He thought about trapping the animal and driving north with it. They would both escape.

The coyote was discussed during Thanksgiving dinner at Miranda's parents'. Mrs. Raynart told what had happened to a friend of hers. "Jeanie's miniature poodle was out playing in their yard and Jeanie heard these horrible squeals. She ran out and scared the creature off with a broom. The poor little poodle had to have stitches."

"Coyotes are varmints," Mr. Raynart said. "The police ought to hunt the animal down and shoot it."

Miranda gave Luke a satisfied, superior look, but didn't betray him. The evening before she had discovered the dish of dog food Luke was leaving out for the coyote. "You're feeding a killer," she accused. "You're encouraging it. It's like leaving the phone numbers of little boys for perverts."

"That's an absurd comparison. If the coyote has enough food, it'll leave dogs alone."

There was talk at the Thanksgiving table of summer plans. Mr. Raynart had retired, and the Raynarts now spent the entire season at Arcadia. "I suppose you won't have too much vacation your first year," Mr. Raynart said to Luke, "but I hope you'll manage a week or two with us."

Before Luke could give his eager assent, Miranda said, "Dad, I've spent half my life up there. I want to see a little of the rest of the world. Mary Lee and John bought a place in the Dordogne. They want us to visit."

Luke hadn't heard a word of the Dordogne, wasn't even sure where it was. He considered sending Miranda off to this Dordogne place and going up to Arcadia by himself, but the Raynarts would not welcome that. Even if they did, without Miranda he would once again be the caretaker's son.

He felt betrayed, and when they returned home after the dinner he made a point of letting her see him empty another can of dog food into an aluminum dish and put it outside. Miranda marched upstairs, gathered her down pillow, and slept in the guest room with Sip.

Luke felt the emptiness in the bed. He regretted what he had done. His dream of returning to the woods was slipping away. Recently he and Miranda had gone to a concert. The choral group sang Juris Karlsons's *Mans Ezers*, My Lake. "How the sun shines, my lake glitters; but in the depth itself lies my heart, and throbs, and throbs, and throbs." Even if they made occasional visits to Arcadia, Miranda's reluctance would be everywhere, in the woods, along the shore of the lake, spoiling it for him. Minders, not he, would be the ones to teach the lake and the woods to his children. He had to win Miranda over.

Luke hurriedly dressed and went downstairs. It had started to snow. By now there would be twelve-foot-high drifts up north. The eerie ice volcanoes would be building out on Lake Superior. His father's hunting rifle was in the basement. Like some Neanderthal huntsman, he would kill the wild animal and bring it like a trophy to his woman, who would praise his prowess. She would love him again. She would forgo this Dordogne place.

Neighbors reported the sound of the gunshots. A squad car pulled into their driveway. When the policeman shone his flashlight on the dead coyote, Luke was shaken by the slightness of the animal he had lured to its death. The policeman appeared pleased. "We've been after that bastard for a couple of weeks. We get calls all the time from ladies with little dogs. Actually I think we got one from around here. I should thank you for doing our job for us, but laws are laws, and we're the ones who can use a gun, not you."

All his life Luke had been scrupulous in his relationship with his prey. It was catch and release with trout, deer were taken in the proper season, he had never treed a bear with a dog. He was overcome by the enormity of his betrayal.

Miranda, who had thrown on a coat and hurried out to see what was happening, had been disgusted, and embarrassed for Luke. The rifle was confiscated, and Luke sentenced to community service at a senior citizen health clinic, his medical education saving him from picking up trash in the local park or giving lectures in the schools on gun safety. When the local paper came out there were quotes from the police and the judge. It was against the law to discharge a firearm in the suburb. A rifle shot could travel a couple of miles and might ricochet into someone's home.

In the article, a professor of animal behavior was quoted, "You get rid of one coyote, and another one moves right in." It was reassuring to Luke that in this place he would not be alone.

COSTUMES

"Those fingers of yours are rather like clever mice running up my legs." All the while I was designing the costumes for Chekhov's *Seagull*, I gorged on the anticipation of having my hands on Nicholas Kendell. Kendell is a legend and the most celebrated actor our Canadian Shakespeare festival has attracted. In photos he was the center of any gathering. People clustered around him, waiting, hoping for some grand gesture or fatal slip. He had run away to us from England, where last winter he passed out while being presented to the queen. The official explanation was that he had a virus, but word went around he was drunk again. I wondered if the queen just stood there while a footman saw to Kendell, or had she knelt down, perhaps brushing the hair from his forehead, and cradled him in her arms?

Kendell wasn't expected to last the season at the Glencarden festival. He argued savagely with Rennier, our artistic director, and worse, he disappeared for two days. Someone reported seeing him in New York, someone else had a story about his being sighted at the Mayo Clinic.

It was only eleven in the morning, and I could tell he had been drinking. Kendell looked down at me, the famous green pupils caught in a red net of veins. Distracted into clumsiness by his one eyelid's rhythmic twitching, I stabbed him with a pin. This time his voice was cross. "Heavy tweed may be the thing for Russian steppes, but it's going to be hell under the lights."

"It has to be authentic," I murmured.

"Authentic." He made the word sound ridiculous, even impossible. "Then where are the stains? A little dried sweat and semen would be authentic. There were no dry cleaners, you know."

"I'll dirty it up a bit and we'll try it again." I was miserable at having to let go of him and eager to make him return. "You can go into the dressing room and change," I said. Still on my knees, I glanced up at the unruly hair, the high cheekbones, the down-slanted Celtic eyes, the mouth that seemed out of control. He was a damaged sixty-six-year-old. I tried to match this Kendell with the notices of him in my scrapbook, scrupulously kept all through high school. Kendell in *Jumpers*, *Equus*, *Rosencrantz and Guildenstern*, *Long Day's Journey*, *Hamlet*, and *Heartbreak House*. Pasted into the scrapbook were articles about his many divorces and his outrageous behavior.

Not bothering with the dressing room, Kendell was trying to unbutton the fly on his trousers. "I don't seem to be able to grapple with small buttons this morning." He shot me a wicked grin. "I don't suppose you'd give me a hand?" My imaginings had not gone that far. I didn't move. "No, I thought not."

His authentic trousers slipped to the floor, revealing tattered shorts. He put a hand on my shoulder and attempted to step out of the tweed puddle. "A little shaky this morning," he said. As he tentatively raised one foot, he lurched against me, knocking me over and landing on top of me.

I scrambled to my feet. Everything I knew about Kendell suggested that I should toss him his clothes and run. Living in Glen-carden, I had seen every play Shakespeare had written. The great tragic figures on their way down were the ones to touch my heart.

He sat there smiling up at me. "Low comedy. Farce actually. I'll tell you what; if I show up like this at rehearsal, they'll send me back on the first plane. I'm finished in England if I don't stick it out here." Tears rolled down his unshaven cheeks.

I helped him up and asked, "When did you last eat?" I have always felt many of the world's problems have come from statesmen sitting for hours at long tables with nothing before them but pencils and glasses of water.

"You would find in my fridge nothing but cartons of yogurt with slimy fruit cowering on the bottom. Rosemary doesn't eat." Rosemary was the young actress playing Nina to his Trigorin in *The Seagull.*

Kendell missed a button on his shirtfront. When I pointed it out, he stood there waiting like a toddler.

I willed my hands not to tremble. When I finished I mumbled, "You could come home with me. I could make you a quick lunch." I wasn't motivated by a desire to take home some lost and hungry animal, but by something atavistic and grasping. For years I had made do with very little; now my own hunger was making me greedy and careless. I don't know where I got the courage. By nature I'm reserved, even shy, but I had my hands on Nick Kendell and I couldn't let him go. I expected an incredulous look, even a sneer, certainly a refusal, probably not a polite one.

"That would be lovely," he said. He looked genuinely pleased.

I thought of Nabokov's joy in netting his first rare butterfly. "Ecstasy," Nabokov had said, and "the thrill of gratitude."

There were logistics to consider. I would be transporting some rare and dangerous cargo, something between a precious jewel and a viper, but first there was the walk through the wardrobe rooms with Kendell a meek step behind me like a queen's consort.

I had worked in those rooms for fifteen years, ever since I had returned from university in Toronto with a degree in art history. I loved costume design, I loved the way it got a jump on the characters, defining them to the audience before they spoke a word, the costume's transformation the very opposite of the invisible cloak. I believed you hardly needed the play and that actors were merely forms on which to fit costumes.

It was heaven to work with fabric, slippery silks, thick woolens, laces, jeweled silks, and furred velvets. I loved the research, the immersing myself in other times and other places, in the living of other lives, so much more interesting than my own.

I started out as a seamstress, became a cutter, and last year I did my first designs. I knew all the seamstresses, the tailors, the milliners, jewelers, dyers, and cobblers. I knew Ellen who did lingerie, Marilyn who decorated hats, and Liz who helped me with research and could tell you the diameter of hoop skirts in 1860. We were maidens, stitching away our lives; the Glencarden Festival our medieval castle.

As I left with Kendell there were curious glances, but the seamstresses must have supposed I was going off with him to settle some question with the stage designer. Still I sensed their envy. Kendell had just that touch of risk, of imminent danger that's so beguiling when your days are measured in neat stitches.

Once outside I asked him to wait for me while I got my car from the parking spaces reserved for festival employees. The car, a five-year-old Subaru that I had grown as attached to as a sibling, now appeared shabby to me, insufficient for its task. I hastily brushed away cookie crumbs from the passenger's seat and headed for the entrance, certain I would find Kendell gone, a clever prisoner who was sure to have the key to the cell in his pocket before he submitted to arrest.

When I pulled up he was sitting on a bench surrounded by an artful planting of early daffodils and tulips. He looked chastened and a little too aware of the charm of his setting. Folding himself into my car he let out a long sigh, like a sleepy child who has been lifted into his crib. I resisted pushing the door locks.

"You're being awfully kind to me," Kendell said. "I've noticed a faint smell of manure hanging about the town. Can that be?"

I winced. "Yes, I'm so sorry," I apologized as if I had been the one to spread the muck. "There are cornfields just outside of town and this is planting time."

"How bucolic, but appropriate, surely. Old Will grew up a stone's throw from cows and crops." He fell asleep, his body lurching against me. There were muffled snores. Overwhelmed by the value of my parcel, I drove cautiously. When I eased into my driveway Kendell awoke and looked about.

"Where are we, my dear? Surely no one lives here?"

It was a neighborhood of substantial homes with gabled roofs and generous porches, constructed of two courses of pale ochre brick made from local soil. Many of the homes, like my grandparents', had been built by successful farmers leaving behind acres of windswept prairie to huddle companionably together in town. Those early settlers couldn't have guessed Glencarden would one day become a Shakespeare mecca. In spite of the cold Ontario winters, all the houses had brave gardens. Soon there would be daisies, delphinium, meaty peonies, and old-fashioned single-petaled damask roses. The settlers had been Scotch and English, and they knew a thing or two about gardens.

I was welcome at any door on the block. I had played hide-and-seek in the back yards and in all the seasons walked beneath the oaks and maples. I knew the routines and customs. Dinners were at six and Sunday mornings were for worship at an Anglican or Presbyterian Church. I felt a traitor to the neighborhood for bringing Nick Kendell into its innocence, for he seemed to carry about with him a heavy burden of sins of both commission and omission.

I was four when I came to live in the house. My parents had been killed in an automobile accident. My grandparents could barely climb out from under the heavy stone of anguish that crushed them. They spoke to me from a terrible distance, never treating me as the child I was. The furniture, massive sofas, armoires, and beds, much of it handed down from my great grandparents, loomed over me so that I had the idea my forbears were giants. When I was fifteen, my grandfather died, and there was just my grandmother and myself. We clung to each other for dear life.

"This was my grandmother's house," I explained to Kendell. "She left it to me." It had seemed a grossly uneven trade: the house for the grandmother. When the lawyer informed me, I wanted to refuse the legacy out of some wild idea that if I did, I would find my grandmother sitting beside the fireplace while the winter interfered with the prairie town, and I read aloud to her another chapter of Trollope. She had chosen to live immured in the glass bell of another century. After my grandmother died, I had trouble finding my way back.

Kendell hesitated and then with reluctance eased himself out of the car. I kept looking over my shoulder, afraid of losing him, but he was following me up the walk, his mouth open a little, like a gullible child's. Once inside Kendell seemed relieved. "I thought you were going to have all kinds of horrors," he said, "Little china animals lolling about on crocheted doilies. Much too orderly, though. You might as well have velvet cords across the entrance to these rooms; they're like stage sets. They need living in." It was too much to hope he would volunteer. Soon be would be gone like a present sent by mistake.

While I fixed his lunch I could hear Kendell's footsteps overhead as he explored the house. It was unsettling, for he had so much magnetism, so much authority I felt anything he touched would become his. I imagined him wandering from room to room, like Goldilocks in the house of the three bears. Perhaps he was trying the beds. I thought of stories in which someone is captured and held against their will: "The Collector," or "The Cask of Amontillado." The same wild impulse that I had in the car to lock the doors returned.

I had a poor appetite and so was a good cook, always having to tempt myself. There was a wild rice and morel soup left over from the evening before. I made a shrimp salad and trimmed it with smoked salmon rolled around florets of watercress. I warmed a baguette. Nick Kendell sat across from me, eating in a way that made you understand why gluttony was a sin.

I've never been able to eat with someone watching; it makes eating an indecent act, like the dinner scenes from *Tom Jones*. My hesitation didn't bother Kendell in the least. When he finished his plate, he reached for mine. When he had drunk his fourth cup of coffee and finished off a batch of dried-cherry-and-white-chocolate-chip cookies, he wiped his mouth and looked at me as if he had made an unlikely discovery in an out-of-the-way flea market and was considering how little he could safely offer for it.

"I hope you'll let me return." He threw some small white pills down his throat and pushed back his chair. "I'm afraid we had better get back," he said, as if we had gone on a leisurely row on a lazy stream or had spent an afternoon hiking over the green hills of the Lake District. "Rennier has called the company for one thirty. He couldn't wait to get his hands on *The Seagull* and muck it up. He's turning Chekhov into Tennessee Williams, wanting us to be neurotic when we are only Russian; his Nina is all innocence when there should be complicity. And there's no humor. The Russian audiences used to laugh aloud at Chekhov's plays."

As we left, Kendell paused to watch me close the front door. "You don't lock up?"

"No. Nearer the festival they do, because of the all the visitors from out of town. We're not bothered here."

I released Kendell at the rehearsal hall, parked the car, and sat there for a moment. Never had an empty seat seemed so occupied. I could imagine him now regaling the cast with his little adventure. "Rather a pathetic sort," he would say, "no one you would have noticed. Works in wardrobe. Took me in like a stray tomcat. Fed me up and dusted me off and all the while terrified, but clearly half-hopeful I might ravish her. The house looked like a set for *The Chalk Garden* or one of Priestley's plays. I couldn't get out of there fast enough. Well, that will be one for her grandchildren, though I doubt she'll marry." The others would snicker.

I left work early. Spring had settled over our Canadian town with the festival's opening of its first two plays. Only the reluctant leaves on the oak trees held back, stubbornly giving nothing but hints. There was the usual parade of visitors on the main street, jaunty in the costumes they had fashioned for themselves, boots and trailing scarves, disguises even they saw though. Drivers had their car windows open so that music and snatches of the evening news accompanied me. The drivers would be welcomed home while I was going back to an empty house. I hoped that some faint trace of Kendell remained and remembered happily I had not washed his dishes.

When I opened the door I heard loud music coming from the upstairs, where I found Kendell lying on my grandmother's bed, scattering cigarette ashes on the pristine white candlewick spread. A jumble of Kendell's clothes spilled out of a duffle bag and appeared in cunning possession of the room. The air was perfumed with Scotch and a portable radio was tuned to a French-language station playing the "Marseillaise." Kendell was singing along in a rich bass.

He motioned me graciously into the room, patting a place next to him on the bed as if I were a compliant dog. I dropped onto a chair.

"Don't want to be cozy? Understandable. My presence must be something of a shock. The fetching Rosemary has taken over my apartment. Her demands, sexual and emotional, are keeping me from concentrating on my lines. Also she has nasty little hunches about me. 'The trouble with you,' she says, 'is that you're afraid to admit what a sensitive person you are. Your macho behavior is all a sham.' She wants to deconstruct me, castrate me is more like it. I hate pop psychology: everyone understood in two minutes and then dismissed. The difficulty is I never know how to get rid of women once they've moved in." He stubbed out a cigarette in my great grandmother's Royal Dalton hair receiver. "I hope you don't mind my camping out here for a day or two until she takes the hint and leaves."

Kendell fell back against the pillows, the ruffled sham making an innocent halo around his head. His shoes were off and I noticed with a stab of pity and a professional urgency a large hole in one of his socks. I wanted to tell him that my grandmother had taught me many things. I could darn socks and I knew how to iron shirts: wrong side of collar first, than right side, sleeves, yoke, fronts, and back. I wanted to assure Kendell that he was in capable hands, but I had no chance, for his immediate need was to be listened to. He was telling me the story of his life, pausing for a drag on a cigarette or a sip of Scotch from the toothpaste glass with its all-over pattern of violets that matched the bathroom shower curtain.

The late-afternoon sun fell upon Kendell as if he were lighted for the part of the stage manager in *Our Town*, or the master of ceremonies in *Cabaret*. While he was saying his lines, I imagined scenery being shifted downstage. "My father," he began in a tone

I associated with the opening pages of *David Copperfield*, "was Head Master at one of those schools for boys who cannot aspire to, or afford, Eton or Harrow; Father's school was second best. The buildings were falling to pieces, the food inedible, the tutors pederasts. What the school, Lexham, lacked in prestige, my father tried to make up in academic excellence. There he was successful. His boys regularly got into Oxford and Cambridge. Still, the boys from those families he most hungered after went elsewhere.

"He hoped to make a scholar out of me. I was not disinterested in books. I read a great deal when I was out of my father's sight. I was drawn to words and, when young, did well in Greek and Latin. I knew parts of *The Odyssey* by heart, and years later when my first wife and I chartered a yacht with friends to cruise the Greek Islands and stopped at Crete, I remembered Homer telling of the island in the middle of the wine-dark sea and of its men beyond number and its ninety cities and the Babel of tongues and the Achaeans and brave Eteo-Cretans, and the wavy-haired Doreans. And there in the hot sun my winter classroom came back to me."

Listening to him I felt I was tuned into a BBC interview. Why was Kendell telling me this clearly packaged story? What was he auditioning for? How involved in his life was I to be? Would there to be a day when we strolled together on the grounds of Lexham? Would Kendell say, "Remember when I first told you about the school?" Was this leading up to a request for a loan or an excuse for his drinking? Or were these favored lines he practiced from time to time. Had I not understood a word, I would have been spellbound by the rise and fall of the celebrated voice, the vowels drawn out, certain words in each sentence cherished more than others.

By the time the sun weakened, Kendell had fallen into shadow and silence. I thought of various responses: interest, pity, amusement, but I was afraid that by inching into his life I might make Rosemary's mistake and be seen as intrusive. It was Kendell who broke the silence. "I'm famished." The performance was over.

With Kendell watching I got out flour and eggs and a great hunk of good Parmesan, garlic, and some cans of baby clams. I rolled out dough and went out to the garden to clip parsley and tarragon. He opened a bottle of wine with a practiced hand and we settled down to huge bowls of pasta. All the while I cooked I had been making up grocery lists for the future: slabs of fresh tuna, tenderloins, thick lamb chops. I knew a farm where you could still get capons and another farm with a greenhouse where adolescent lettuces and miniature vegetables were grown. The way to a man's heart.

I was only a little disappointed and not at all angry when Kendell grabbed his jacket the moment dinner was over.

"Don't wait up for me, I'm meeting some of the cast for a drink after the performance." Kendell appeared to see me for the first time, and for the first time I was frightened. He wandered back into the kitchen and sat down on a chair to watch me scrub a kettle, staring at me with such inquiring intensity that rather giddily I tried to think if there was a scene in Shakespeare where dishes were washed and he was looking for hints on how to play it.

"You've been very kind," he said. "You must wonder what I'm doing here, settling into your house like a squatter and boring you with endless tales."

"Oh, no." Surely he saw how pleased I was to have him there, how much I was like a hotelier in some remote and uninteresting town, desperate for a guest.

"You're a very charming young woman, but I have to be honest and tell you it's the house. I haven't lived in a house since I left Celia and the children ten years ago. It's been apartments and hotels, waking up to unfamiliar rooms, even hostile rooms that don't want you in them. The heating contraption rattles all night and there are oddly colored pubic hairs in the bathtub. It has been a great pleasure to walk from room to room here and to go upstairs and downstairs. I'm very grateful to you. If you agree, I'll get rid of Rosemary and my apartment. Of course I mean to reimburse you. You must tell me what I owe you for your trouble."

I blinked away tears.

"I didn't mean to offend you," he said hastily. "I know you would put up with me out of kindness, but even so we must be businesslike, must we not?" He stood up. "Superb dinner." He was out the door.

Of course he would want to pay. That way he would be under no obligation to me. My home would be a sort of boarding house or upscale bed and breakfast. There would be a paragraph in his biography, "It was at the Glencarden Festival that Anne Irwin rescued Kendell from his demons, seeing that he ate properly, giving him the courage to stop his destructive drinking, providing the selfless stability that Kendell had long been seeking." Perhaps I would be quoted—something modest but trenchant.

I wandered up the stairway and into Kendell's room, already missing him. Should I hang up his clothes and fold down the spread like a chambermaid doing the nightly turndown? Perhaps put a chocolate on his pillow? Or should I leave everything just as it was? I had once read that in bringing Arnold Bennett tea, his maid would have to tell him the exact moment she had poured the boiling water into the pot. He would then pull out his watch, and in precisely four minutes' time the tea would be served. Any alteration infuriated him. Suppose Kendell had imposed on the room some subtle invisible order that must not be disturbed.

In the bathroom there were swags of damp towels on the tub and puddles deep enough for frogs on the tile. Only the violet patterned shower curtain was dry, it's purpose having been ignored or perhaps misunderstood. On the sink was a frazzled toothbrush, a straight-edged razor, a pot of soap, and a shaving brush that looked like a small, drowned animal. There was a pillbox with the days marked out and a plastic container, like a little house, that must have held, overnight, some arrangement of teeth. It was a relief to know he was mortal.

I spent a long time preparing for bed that night, for Kendell had seemed ready to help himself to anything in the house. I told myself all the charm in the world would not make me go to bed with Nick Kendell, and then I put on the silk nightie that my grandmother had kept in a drawer wrapped in tissue and had never worn. I skipped the night cream. I imagined him standing at the entrance to my bedroom, perhaps whispering my name to see if I were awake. Or would he go directly to his room and then in the early morning hours, troubled by bad dreams, stumble into my room and the comfort of my arms?

At midnight I awoke to the sound of clumping thuds and shrill whispers on the stairway. I kept a consoling nightlight in the hall so that I had only to open my door a few inches to discover Rose-mary dragging a drunken Nick Kendell up the stairway like a mammoth pull-toy. She headed for the open door of my grand-mother's room and, catching sight of me, gave a complicit wave before she pushed Kendell inside.

I had thought of sex as accompanied by whispers and sighs, not the shouts and grunts I now heard, creating in my mind images of slippery bodies, gladiators, warfare, winners and losers, and death. Even with a pillow over my head I heard the scrimmage that came afterward, the crash of a heavy object heaved against a wall, the breaking of china, someone stumbling down the stairway, a slammed door.

In the early morning there were sounds of retching. I opened my door to see a naked Nick Kendell emerge from the bathroom. It was not his nakedness that shocked me but how real, how alive he appeared with no costume. When he gave me a hungry look, I slipped out of my nightie.

Claudia turned from her painting to find Ralph, her husband of fifty-two years, in her studio. All the way through the door. Seven years ago, after a critical remark about her work, she forbid him entry, so his presence on this morning was more assault than trespass. At the time of his exile, Ralph retaliated by denying Claudia his study. Boundaries in their spacious home in a suburb of Detroit were marked like the invisible fences put up for confining dogs. They were startled at what they had done and wanted to undo it but didn't know how.

The no man's land between the study and studio, once a showplace of ordered bookshelves and carefully chosen art, fell into chaos. The crises in the newspapers had long since been resolved. Tables were littered with unpaid bills for which neither of them would accept responsibility. Dishes, clotted with moldy food, hadn't made it to the kitchen. Clothes Claudia meant to give away lay on the sofa in a heap of past events.

A maid came in once a week for a few hours. Actually the maid was many maids, whose various names neither could recall. The women never lasted long and all developed ways of working around the disorder. Sometimes they took a maternal approach, bringing cakes and cookies baked with their own hands, but when they returned the following week the offerings were still there, untouched. Occasionally they would sweep away the disorder only to be dismissed for misplacing some scrap of paper Claudia or Ralph insisted they could not do without.

The winter had been long and Ralph felt in these first days of spring that he had crawled on his hands and knees through a long and endless tunnel. He headed for Claudia's studio because something in the encroachment of the sun onto his study floor, his chair, and then as a gentle hand on his shoulder gave him a terrible hunger for a human voice. They didn't own a television, and the cleaning lady would not be there for another day. Even their latest conflict, the battle of the thermostat, was wordless. Ralph had years of broodings about the universe and the future of mankind to communicate, but, unable to help himself, his first words on entering Claudia's studio were a complaint, "We don't have any tea."

He looked around the studio to see a gallery of unfinished paintings, his wife's work of fifty years of indecision and discouragement. She had never developed her own style, but had promiscuously embraced the work of first one artist and then another, her perception always a little off as she punished herself for encroaching on someone else's vision.

Seeing Ralph, she was alarmed. *Was he ill?* No, he stood upright. Quickly she hid her worry. "You don't know where the store is?"

"I thought you might have some here."

"Are you suggesting I'm stealing from the kitchen?"

"It hadn't occurred to me that you knew where the kitchen was."

Their meals were taken separately. When he thought of it, he grilled a burger. Usually he made do with a can of soup and those little round crackers that bobbed so merrily about. Claudia ordered out, regarding women in the kitchen as stereotypical. Due to arguments with restaurants over the quality of the food, the time of its arrival, and its cost, her rotation of take-outs had come down to a Korean place, which had the advantage of not understanding a word of her complaints. In turn she didn't understand the woman who took her order, so Claudia was reduced to dining on whatever they sent; lately it had been mung bean pancakes and seaweed soup.

Ralph had meant that afternoon to remain if not cordial, at least neutral, but he had fallen into the usual, and he retreated to the silence of his study. It wasn't always like this. There were occasions when they came together, bright, silvery drops of mercury that rolled beside each other, never touching. Ralph, now retired, had headed the English department of one of the city's smaller colleges. From time to time he and Claudia were invited to department functions. Or there might be an invitation to the opening of a gallery where Claudia had been an exhibitor or, more often, a client.

When the head of the English department where Ralph used to teach retired, Ralph sent Claudia the invitation he had received to Gregory's retirement party. On it he scrawled, "Do you wish to go?" Notes flew back and forth.

"I don't care one way or the other."

"We should leave by six."

"Six is too late. The expressway will be crowded."

"We don't have to take the expressway."

"It's much shorter."

And so on.

Once at their destination they simply wandered away from each other, flotsam on a wide sea, and then at a predetermined time came together as if their confluence was a matter of currents and feckless breezes. The invitations became increasingly rare as their friends were driven to take sides.

There was the rare visit of one or the other of their two daughters, who came more and more infrequently, uncomfortable with their parents' attempts to suborn them. They were big healthy girls. Diana was a rheumatologist occupied in research rather than engaged with patients. She lived every day on the cusp of discovery. The other daughter, Lydia, headed the legal department of a large company where she fended off suits brought by dissatisfied customers looking for a buck. Throughout their childhood they were regularly reminded by their parents of the importance of work; how their mother's painting and their father's articles must come before a swimming meet or a class play. They believed their parents when they looked up from the desk or easel to say, "Not now, dear, this can't wait." Both girls were outgoing and cheerful with many friends and parent surrogates. Having seen what distance and isolation had wrought, they took another way.

Claudia's taste exceeded her talent so that she was never satisfied with her paintings, and one day she awoke to discover art had become ephemeral. It was no longer hung on walls but was created by videos or flashing lights or designed after a designated time to disappear all together, the gallery director explaining how much greater the impact was of a piece of art that was destined to be destroyed. The moment of the destruction was also a work of art.

"And if they had burned *War and Peace* so that no one in the future could read it?" Claudia asked, thinking she had the clinching argument.

The face of the gallery director flushed with excitement. "Just imagine being there for *that!*"

Ralph had spent the last twenty years on a book about Emerson only to find he had bet on a loser. Emerson with his concept of *Bildung*, the reformation of the individual over the reforming of a nation, was no longer a popular concept. Everyone liked the way they were.

Each day for Claudia and Ralph began with the wisp of an idea, but when they put out their hand to grasp it, the notion would not be handled. In isolating themselves from each other, they had become like the experiment in which the subject is hung suspended in the darkness of a tank, all sensory stimulation removed. Nothing occurred to them and they couldn't even talk about that. They reworked old ideas and followed the careers of people whom they had known and who were now successful. They reread favorable reviews of their work in yellowed newspaper clippings.

Ralph considered how his career might have blossomed under a wife who believed in him and who devoted herself to his care. Claudia had dismissed his Emerson: "A ghoul who dug up the corpse of his wife and son from their graves." Claudia was convinced a trip to New York instead of down the aisle would have changed everything for her.

Twenty years earlier it was a different story. On a trip east, Claudia had dropped Ralph off in Boston to research his Emerson book and to present a paper at a meeting of the prestigious New England

Followers. Claudia went on to Provincetown for a workshop led by a well-known artist. Traveling with her were Diana, eight, Lydia, ten, and Helga, an au pair from Germany. Ralph and Claudia parted with affection, convinced the recognition they craved for themselves and for each other was within grasp. Everything back home was temporary, a springboard. He had avoided close friendships and involvement in the city's organizations, for he anticipated an appointment at a prestigious university. Ralph regularly checked real-estate listings in the promised land of Cambridge and Princeton, even researching schools for the girls in those cities, keeping in mind Claudia's insistence on his settling at a university close to the museums and galleries of New York.

In Cambridge the library informed Ralph that much of the material Ralph needed would not be available. A member of their own faculty had requested it.

"How long is it checked out for?"

"Oh, at that level books aren't checked out, they're lent."

"So for how long is the material lent?"

"When it's lent there is no specific time."

"You just say good-bye to it?"

"We encourage research and publishing by our faculty and do what we can to facilitate it."

"What is he publishing?"

Ralph was left with the knowledge that a recognized scholar was coming out with a book on Emerson that would surely trump his. He transferred his hopes to the paper he was to give the next morning, gratified to see on the meeting's registration list representatives from several prestigious universities. In the *New York Times* and the *Times Literary Supplement* were advertisements for positions in those universities. Unfortunately the ads in the *Times* dwelt on equal opportunities, and in *TLS* the UK was designated as "a very high target" in recruitment, so two strikes against him. Maybe if his ancestors had just stayed in England.

Like a college freshman studying for his first exam, Ralph stayed up all night going over his paper, crossing out and putting back. He used up all the little packets of coffee in the hotel room and at about three in the morning opened the minibar, downed a Scotch, and selected a packet of chocolate raisins. Early in the morning he took a cold shower as if he were facing a licentious temptation instead of giving a paper on "The American Mind, a Wilderness of Capabilities," the quote borrowed from Emerson.

The Followers had scheduled his presentation for eight in the morning. Ralph imagined a large audience eager to begin their day, and indeed the crowds in the hallway were promising, but by eight fifteen there were fewer than a dozen people in his room. Two of them came up to ask if there were any openings in Ralph's department and, when told no, drifted out of the room. Ralph had neglected to look at the schedule. At the same time he was giving his paper, a professor rumored to have engaged in hand-to-hand combat with a prominent author was speaking in an adjoining room to an overflow audience.

In Provincetown Claudia attended a workshop each day, and Helga took the girls to the beach, where she painted her toenails and wrote long letters to her boyfriend, who was working as a waiter at a resort in northern Michigan. After staring it down for an hour, the girls ventured to the edge of the sea, tempting the waves and collecting shells and gull feathers.

Claudia painted, and one day the famous artist nodded approvingly at her work. That was the day Diana and Lydia complained of headaches. Claudia blamed the sun. When a rash developed on their chests and arms and even their scalps, Claudia took them to a local doctor, who diagnosed chicken pox and gave them shots to minimize the illness.

Hearing the diagnosis, Helga said, "What if they get on my face?" When Claudia refused to give Helga money to fly to Michigan, she stole it from Claudia's purse and left a nasty note.

The girls could not be left alone. Claudia called Ralph. "Couldn't you come down for a few days? You said the research you wanted wasn't available and you've given your paper, so why do you need to stay there?"

He could not abandon this center of learning to be a nursemaid. He couldn't face Claudia. She would see at once that his hopes had slid away, that nothing in their lives would change, that they would always be where they were. He couldn't move out of his hotel room. He was ordering room service, unable to handle the logistics of getting to the hotel dining room, much less the Cape. "I'm afraid it's impossible to get down there just now," he said. And it was.

She heard the desperation in his voice, but what could be more desperate than her own situation with the famous artist just down the road and two sick children on her hands. She tried to get a babysitter, but one look at the girls and the applicant fled. Desperate, she bought the girls sun hats, long-sleeved shirts, and slacks, and took them with her to the workshop, which was held *en plein air.* The girls dug listlessly in the sand, their wide sun hats drooping over their flushed and spotted faces, their slacks and buttoned shirts incomprehensible in the heat. When one of the students, taking pity on them, offered to share a cold drink, Lydia politely refused. "We've got chicken pox and the doctor says we ought to keep away from everyone because they're catching." The student spoke to the famous artist, who gave Claudia a furious lecture and sent her back to the cabin with instructions to stay there.

When they returned home, Claudia and Ralph were barely speaking, leaving the children to act as intermediaries. "Ask your father." "Tell your mother." The parents were immigrants from two distinct foreign lands, their language intelligible only to their children. They had failed, but what hurt most was that they had failed each other.

Returning from the attempt to breech Claudia's study, Ralph watched a little flurry of letters drop through the mail slot. There was a letter from each of their daughters. He thought it must be something in the juxtaposition of the planets causing the daughters to announce simultaneous visits. It was not the planets at all. The daughters had received notes from their parents' last maid, who had copied out the daughters' addresses and written identical letters to both of them: Dear daughter, I used to work for your folks and I think you should know the house is a mess and they don't eat. Also they act strange. Please don't say I wrote you.

The letters were not signed. As in so many urgent acts it was difficult to deduce whether the deed was born out of love or revenge. The daughters, who were not close, but who were fond of each other, got on their cells. Their first impulse was to delay, for they were both engaged in important work, but something about the very phrase "important work" nagged at them, having heard it often as children. They found a time.

Diana arrived first. The vulgarities of the airport left her with what she knew was the unrealistic hope of walking into a home where some scrap of parental care would be exercised. She wanted to be welcomed and cared for, relieved of her suitcase and led to a comfortable chair. A cup of tea would be offered and thanks given for her efforts in getting there. She skipped over her experience of recent years to recall the living room of her childhood with its art and books; its chintz-covered sofa and yielding pillows, the Oriental carpets worn to muteness. Into this room she placed her parents; her father, hair tousled, wearing his Irish fisherman's sweater, tortoiseshell glasses slipping down his nose, red-faced with eagerness to tell her of how a work of his had been cited in a popular book. Her mother in a painter's smock, a bright scarf wound around her throat, bracelets sliding on her arms, her hair pulled back by a band and gathered into a tentative chignon, eager to show her cuttings from a recent exhibition.

Or even earlier. When she and Lydia were children, their mother hired a nanny to take care of them during the day so that she could immure herself in her studio with no childish interruptions. Late in the afternoon the nanny would leave them with the admonition not to bother their mother, but heedlessly the two girls would open the door to the studio with its rich smells of paint and turpentine and creep inside. Often they were chased away, but if her day had been productive, their mother would welcome them, eager to show off her work, pleased to explain what she was attempting. There were days when she dressed them in old shirts of their father's and gave them scraps of canvas, paints, and a brush and cheered them on, saving their efforts to show to their father, who was sure to lure them that evening into his study, usually forbidden, to read to them scary bits of Hawthorne or Poe, making sure they had words as well as pictures.

The two wraiths that greeted Diana put an end to fantasy. She was no longer a daughter but a doctor. She saw evidence of old age and severe malnutrition: petechial hemorrhages, ecchymosis, thin and scaly skin, osteopenia, hair dry and sparse, and protruding bones. They had both lost height, causing her to feel too large, a changeling in some fairy tale of misplaced identity.

Her father took her hand in his hand, with its bruised skin and veins like blue rivers flowing to secret places in the heart. "Diana, come into my study. I need to talk with you."

Her mother took her other hand in a powerless grasp. "First, come into my studio. There are things you need to know."

"Let me get off my coat and shoes. Then we'll sit down right here. I want to talk with both of you." She cleared a chair and then watched as her parents settled down on the sofa, leaving a cushion between them. She tried to guess the nutritional value of the dried food on the plates that were scattered around. "You're both so thin. What are you doing for meals?"

"I have no idea what your father is doing. I have my own sources."

"I grill a burger."

"There have been no cremations in months."

"Since when have you been concerned about my food habits?"

"Curiosity, not concern."

"I have certainly been curious about what it is that smells like low tide in those paper cartons you leave about."

Diana broke in, "When Lydia gets here, we'll have to find a way to put some weight on you. You can't go on like this. You're fading away." Indeed they looked to her like revenants in need of luring back into the corporeal world.

Sensing the threat of being handled, Ralph was firm. "I'm getting on very well. Of course I can't speak for your mother."

"Of course you can't speak for me. I can speak for myself. I don't need fattening like some force-fed goose. Georgians who eat nothing but yogurt live forever."

"Another of your gross exaggerations."

"You don't exaggerate when you say you are getting on very well? You haven't mentioned your fainting last week."

He was silenced by surprise. How had she known that? He was left with a novel crumb of pleasure at the thought of her fretting over him.

"I don't suppose you have a doctor?" Diana asked. "Never mind. I'll give you both a good going over. Right now I'm starved. There must be something in the kitchen I can fix."

Later that evening when Lydia arrived, Diana walked out with her to her SUV, ostensibly to help with luggage. "We got here not a minute too soon. Not a bite of food in the house. They're at each other's throat. This can't go on. We've got to find a place for them." For years their parents had arranged for their young daughters' care, with little trouble to themselves. Now it was the daughters' turn.

The next day Ralph and Claudia watched their daughters sweep through the house like lumbermen clear-cutting a forest. They scraped down the kitchen and brought in food. They cooked a dinner with lamb chops, two kinds of vegetables, and a salad.

Claudia and Ralph were wary in each other's presence. They picked at the food. "Your stomachs have shrunken," Diana said.

Lydia said, "For dessert there's chocolate ice cream."

Considering how treats were offered to serve a purpose, Claudia and Ralph were driven to exchange glances, startled to find themselves in touch.

When their parents retreated to their separate rooms, the daughters murmured together, commiserating with each other, for each of them had her own problem. Diana was in a relationship with the head of the dermatology department who had a wife. "It's going nowhere," she confessed. "I sometimes think it's just an excuse to keep from getting married. I worry I'll end up like Mom and Dad."

"It doesn't have to be like that. Nick and I are fine. Unfortunately he came with a fifteen-year-old step-troll who would like to poison me."

The next day the daughters took off together in Lydia's SUV to visit assisted-living facilities and picked The Olive Tree. The director said, "We want our residents to know that just like an olive tree the most succulent fruit is born after many, many years of growth."

Succulent was not the adjective the daughters would use for their parents, but the home was clean and bright, the employees pleasant, and there was no odor. The residents camped out in chairs in the hallway were disconcerting with the insistence of their presence, as if they wanted all the world to see what they had come to, however, the day's menu tacked on the door of the dining room was reassuring with its attention to all the necessary food groups.

They signed papers and made a substantial down payment. As they walked out into the open air Diana said, "I hate to force them, but if they go on like this, they'll be dead in a year." She had seen vagrants wheeled into the emergency room and wondered why they had no one in their lives to see to them. She did not want her parents making an appearance in a hospital in a state of starvation. She was troubled, though, by a doubt as to the value of food. They had provided food for their parents these last days and seen little change. Was there something else that was causing them not to thrive? Their hearts beat and their lungs worked, but when she expressed her doubt to Lydia, her sister spoke only of next steps.

"I've drawn up the guardianship papers. We own the house, so selling won't be a problem." Some years before, their parents, unable to agree on financial decisions, had elected to set up an irrevocable trust, each happy the other was shut out of further decisions. "If we can get the house in some sort of order, it should bring a decent price. Certainly enough to pay for their care. I've got a realtor coming tomorrow."

Ralph and Claudia, from the fastness of their own rooms, watched the house stripped. Every item carried out was an event erased from their lives. Never again would they be able to put their hands on their past.

There were sops. Lydia offered, "You can pick out a dozen or so books, Dad. The local library has a mobile that stops at The Olive Tree if you need anything else." A dealer came and selected several boxes of Ralph's books, happy to see first editions, but disappointed that they were by less desirable authors, no Hemingway, no Fitzgerald, lots of New England writers whose poems had been memorized by schoolchildren long dead.

There were no pleasant surprises on the walls. The paintings their mother had purchased long ago were those of obscure local artists who never made it. The disposition of their mother's own paintings was more difficult. A cursory inquiry indicated dealers were not interested. "We can't tell Mom that," Diana said. "We'll say we love them and we're going to split them between us. I really would like to keep a couple of small things. The rest we'll load in your wagon and you can get something for the frames."

At dinner that night, Claudia looked past the Cornish game hens, the buttered corn kernels, and the baked squash, and, for the first time in many years, caught Ralph's eye. She wanted him to do something. Her appeal with its suggestion of an affirmation of their connection shocked and then thrilled him. Alone in his study he considered whom he might call. Their close friends on the faculty who were not dead had retired to Phoenix or Fort Meyers. In the phone book was an ad for an attorney with an 800 number. When he called, some nice woman listened patiently until she learned their money was all tied up. "It's probably for the best," she said and told him to have a nice day.

On the afternoons the house was being shown, Lydia took them for rides up and down the suburban streets where people their age were out exercising small, feisty dogs. Ralph in the front seat and

Claudia in the back tried to guess when they had fallen out of the parade. When the prospective buyer was gone, Diana would text Lydia and Lydia would drive them home.

The day they moved into The Olive Tree, their possessions fit into the station wagon. They were introduced to the director, who welcomed them. "Your daughters have told me all about your distinguished careers, and we feel very honored to have you with us." She smiled reassuringly at the girls and addressed the rest of her remarks to them, a principal addressing parents while the children looked on. "Your father must join one of our book clubs, and we have a craft club that I'm sure would suit your mother."

Once their parents were settled in, the daughters kissed them good-bye promising to write and visit. They left their landline but not cell numbers. Then they were gone.

Ralph and Claudia shared a bedroom and a sitting room so small they saw it could not be divided. The sitting room was furnished with two comfortable chairs, each with its own lamp, a coffee table, a small desk, and a bookshelf on which the girls had set pictures of themselves. Ralph thought of their first apartment, not much larger than this. He was a graduate assistant and Claudia was getting her masters in fine arts. He remembered a party they had given. He invited some other graduate assistants and, full of himself, the head of the English department who was guiding his thesis. Everyone told him it was unheard of for an assistant to reach that high, but the great man came, drank their cheap wine, took off his necktie, and did his imitation of the university's president. Claudia invited a group of women painters who, after seeing her work, accepted her for membership in their organization. That was before Claudia rose up against the hiving off of women into seg-regated groups.

There were heated arguments at the party. Sides were taken, Claudia supporting art and Ralph standing up for the written word, but after their guests left they made love.

Wrenched from their home Ralph and Claudia felt vulnerable, like turtles or mollusks pried from their shells, every inch exposed and undefended. Ralph recalled a famous writer who shot and killed his wife and then turned his gun on himself. The note he had left behind spoke of old age and an unworthy world. Kindness was implied. Ralph extracted Claudia's easel from one of the still-unpacked boxes and set it up next to the window. "The light's not bad," he said.

Claudia took down the pictures of the girls and put out Emer-son's complete works. They would not kill each other after all.

TRAVELOGUE

wasn't happy at the thought of three of us in one room, but New York hotel rates and Tim's enforced four-day workweek said that's how it would have to be. My twenty-year-old daughter and I had roomed together at her high school softball tournaments and on trips to audition universities, but I worried Emily would be uncomfortable having her father at such close quarters. The arrangement was that Emily and I would sleep in the king-sized bed while Tim thrashed about on a cot we had to maneuver around as if it were a large sleeping dog. Tim complained. "Why doesn't Emily sleep on the cot? She's the thinnest."

"Dad, that's disgusting. I'm not going to spend one second in a room where my parents are together between the sheets."

I knew how she felt and wondered why I hadn't I been able to say that to my parents on a trip we took together when I was Emily's age. It was the semester break of my junior year at college. As a treat my mother and father took me to an upscale resort in Hawaii, the last place I wanted to be, but I relented when I stepped off of the plane. The air, velvet or cashmere, made me want to stroke it. I remembered my philosophy professor quoting some Greek who said air was the first cause of all things. I became optimistic.

The resort had loggias and pillared passageways with glimpses of gardens and the sea. There were primitive totems set around and on the walls, subtly colored Hawaiian quilts. I thought I might be happy there until we were shown to our room. It was spacious with louvered doors that slid open to give a view of the ocean. I waited to be taken to my own room, but a cot was rolled in.

"Am I staying with you?"

Dad said, "Have you any idea what a room at this place costs?" Mother looked hurt, as if I had returned a carefully chosen present.

I didn't see how I could manage both days and nights with them. I was always a secret child. I had been ill when I was young, and months in bed made me feed on my imagination, an imagination that vied with the world in which I had to do my living. When I was too much with people, they challenged what I had concocted. Immediately I thought of ways to be by myself; I'd spend the days on the beach or in a remote part of the gardens.

Mother assigned each of us a dresser drawer and place in the closet to hang our clothes. In the bathroom she set out three glasses. Seeing how there would be separations, I felt a little better. We dressed for dinner, which was a formal affair as if the hotel were a cruise ship floating on an imaginary sea. The maître d' had a British accent. He introduced himself as Alex. He was a young James Mason with the same lock of dark hair falling over his forehead and Mason's jaded look that suggested he saw much farther ahead than other people did. I guessed Alex was in his late twenties. As he seated us I gave him a complicit smile to let him know that I understood how painful it must be to toady to tourists like my mother and father.

The minute he heard an unfamiliar accent from a taxi driver, a waiter, or, for that matter, a fellow guest at a party, Dad wanted to know where the person came from. He wasn't hostile to foreigners. He wasn't prying. It was a geography lesson, but it embarrassed Mother and me.

"You sound like you come from England," he said to the maître d'. "What part?"

"I'm from London."

I was thrilled. It was as if the authors I loved: Woolf, Forester, and Graham Greene had suddenly materialized right there before me. I wondered how I could let him know I was familiar with his world.

Dad wasn't finished with his quiz. "What brings you all the way to Hawaii?"

"I'm hoping to learn something about the food industry."

It was hard to get around the pedestrian "food industry," but I understood that he couldn't be reading all the time, he had to make a living. Alex looked around as if he were afraid of being overheard. "To tell you the truth, I would have preferred a city on the mainland, but there wasn't anything available."

"You must not have looked in the right places. I'd be surprised if you couldn't find something in our own city."

"I'd certainly welcome any suggestions." Alex reverted to his more formal manner. "Please let me know if there's anything I can do for you."

There was an orchestra, older musicians staring off into space as if they had nothing to do with the music they were producing. Mother and Dad put their napkins on the table and headed for the floor. They had joined a dance group at our club and were pleased with their extra little steps and their daring separations and coming together. Dad had a flirtatious look on his face and Mother did a little wiggle of her hips. I thought it was sickening. When they came back to the table and Dad asked me to dance, I demurred. He was hurt by my refusal.

"I suppose you think I'm not up to date enough for you."

"No, you and Mom are great. I'd just rather not."

Mother said, "I hope you aren't going to be in one of your moods on this trip. Your father's gone to a lot of trouble, to say nothing of expense to bring us here."

"No. I really don't feel like dancing. I like watching the two of you."

My refusal spoiled things and they didn't return to the floor.

Our courses were garnished by tiny orchids and described to us in detail by our server as if we couldn't see what was before us. All the while I watched Alex. A couple of times he noticed and looked quickly away. I wondered when he was off duty and where he lived. I imagined him in an austere room writing a novel about American tourists in Hawaii, something along the lines of Evelyn Waugh.

By the sixth sense that always brings bridge players together, Mother and Dad found another couple, and went off with them to a room where tables were set up. I settled on a terrace chair with a view into the dining room. I had the self-importance of an only child, seeing myself the center of the universe, imagining because I was thinking of Alex he must be thinking of me.

Looking back I'm embarrassed by my self-absorption, but my greatest regret is my inability to see how pale was the fiction in the books that consumed me beside the stories of my parents' lives, which at that time meant nothing to me. My father came from a small farming community. When Dad was in the eighth grade, his father was killed in a fall from a silo. Dad had to leave school to help his older brother with the farm. There were fourteen-hour days and long winters, when the chill of the farmhouse with no heat but the kitchen stove sent Dad to the animal warmth of the cow barn to study his brother's old schoolbooks. When he was eighteen that brother married. When he and his new wife went on their honeymoon to Detroit, to give Dad a treat they took him along. Dad found work in a tool and die company and never went back to the farm. Now he owned the company, but he believed his lack of schooling and his years of working with his hands created a barrier keeping him from rewards he was due.

Mother had grown up on the edge of an exclusive suburb. Her own mother had been eager for her daughter to make friends with the wealthy children who lived nearby. My grandmother was a seamstress and was sure that if only she could dress Mother as expensively as she believed the other children were dressed, Mother's acceptance was assured, but Grandmother's template of old *Vogue* magazines was disastrous: too many ruffles, pleats, and dressy fabrics just at the time children who could afford all of those things were turning to jeans and dressing like workers. Mother once told me, trying to make a joke of it, that when she was finally invited to her high school prom, her mother spent hours sewing pearls on her dress. Mother lived her entire childhood in costume.

All this was known to me, but at the time, instead of entering my parents' lives, I only wanted to get as far from them as I could so my own life could begin.

Getting ready for bed that night with my parents in the same room was like preparing for a doctor's exam, only small pertinent parts of our bodies were exposed. The new setting gave to Dad's familiar pajamas and Mother's peach silk gown a surprising eroticism, so that seeing them climb into bed together, I felt like a voyeur. I tried to formulate words I would use to ask Mother if we could share a bed, but the words all implied my mother and father ought not to be sleeping together, or worse, that their sleeping together suggested something more, as if my middle-aged, reserved parents had become libertines.

When I was young, sleeping near my parents was reassuring. Still stored in the attic was the crib that once stood in their bedroom. I remembered Sunday evenings when we returned from a long drive to my grandmother's farm with me curled up on the back seat among baskets of sweet-smelling pears and peaches from the farm's orchard, my parents' presence a safeguard against the dark through which the car carried us.

In the hotel room their presence was massive, a stone king and queen stretched out on a tomb. In the early morning hours I slipped out of the room onto the balcony, where I finally fell asleep on a chaise, and where my distressed parents discovered me and my urgent need to separate myself from them.

I was to go fishing with my father that morning. He had arranged to charter a boat and engage a guide. There were two other couples sharing our trip, Marilyn and Jack, and Kay and Alvin. I don't remember their last names. They were in their thirties, friends traveling together. The women were in shorts and sandals. They brought suntan lotion, nail polish, postcards to write, and copies of *Harper's Bazaar* and *Vogue*. The wives had no intention of fishing. Jack and Alvin had a good-natured rivalry going on between them and were eager to get a rod in their hands and start competing.

Dad questioned Captain Spence about the chance for marlin and was disappointed to learn we would be fishing for tuna and shark. My father explained to the captain that it was the first time I had been deep-sea fishing. "I want her to have a successful day." Dad was used to giving orders.

"We're all looking for a nice day," the captain said and went about checking the sea surface temperature in a business-like way to let us know he knew what he was doing. "We'll troll the W pattern, two long on the outriggers and two short on the flat lines." The men watched the captain bait my line and then baited their own.

Once the lines were out, it was hard not to feel expectancy. Even Marilyn and Kay, busy with talk of who was staying at the resort, broke off to check the tension on their husband's lines. Dad watched my line, not his. He had talked me into coming on the boat and he meant for me to catch fish. I was glad I had come. The sun on the water would give me the tan I was hoping for. The two women included me in their talk, holding up fashion illustrations from the magazines for me to see, and asking what I thought of them, Marilyn assuring me, "With your slim figure you could wear anything." I'm embarrassed now to remember how indifferent I was to their friendly overtures. I thought it was my due. I considered their lives idle and pedestrian, representing everything I intended to elude. I think now that to a casual observer, as I had been at that time, my life today would look very much like theirs.

Jack hooked the first tuna, Alvin the next. The captain put down his rod to handle the gaff. He cut into the gills of the fish, "to bleed them," he explained, and then threw them onto ice. After Dad pulled in his second tuna, he exchanged positions with me. "See if this isn't a better spot." I was embarrassed because Dad made it sound like the position assigned by the captain had been done on purpose to thwart me. The captain didn't miss the inference.

By noon all three men had pulled in several fish, but I hadn't had a bite. I didn't really mind. There was enough going on in the boat to keep me interested. Jack caught a shark, and when he slid the fish in their direction, the two women jumped up with unconvincing screams.

The captain produced a picnic. The men and Marilyn had beer and Kay and I, Cokes. President Reagan had just announced he was running again and we got into a lively discussion with the captain, Jack and Marilyn on one side and the second couple and myself on the other. Dad was uncharacteristically quiet. When the leftovers were cleared away he went up to the captain. "My girl's not getting any action. I didn't pay a child's rate for her. I paid the same as those two men and myself."

Everyone heard him. If land had been visible, even after seeing the shark at close quarters, I would have jumped over the side of the boat. The others suddenly got busy, the men baiting their lines and the women turning pages.

"There's a lot of luck in fishing," the captain said.

"Dad, I'm having a great time. I don't care whether I catch a fish or not."

I could see from the set of the captain's chin he was furious. To make things worse, Dad refused to pick up his rod and just stood there staring out at the ocean as if his not fishing would increase my chances. It was late in the afternoon when I finally hooked a fish. The women put away their magazines to stand beside me; the men coached me. Dad had an enormous smile on his face. The captain gaffed the fish, a forty-pound tuna, and complimented me on bringing it in by myself, though he had given me a lot of help.

Later, when we got off the boat, everyone shook hands and said their good-byes. The captain avoided Dad's hand, but he shook mine and looked like he felt sorry for me. All I felt was embarrassment and anger with my father. I was too young to understand how obtuse love was.

Getting ready for dinner that night, I relished the feeling of my silk dress slipping over my burning shoulders and back. I took trouble with my hair. Alex was at the entrance to the dining room looking for us. He greeted us by name and led us to a choice window table with a reserve card on it. After the captain's studied indifference my father relished the special treatment. He liked the deference Alex showed him and wanted to give something back. He wanted Alex to know that he had influence in high places. "What kind of job would you like if you could find something back on the mainland?"

Alex was prepared, his words so carefully crafted I was sure the special treatment he gave us was the result of his thinking about Dad's casual mention of the ease of finding a job in our city. "I enjoy the work here, but of course it's seasonal. The resort has to let staff go in the summer. Actually I'd like the security of year-round work, and then anything that gives me a chance to engage with people. I think that's something I'm rather good at."

Dad understood and appreciated ambition. He looked at Mom. "I might have a word at the club." He turned to Alex. "Our country club is looking for a maître d'. They've interviewed a couple of applicants, but I'm on the committee so I know they haven't settled on anyone. Give me your résumé and I'll pass it along."

As he left Alex gave a little bow and said, "Madame," to Mother and "Mademoiselle" to me, giving me a shy smile.

"Well," Mother said, "it looks like you've made a conquest."

"Don't put ideas into her head, Elly. The man is just trying to be courteous. That English accent would lend a little class to the club. Certainly would be an improvement over Robert."

Robert, the current maître d', was on his way to retirement because he had taken to calling a couple of the members, members he had known for twenty years, by their first names.

Mother and Dad were playing a final rubber of bridge. I was settled in the lobby with a book keeping an eye on the dining room. The orchestra was packing up their instruments and Alex was saying good-bye to the last party. A couple of waiters were setting up for breakfast. One of them came over to Alex. The waiter was young with a dark tan and shoulder-length blond hair bleached by the sun and pulled into a ponytail. At first the two of them appeared to be having a friendly conversation, but something changed, and whatever the waiter said made Alex turn and walk away. He was about to head out the service entrance when he saw me.

He came over and asked, "You didn't go to the movie?" There

was a movie every night. Tonight's film was *Tootsie*. I told Alex I went only to foreign films.

"I'm afraid you won't see any foreign films here. They have to cater to a larger group."

"Are you finished for the evening?"

"Yes, I'm going for a walk on the beach. I need to decompress." Of course it was an invitation. How could someone who had been on his feet for five hours look forward to a walk? I wished he hadn't used the word "decompress."

"I was just thinking of doing the same thing. Would you mind if I tagged along?"

"What would your parents think of you with an employee?"

"My parents are in a killer bridge game."

"I have to go out the service entrance. I'll meet you down on the beach."

I was in a movie of my own making, walking along a tropical beach in the moonlight, carrying my sandals, my silk dress blowing in the soft evening breeze, Alex barefoot in a dinner jacket, his trouser cuffs rolled, the tide coming in so that we had to keep moving up on the sand to escape the licks of water that chased us. Nothing that romantic had ever happened to me.

"I envy you living in London," I said. "My favorite writers are there. You English are so good with words. It must be all the Latin and Greek you learn." I was heavily influenced by *Masterpiece Theatre* scenes of elderly British schoolmasters instructing reluctant students.

"I went to a comprehensive. No Greek and not much Latin."

I had hoped he had gone to Eaton and Cambridge and was just

playing at being a maître d'. But maybe it was not a novel he was writing, but a memoir like Orwell's, although an elegant resort in Hawaii was not quite like the underground hell of Orwell's London restaurant. I put Alex with the angry young men, Osborne and Amis and Alan Sillitoe. What better way to see the foibles of the upper class than to serve them? "You must hate your job."

"Why would I? I thought it was a bit of luck to land here. A man came recruiting and hired a friend of mine as a waiter. Because I had been the maître d' of a private club in London, they took me on. If I tell your father about working in a private club, would that be a help? I could mention it tomorrow night."

I was disappointed with the talk of jobs. I didn't want to think that was why he was interested in me. I asked, "What do you do all day?"

"If there's going to be a private party, I make the arrangements, and I take over at lunch on weekends when we get people from the other hotels who come here for a taste of luxury."

"No, I mean when you're not on duty. Don't you ever go into town? I'm trying to find something to do to get away from my parents."

"Nothing much to do in town. There's a park and a zoo where I went once. Not like the zoo in Regent Park, no lions or elephants, lots of snakes and pretty birds."

Alex turned back toward the resort as if we had come to a barrier when there was nothing there but endless beach. I said, "I don't suppose you'd show me the park?"

"Sure. I have tomorrow off. One of the staff has a car they'd let me borrow. What about your parents?"

"They're taking a tour to see the Pearl Harbor Memorial."

Later I explained to Dad, "I'm not being unpatriotic. I just want a day to wander on my own."

When Mother and I were alone in the room for a moment she said, "Your father is very disappointed with you, Beth. He can't understand how you could come this far and not go with us to see something so historical. What exactly do you have planned?"

I was always taken aback when Mother understood me. I considered myself scrupulous, but I exempted parents from the truth because of their unfair power. "I don't have anything planned. I just want to soak up some atmosphere. I haven't been anywhere but the resort. I want to see some Hawaiians. I want to see the real Hawaii."

I slept well that evening. I was no longer an uncomfortable part of a threesome. I had my own partner.

It was the first time I saw Alex in something other than his dinner jacket. The Hawaiian shirt and the slacks that were a little too short were disappointing. I would have loved jeans and a scruffy T-shirt. Alex looked too much like my father on his day off. There was an awkward moment when I tried to pay the admission to the park and Alex insisted. The park appeared unsettled, the plants new, the trees too young to shade us from an insistent sun. The birds were bright colors, a red I'iwi, an elepaio like a blue ghost, bright orange and yellow birds. All by itself in a cage was a robin, its name carefully printed, its habitat North America.

What was he reading? I asked Alex. Was he as disappointed as I was with Graham Greene's latest, *Monsignor Quixote*? Had he read the review of it in the *Times Literary Supplement*?

"I don't get much time for books. I've been trying to read Michener's *Hawaii*. With all the families and the generations, it's taking forever. My roommate who's a waiter here at the resort is reading Michener's book about space. He says it's actually pretty good."

What Alex wanted to talk about was Detroit. "Where was the country club located? How much were apartments in the city? What were salaries like? What could you do in the town? What did I think his chances were? Would they be hiring waiters?" His friend was looking for a job, but if that weren't "on offer," it wouldn't keep Alex from taking the job. It was obvious Alex was interested in a position at the club, not me.

It wasn't even noon, and we had said to each other all we wanted to. Alex seemed eager to return the car. I said I had some shopping to do and I would take the bus back.

I wandered around town and got back just in time to change for dinner. Mother and Dad were unusually quiet. I thought they were still disappointed I hadn't gone to the Memorial with them. When Alex greeted us, Dad didn't say a word to him. As soon as he left us, Dad asked, "You were running around with him today?"

When I was silent, he said, "You may as well tell us the truth. Someone left a note in our mailbox. They saw you at the park and thought we ought to know. I don't like anonymous notes, but in this case, they were doing us a double favor."

"Jim, don't make it sound more than it was," Mother said. "They might have just run into each other."

I didn't use the excuse Mother offered. "Why shouldn't I have spent time with Alex?" I hated my father's snobbishness. "He was just showing me the zoo."

"He was cozying up to you to get that job, which he certainly won't get now. The last thing we need is another club manager who doesn't know his place."

Across the room the blond waiter was watching us. I didn't like his smile.

Dad decided in the days we had left that we ought to see the other islands. In Maui and Kauai we stayed in less expensive resorts and I had my own room. I loved the privacy, but walled off from my parents I felt exiled and looked for excuses to wander into their room.

In New York our daughter, Emily, stretched out on the king-sized bed and regarded us fondly. "We've got to do this more often. I feel like I'm five years old again, no responsibilities, no decisions, no trouble I can get into, just the two of you doting on me. Heaven."

When I was seventeen I started feeding babies at night. For three or four months at a time I'd stay in someone's home. While the mother slept I'd prepare the formula, hold the baby, fill the bottle, and pop the nipple in the baby's mouth, and the mother would sleep. My presence in the home was minimal: a toothbrush, my nightgown, and the robe my dad gave me for my birthday, picked out I was sure by his girlfriend. I had to sneak into the family's pattern, and it always took a while. Some families said everything, their lives spilling out. I'd know what they were thinking, and they'd encourage me to speak up. They had nothing to hide, and they believed I didn't either.

The Raychers were my third family. At first they hardly noticed me. Their computers were always alive, the house quiet but for the little ping indicating a new e-mail or the ring of a cell, hers "Can't Cry Any More" and his "Something's Always Wrong." Sheryl Crow was about all they seemed to have in common. They didn't have much to say to each other. I sensed words stockpiled in all the rooms like ammunition awaiting a great war. It could have been my own home two years ago.

By ten the Raychers were on their way to their bedroom, and I was in the nursery with Nicki. The first time Mrs. Raycher handed over the baby, she told me, "I really didn't want someone else caring for her," as if it were all my idea. "My husband says babies don't mind who feeds them." Which wasn't very flattering to me.

Even early in the mornings Sophie Raycher was always perfectly put together, as if she used hair spray all over. The sad thing was she never seemed pleased with the result.

When I asked how long she would need me, she was vague: "I can't say. You know how things can happen." It was said in an expectant voice, as if she saw something good might come from a hurricane or an earthquake.

Each night before taking off for the Raychers' I'd have dinner with my mother. Since the divorce, Mom had more or less stopped cooking, as though the preparation of meals was part of a contract that had expired. She'd pick up something on her way home from work, pizza or an ethnic thing, Middle East, Chinese, or sushi. Sometimes she'd wander into the past and happier days, and serve me SpaghettiOs and carrot sticks. I hated the nights she had wine with dinner. By the time we got to dessert she was insisting that although Dad had done unforgiveable things she would never say a word against him to me because he was my father and it was important to preserve my relationship with him, as if I could have a relationship with someone who wasn't there.

After supper I'd leave for the Raychers'. It was late April, but the leftover winds of winter whipped around the corners, taking you by surprise. Walking along the dark streets I'd check the houses, where often the only sign of life would be the glow of a television screen connecting the world to the house but no one in the house to one another. I wanted to think that inside those homes everyone who was supposed to be there was there.

I went from the more modest part of the suburb, where Mom and I now lived, to the Raychers' upscale neighborhood, where instead of numerals the addresses over the front door were spelled out as if the more expensive houses were entitled to words. We had once lived down the street from the Raychers, but Mom and Dad sold that house during the divorce proceedings. Dad moved into the city with his girlfriend, and Mom bought a house a mile and a half away, but still near my high school where I was a senior. Every time I opened the door into our small home, I expected more — more space and more people.

I knew who the Raychers were before I took the job. One of my friends lived near them, and I had seen the pregnant Mrs. Raycher climbing awkwardly out of her car. She had a job coordinating events for the wives of conventioneers. I imagined her ascending and descending the mountainous stacks of escalators at the convention center, herding women onto and off of buses, watching over them like a mother.

Dan Raycher was a member of the law firm where Mom's divorce lawyer worked. When Dad's lawyer said Dad didn't have to pay for the college I had set my heart on, but only a state or local college, Mom got a little hysterical. Her lawyer put her in touch with Mr. Raycher, who was a local recruiter for the college I wanted. He asked about my grades, and after Mom showed him some stories I had written he contacted the university and got me a scholarship. When I told Mom it was the Raychers' baby I'd be feeding, Mom was pleased.

The Raychers' house had all the extras. The kitchen had silver swaths of stainless steel, and a chandelier of pots and pans dangled over a landing field of granite. They must have run out of money, though, because the climate-controlled wine cellar had only a single bottle. In the nursery where I had a cot there was a wrought-iron pumpkin crib like Cinderella's coach with big round wheels and a crown on top. When you got to the little morsel in the crib, it was an anticlimax. In my sloppy clothes I felt out of place, but Nicki didn't care, nuzzling my scruffy T-shirt while she slurped away at her bottle. I had Cinderella dreams for her. She would grow up to be the first woman president and invite me to her inauguration. I had lowered my own ambitions to helping others achieve something.

After Nicki dozed off I'd read myself to sleep with my English assignment. Our teacher gave us a choice of two novels. Most of the boys in class chose *Moby Dick* and most of the girls Hawthorne's *The Scarlet Letter*. I never wanted to hear the word adultery again, so I was with the boys. I read somewhere that Hawthorne copied out *Moby Dick* for Melville. That was such a nice thing to do. I liked Melville and his "watery world." I liked Queequeg and Ishmael sitting cozily together in bed, chatting and napping and sharing a cigarette. I wanted people to get along.

Around one or two in the morning Nicki's mewing and hiccoughing awakened me. I'd pull on my robe over Dad's old boxers and Tiger T-shirt and tiptoe down the stairs. I'd open the fridge, take out a bottle, and put it in the warmer, and, after testing the formula on the back of my hand, return to the nursery. If Nicki was fussy and starting to cry, to avoid waking the Raychers, I'd take her down to the kitchen with me and feed her there.

We watched each other. At her age she didn't have a lot she

could tell me, but I filled her in. "You can't get too attached to anyone," I told her, "especially not me. In a couple of months I'll be gone. And take a look at the divorce rate. You have to keep something back for an emergency." I wished someone had warned me.

Helina took care of Nicki during the day. She was a Polish woman who had recently come to this country and didn't have a lot of English. She wore clothes that must have belonged to someone much larger, making her look like she was waiting to grow into them. She got there before the Raychers left for work and stayed until the Raychers returned. When she arrived in the mornings, she checked the blender, gulping down any leftover smoothie from the Raychers' breakfast. The minute the Raychers were out the door Helina put together an enormous breakfast for herself. Helina had questions for me. How did the kitchen faucet work? It was one of those fancy ones that looked like a piece of sculpture. She wanted the dishwasher demonstrated. "I don't want to bother my lady," she said.

When I mentioned to Mrs. Raycher that there was a lot in this country that was new to Helina, Mrs. Raycher said women new to this country were the only ones who would stay for ten hours at a stretch and Nicki needed the continuity.

Helina didn't approve of Mrs. Raycher working and leaving the baby all day. Her eyes widened and her hands got into the conversation. "No family for the baby? Grandma? Auntie?" Helina had taken a dislike to Mr. Raycher. "He throws my lady out to work. I had a man like that, but he's back in Poznan."

One morning I found Helina in Mrs. Raycher's room trying on her coat, stroking the fur collar and turning around in front of the mirror. She didn't seem at all embarrassed to be caught. "My lady deserves nice things. Mr. Important makes her work hard so he can buy himself a big car."

I knew all about the new car. I usually got to the house around eight. In spite of all the fancy pots and pans, Mrs. Raycher seldom cooked. I would find pizza and Chinese food cartons in the wastebasket still smelling of soy sauce or oregano. The night before, as I let myself into the house, I heard Mrs. Raycher yelling, "That's costing half my salary. You expect me to go out and leave my child to strangers so you can ride around in some goddammed chariot."

"I'm paying for the car. You can pay your Saks' bill; it amounts to the same thing."

"That's bullshit. I need decent clothes for my job. Let me quit and I'll be happy to go around naked."

When they heard me they shut up, but in the middle of the night when I went down to heat a bottle I found Mrs. Raycher in the kitchen having a cup of herbal tea. In her ragged nightie and without all the fixings, she looked half her size. I had the feeling she was waiting for me.

"I hope you don't think I'm abandoning the baby by not doing the night feedings."

I was surprised she cared about what I thought. "No, not at all. You probably need your rest after you work all day."

"But you need your rest, too. You have to go to school in the morning."

"I go right back to sleep." Which was a lie because once I was awake there was a whole slew of things I would think about, starting with the slammed doors and angry conversation I had once heard at home and was hearing now at the Raychers'. Nicki was hearing them too.

"I was sorry to see your parents sell their house. I don't want to pry, but I understand they're divorced."

"Yes," was all I said. The Raychers were buying my time, not my life.

"It must have been hard for you."

"I think I hear Nicki crying." I couldn't wait to get away.

"If you ever want to talk about it," she called after me, "remember I'm here for you. And call me Maida."

Next morning when I arrived there was that loud silence between the Raychers you sense after people have been quarreling. When she heard Nicki crying, Maida brushed past me and started up the stairway, calling over her shoulder to Mr. Raycher, "This is what I should be doing, not running around trying to make the wives of car dealers happy."

Dan Raycher dropped into the nursery that night. It was around eleven and I suppose he saw the light under the door. I was wearing my robe. I had washed my face and had my hair tied back. When he knocked softly, I thought it was Maida and said, "Come in." When I saw it was Mr. Raycher, naturally I was embarrassed, but he didn't show any awkwardness seeing me like that.

He settled on a child's chair much too small for him and watched Nicki for a while as if he had casually picked up a book and gotten interested in it. Finally he said, "Your mother showed me some stories you wrote for English class."

I was angry with Mom about that, but I knew she thought it would help me get the scholarship.

"They were personal."

"I think she just wanted me to know you had some talent along those lines. You say they're personal? I guessed they were. Your parents just got through a divorce?"

"Yes," not looking at him. I was trying to keep my distance. My best friend Tracey warned me I had a tendency to latch onto older men. At school I worked hardest for Mr. Curtis, my math teacher, and I got to choir rehearsal early to kid around with St. Stephen's music director. I even opened the door for the postman when I saw him coming instead of letting him drop the letters into the mail slot. I was in search.

"I don't mean to pry. I know you've heard us arguing, and I know Maida talked to you last night. I wouldn't want you to get the wrong idea about us. It's not only money, though we certainly need her salary. I just don't think it's a good idea for her to be sitting at home all day. She's a very talented woman and energetic. She needs to be kept busy. My own mother never really reached her potential."

What was his mother's potential? Did she know she had failed in her son's estimation? Mr. Raycher had lovely soft brown hair that fell across his forehead, and I imagined his mother brushing it gently back with a secret smile for its waywardness. Didn't that count for something?

"Being your age I'm sure you can see that women can't simply define themselves as mothers. Maida doesn't understand that now, but when she moves up she'll thank me."

The escalators again. I wanted to ask, "Isn't it her choice?" but he had been so nice about getting me the scholarship. To change the subject I brought up the university I would be attending. What had it been like when he was there?

"It's where I met Maida," he said. "I was bussing dishes at her sorority house to help me get through law school. Some of the girls were snotty toward me because I worked there, but not Maida. She admired my ambition, and we found we had a lot in common." He stopped as if he were considering what that might have been. "Best years of your life," he said. "You'll love it there." He glanced at Nicki, treating her as if she were off limits, not attempting to take and hold her. After a little while, he went away. I wouldn't have minded if he had stopped by another evening, just to talk, but he never did.

I had always been closer to my dad than my mother. He was less complicated. I never had to search what Dad said for hidden meanings. When he had to say something he knew would hurt me, he just said it and got it over with. Mom was more given to slow torture, the bad news coming around corners and always with the implication that however bad the news was for me, it was worse for her, so I couldn't really complain without looking selfish.

The Raychers gave me Saturday nights off. You would think I'd be happy to escape the nursery, but I would wake up in my bedroom at home sure I heard Nicki crying. I knew I wasn't supposed to get attached to the babies, but babies aren't all alike. You see the way they change a little every day and you get interested and a little frightened because they're watching you, taking you in, looking to you to show them what it's all about. I even went online and read about what to expect, and Nicki was way ahead, already smiling. She'd reach for things and follow me with her eyes. When I bragged about her to Helina, Helina only said, "Babies, they're all the same."

Maida was in the kitchen again that night. Her eyes were red, and next to her cup of tea was a mound of used Kleenex like a lot of dying doves. She said in a tentative voice, "As long as I'm up I could give Nicki her bottle."

I figured out she was there for just that reason. I didn't want to give up Nicki. I know it sounds selfish, but I felt it was my time, not Maida's. Maida noticed my hesitation and right away she said, "No, you go ahead. She's used to you."

I saw how disappointed she was, and I handed Nicki over thinking it was sad that she had to sneak down to feed her own baby. She took Nicki in her arms, holding her tightly as if I might change my mind.

"You probably wonder why I'm not taking care of Nicki," she said. "I want to more than anything, but Dan thinks we should pay off more of our mortgage so we're secure, and he wants to join the country club. The golf would be good for his business. He says it's better if the baby is more independent, but why should a baby have to be independent?"

She used a damp Kleenex to wipe away tears that were falling on Nicki like providential rain. "Maybe I could get myself fired."

The next morning and for several mornings I noticed that Maida went to work without makeup and that her suit jackets and skirts were mismatched, but her employers must not have noticed because she kept her job.

After that I made a point of bringing the baby downstairs while I prepared her bottle. Maida was there to hold and feed her. It was in the middle of one of those feedings that Mr. Raycher appeared in the kitchen wrapped in a worn plaid bathrobe with a button missing. Without his glasses and suit he looked like he had been thrust unarmored into battle. Maida gave Nicki and the bottle to me as if she had no right to her, explaining, "I just happened to come down for some tea and found Ardis here with Nicki."

"I thought we were paying Ardis to take care of the baby at night."

"Why should we pay someone? That doesn't make any sense."

"You were the one who said you couldn't work and be up all night feeding the baby."

"I said I'd give up work."

"Why should you give up a perfectly good job to do work that anyone can do? It's a question of economics."

"But I want to stay home. I hate my job. You should see what the women do to get front seats in the bus, and yesterday half of them wouldn't get off to visit the aquarium."

"Everybody hates their job. I hate my job. I'd like to stay home and take care of the baby and lounge around all day."

Nicki started to whimper. I gave them a furious look and fled upstairs so they wouldn't see me crying. It was everything I had gone through the last two years. Which was worse, losing your father after you were used to him, as I had, or losing him before you ever got to know him, as it looked like Nicki might? In the morning I waited in my room until I heard Helina arrive and the garage door open. From the window I saw the two cars leave.

When I came downstairs Helina asked, "Something bad happened? My lady was crying when she left."

"They had a disagreement."

As I was leaving I heard Nicki's whimpers. "I think that's the baby," I said.

Helina was busy exploring the fridge. "Good exercise for her lungs." She pulled out the carton of eggs. "My lady forgot to buy bacon again."

Nicki's window was open, and as I hurried away I could hear her wailing.

The next day I received an invitation to my father's wedding and the reception that followed. There was a note from Dad saying how important it was to him and to Julia that I be there. I knew Mom would hate my going, besides, there was Nicki, so I declined. I had met Julia. Dad explained she was going to be a part of both of our futures. "I don't want you to see her through your mother's eyes. She's a wonderful person."

The three of us had dinner together at a fancy restaurant in town. I know Dad was hoping I'd clean up and look like the daughter he probably was selling to Julia just as he tried to sell Julia to me. Instead, knowing Julia was the fashion co-coordinator at an upscale store, I arrived in my usual torn jeans and flip-flops. When I left the house, Mom didn't say anything about the way I was dressed. She must have been thinking, "Let him see the mess he's made of his daughter's life. Let him see what she's come to."

Julia didn't flinch at the way I looked. She knew that, being only a few years older than I was, she couldn't do the mother thing so she chose to be the older sis. "We'll have a shopping binge. You have a fabulous figure with those shoulders and slender hips. I'd love to pick out some clothes for you."

But I wasn't going for that. "Clothes aren't how I define myself," I said. "Maybe we could go to a bookstore and I could pick out some books for you."

School was out. It was daylight now when I walked to the Raychers' through the suburb's parade of blooms: the daffodils, then the tulips and irises, the peonies, and finally the roses, all doing what was expected of them. Nicki slept through a couple of nights. I was tempted to wake her up, knowing I would soon be leaving her. Afternoons I would go out of my way to pass the Raychers' house. Helina was a great one for fresh air for Nicki. If the weather was good, the carriage would be parked in the shade of a big maple tree. Helina would be inside cleaning and doing the laundry or maybe having a snack and trying on clothes. I'd stop by and say hello to Nicki, who would reach out to me, curling her fingers around my finger, holding on tight.

There were arguments now almost every evening. The Raychers were so self-absorbed they didn't seem to care that they were overheard, and I didn't know how to stop listening. When my parents had quarreled, I marched out of the house, slamming the door. Sometimes I thought I might try that and take Nicki with me. I knew babies reacted to things even in the womb, so Nicki must be upset.

The Raychers moved into separate bedrooms. Mrs. Raycher explained that she had her own room because she needed her sleep, as if sleep were a finite thing and, given proximity, her husband might snatch it from her. I worried that they would separate, that Maida would get a divorce. Nicki would lose a father. I hadn't been able to stop my father from leaving, but I was going to do something about the Raychers. I was going to do one last good thing for Nicki.

For the note I used a scrap of newspaper I found on the street.

I held it by the edge of my T-shirt. I printed. The next afternoon I stopped by the Raychers' yard. Nicki was in her carriage and Helina was nowhere to be seen. I had on sunglasses and a cheap wig and gloves. Nicki saw through the disguise right away and put her arms up to be held. It was only a couple of blocks to St. Stephen's. In the middle of the spring afternoon the suburban streets were deserted. I left the carriage at the front door of the parish house and stood a half block away where I could keep an eye on Nicki. I had one of those cells you could buy and pitch. Lucy Eckert answered the rectory phone. She's the secretary who runs the parish office. Priests don't have housekeepers anymore so Lucy also does things like picking up the priests' dry cleaning, and once a week she grocery shops for them. She says rotisserie chicken and frozen mac and cheese are big favorites. She also says they buy their coffee themselves because they don't want the parish to know they go upscale.

That evening when I got to the Raychers, there was a police car parked in front of the house. I wanted to turn and run. I hadn't anticipated the police. I had skipped that step. I made myself walk into the living room. A policeman, not a lot older than me, stood with his hands in his pockets looking around the room like a prospective buyer. He gave me the same appraising look. The older policeman was writing in a notebook like they do on TV police shows. Sitting on the sofa was a whimpering Maida hugging Nicki, and beside her Mr. Raycher with his arm around both of them. He had the shocked look of someone trying to catch up with a life going in a whole new direction. A priest was inching toward the door. I was relieved to see it was Father Schmidt and not Father

Quilty, who knew me. Hovering in the background was a distraught Helina.

The older policeman turned to me. "Who are you, young lady?"

I was too frightened to say a word, but Mr. Raycher spoke up, "That's a girl in the neighborhood who comes at night to take care of the baby."

"Every night? Where are you and your wife?"

"We're right here. But my wife needs her sleep."

"What about the girl?"

"We pay her to take care of the baby."

"When does she get to sleep?"

Maida broke in, "I said the same thing, officer. It doesn't make sense to hire someone to do what I could perfectly well do myself. I'm certainly not blaming Helina, but if I had been here taking care of Nicki this would never have happened." She turned on Mr. Raycher, "I hope you're satisfied."

His face crumpled. "It must have been a crazy person. Thank God they thought better of it."

Father Schmidt gave a marked-down smile. "Fortunately it all turned out very well. I have to tell you, Father Quilty and I were quite excited when we discovered her. We got an anonymous call at the rectory, the voice obviously disguised. The person told us to look out our front entrance and there was the buggy. It was just like stories you hear of babies left at the door of a monastery. Of course I could have brought her right to you since your address was pinned to the blanket, but a priest rolling a buggy might be misunderstood. It's always best to go through the authorities." He had his hand firmly on the doorknob. "You have my name and address," he said to the policemen. "I'm afraid I have to leave. I have a meeting of the finance committee."

Everyone at our parish gives good marks to Father Schmidt as an administrator. Contributions are up. After he left I made myself ask, "What happened?"

Helina said, "It wasn't my fault. I put her out in the yard for her fresh air just like usual. I got the ironing. I got the bathrooms."

"No one is accusing you, Helina," Mr. Raycher said. He explained to me, "Nicki was left at the entrance of St. Stephen's, not that we are Catholic, but I suppose the kidnapper was." He turned to the older policeman. "I wouldn't want too much made of this. In my business, that kind of publicity is a killer."

The policeman flipped shut his notebook. "Probably some eccentric. I'll have to notify Child Services, though. They'll want to check out the home."

"Investigate *us*? That's outrageous!" Maida turned on Mr. Raycher. "You can do the explaining. Leaving Nicki all day wasn't my idea."

The younger policeman informed her, "It's nothing personal. We always have to call them when something like this happens." He turned a little too eagerly to me. "We'll want your address and phone number, Miss."

After Helina and the police were gone, Mr. Raycher explained that they wouldn't need me any more. "We've really appreciated your help, Ardis. You've been like one of the family, but in view of what's happened I agree with my wife that it's best if we make some changes. Helina will be leaving, too."

I never heard from the police, and the Raychers must have had connections because the story didn't make the newspaper. During the summer afternoons, I'd see Mrs. Raycher, her hair pulled back in a scrunchie, no lipstick, prancing along with Nicki in the carriage. On the Fourth of July when I went with my date to the fireworks at our local park, the Raychers were there with Nicki. I wanted to go over and pick her up and hold her, see if she remembered me, tell her everything was going to be all right.

THE ARK

Lisa and Ralph had been married for three years. In the past when Ralph traveled, Lisa remained at home, but these breaks in their relationship had become more and more like putting down an uninteresting book: there seemed to be little reason for taking it up again. They were afraid another separation would be mortal. Ralph suggested Lisa travel with him on his upcoming trip.

Instead of staying at a hotel, they were renting a house while Ralph revised the psychological testing program of a Philadelphia firm. A number of employees of an unacceptable strangeness had slipped past the personnel director. Ralph knew what cunning questions might be asked to keep from the sales departments employees who set fires in wastebaskets or whose obsessions would not allow them to ride in elevators.

Lisa, a freelance interior designer, had hoped their quarters in Philadelphia would be sparsely furnished. She could then add a few touches. The white canvas sheets painters used could be thrown over the sofa, a cheap straw rug, and a pillow or two in a rough hand-loomed fabric of no color would work wonders. Among these light furnishings they might survive, like butterflies loose in some airy enclosure where there was no danger, the fine, necessary dust of their wings rubbing off on each other.

Perversely, the company settled them into a cluttered house, which had been lived in by the same family for years. Lisa found the presence of the family stifling. There was not a square inch of the house on which she could make an imprint. Chairs awkwardly placed looked more awkward when she tried to rearrange them. The house refused to submit to her. It had a stubborn rhythm of its own that waited for her to take up.

Everywhere she looked she was confronted. Tables were littered with bits of puzzles, coy china animals, vases of dried flowers faded into ghost colors, dog-eared playing cards, and half-finished needlework. Everything was ordinary—or worse. There was actually an ashtray in the shape of a bird whose crest was made up of safety matches.

Discarded dog collars lay about. Old knobby bones turned up under the couch cushions. Their books were hopeless: Louis Bromfield, Edna Ferber, *Readers Digest* condensed novels, a heavily underlined chemistry textbook, copies of *Black Beauty* and *Eight Cousins* with free pages.

The children of the house had evidently grown and left—but not entirely. In one bedroom she found a shell collection leaking sand, in another, tennis and swimming trophies.

In the kitchen, hardly anything was whole. Spoon handles had been bent in the disposal. The glasses were chipped. The teakettle was scorched and the counters covered with indelible rings. Looking through a card file, Lisa found recipes for Jell-O salads with marshmallows and casseroles made with canned soups.

A river had surged though the rooms, leaving behind the detritus of years. It was painful for her, committed as she was to the irreducible. She wondered how people could live in a house and not be crushed by so much evidence of one another's presence.

It was high summer and she thought to escape into the yard, but the disorder pursued her. Violets and lily of the valley crept into the flower beds. Wild grapevine twined around the roses. The lawn was weedy and there were worn patches to mark the spot where on summer afternoons a perpetual baseball game must have been played. A swing with a broken seat dangled from a tree branch. A rusted rake lay on the ground next to a deflated inner tube.

The house itself was substantial, but Lisa could see no grace in it and nothing but ugliness in its miscellany. In Lisa and Ralph's New York apartment, she had placed everything so carefully—the movement of a single ashtray resulted in instant disorder. In this house, disorder, even chaos, might exist undetected for long periods of time.

One evening she found Ralph looking into one of the boys' rooms. He appeared interested. She and Ralph decided before their marriage not to bring children into so unpromising a world, a world that any day might be destroyed by a tyrant's short temper. Lisa felt betrayed. Why didn't he look around the house and see the mess that became of two lives when they expanded?

She fought the home's disorder by keeping to a rigid schedule. She worked all day on a commission to decorate the condominium of a wealthy man who had just been divorced, a man who shared her taste and with whom she had too many lunches. But her sketches would not come out right.

When she awoke in the morning she was exhausted by the richness of her dreams, and she worried that the confusion of the house's disorder had found a secret entrée into her consciousness, like a mouse silently moving its collection of acorns through a tiny chink.

While Lisa felt like an interloper, the house didn't trouble Ralph. He seemed to belong there. She saw criticism of herself in the grateful way he sank into the ugly, overstuffed furniture. At home he disapproved of the contemporary Italian chairs she picked out. "They're so sculptural," she had pleaded.

"But you can't get your ass into them."

There appeared to be some system beneath the shambles to which Ralph had the key and she did not. He could put his hand on a pair of scissors or a screwdriver.

"How did you know it was there?" Lisa asked.

"If it were my house, that's where I'd keep it."

They seldom talked to each other about their feelings. It seemed useless, a waste of time, like reading a travel book for a trip you never planned to take, but now she asked, "Doesn't it bother you? The house? It's like wearing someone's unwashed clothes."

"I don't know. They were probably decent people."

She felt a rebuke and wondered if he believed as she did that good taste was a moral quality. Then something occurred to her. "Why did you say 'were'?"

"I wasn't going to mention it. You seem bothered by the house."

Lisa resisted Ralph's watchful solicitousness, a trait borrowed from his father, who had been a doctor in a small country town. "Don't be silly, just tell me."

"The reason the house was for rent is that the owners were

killed a month ago in an automobile accident. Their kids are grown and scattered and need time to make plans. They'll be getting together to divide the stuff after we leave. For now they're renting the house; an empty house is an invitation to vandals."

There was no reason for her to be upset over the death of two total strangers, but later in the kitchen Lisa's hand trembled as she picked up the dead woman's salt cellar, opened the dead woman's refrigerator, used the dead woman's stove. And those were only three of the things the dead woman had relinquished.

In bed that night she thought how, in some countries, the dead were laid out in beds. She and Ralph lying there inert, not touching, were light as ghosts. They had always been scrupulous in the way they allotted space to each other in bed. But Lisa could not keep herself from moving close to Ralph. The warmth from his body seemed the last warmth left on earth. Ralph welcomed her. Their lovemaking had become increasingly rare. Tonight it proceeded cautiously and with a certain resignation, as a present is opened when you think you might return it.

Lisa dreamed the flower beds on either side of the yard were parched and the grass brown with drought. She was standing under a darkened sky in that moment of abeyance when a drenching rain might come or might pass over. Both possibilities seemed to lie in her hands.

In the morning they were shy with each other, diffident as they passed the toast and butter, speaking only words that were absolutely necessary but wanting to say more. As with prisoners who tap messages to one another through thick cell walls, there was an urge to communicate beyond their means.

After Ralph left she examined the photograph albums, anxious to restore the house to its owners. Until now, mortality had not touched her. Her parents were alive and well. Her father was a CPA in La Jolla and played eight holes of golf every morning before breakfast. Her mother edited a newspaper in a small Oregon town and had a young lover.

She opened an album and was disappointed to find the family ordinary. It was like seeing a choir descend from the loft of a church and come among the congregation only to find the makers of the glorious music were commonplace: young men with acne, women in uninteresting clothes.

In the first volume were pictures of a young couple, the man in the uniform of a naval lieutenant, the woman in a full skirt and short, chunky fur jacket. A few pages later a baby appeared, large-headed, fish-mouthed, lying on its stomach, its head propped up on bowed arms in a first attempt at assertion.

She hurried through the albums, flipping the pages. More babies, and then a picture of the house in which she and Ralph were living. She was startled at how the trees that now soared high above the roof had once been no more than saplings. All that uncurbed growth disturbed her.

The family traveled. They posed in front of the Lincoln Memorial, the Capitol Building, Mount Vernon. Their faces looked smug, as though the monuments were a result of their own cleverness. Numerous Christmas and Thanksgiving celebrations were recorded. In one of the pictures she recognized the very chair on which she was sitting. It was unnerving. She felt the family materializing along with their furniture.

She put the albums aside. Soon the snapshot children would come and take into their own homes the furniture and china, the knickknacks and photograph albums. Family stories would be repeated. Even the hideous bird with its crest of matchsticks would be fondly exclaimed over and carried away.

In Lisa and Ralph's apartment there were no family mementos. She had expressed a firm disinterest in Ralph's parents' things, so his brothers and sisters had taken them. When Lisa's mother and father divorced, they simply discarded everything to begin new lives. If tomorrow she and Ralph were killed in an automobile accident, their possessions would enter the world anonymously.

The house encroached on her work. She found herself adding fussy touches to her sketches for Walter's condominium. Right in the middle of Walter's elegant silver-and-black entry hall she put a grandfather clock exactly like the one in the house. In Walter's nutmeg brown-and-flax study she sketched a braided rug, identical to the worn one on which her feet were resting.

She heard doors slamming, the sound of a stereo coming from one of the bedrooms, a motor revving up in the driveway. Once she was sure someone had called down the stairway to her, and she had nearly answered before she recognized it as another trick played on her by the house, another ruse to pull her into its possibilities.

Her struggle with the house was lost in the kitchen. They were going out to dinner and afterward to see a new French film, but late in the afternoon a summer storm broke. Plumes of rain fanned across the windows. Puddles grew in the bare depressions of the yard. Water sluiced along the gutters and bubbled up from the storm sewer to flood the street. It seemed foolish to venture out. She thought she would make a frittata or an omelet *pipérade*. But when she looked in the refrigerator, she was surprised to find, where she had remembered several, only a single egg. She explored the cupboards and found a package of dried noodles, cans of mushroom soup and tuna. She consulted one of the dreadful recipes and put together a casserole. For a joke she decided to use another recipe from the file—a dessert concocted of cookies and whipped cream. The card on which the recipe was written was smeared with chocolate fingerprints. She would make Ralph— who often praised the refinement of her cuisine—laugh at these people. They would eat a ritual meal and break the house's spell.

Ralph grinned at her as he asked for a second helping. "Would you believe my mother used to make this stuff?" He attacked the dessert with the same relish, turning her practical joke into a celebration.

They sat at the kitchen table together talking long after it grew dark. Ralph became effusive, even garrulous. He spoke of his childhood. She was amazed to learn he was fluent in Italian. How could she not have known that? He told her of a great aunt who, on a visit to Bermuda, had danced with the Duke of Windsor. He said he hated his high school basketball coach's guts because he played one boy against another. When his dad had taken him hunting for the first time and had left him sitting on a stump, an eight-point buck had passed right by him and he hadn't had the heart to shoot it. Sometimes he was sorry he was keeping all the weird people from getting jobs. What difference did it make if you were afraid of elevators? Didn't she think it was possible eccentric people might know something other people didn't? He said he would like to have a back yard and build a sailboat in it. On summer nights when it rained he recalled the shiny wet poplar leaves that shook against his bedroom window when he was a boy.

She told him when she was thirteen years old and baby-sitting for their neighbors, the husband tried to seduce her. Once she spent a week on a farm, and the butter was white, the bedrooms unheated, and the bathwater shared with her cousins. She said she thought Picasso's pottery was not altogether successful. She wished someone would explain to her the unlikely relationship between mathematics and music. On rainy summer nights, she said, she thought of lighted cottages on little lakes.

They went upstairs, leaving the dirty dishes on the table. Lying in one another's arms, they listened while sheets of rain washed over the house. She knew it would hold because of the weight of all that was in it.

MIGRATING

"**W**e're out of our minds to drive into Detroit at night." Liz
Grayton was waiting for her husband, Tom, to fasten
her bra strap; something her own fingers, stiff and
knobby, could no longer do. She was cautious, less trusting than
her husband. Her family had been larger than his, and so she had
endured more deceptions and deaths; repetition had its impact.

"I don't like being a prisoner in my own home." His voice was
mild, amicable. His appearance was relaxed; age and gravity loos-
ening all that could be eased on his portly frame. This temperate
manner combined with an artlessness allowed him to be candid,
even blunt, without offending. In the trust department, he had
been assigned the difficult accounts—women wanting to invade
capital to redecorate their homes, men insisting their portfolios be
jazzed up with glamour stocks. He treated them like willful sons
and daughters, correcting but not scolding. They sensed his benevolence and responded.

"We aren't prisoners," Liz said. "We were out all day yesterday."

"So why not tonight?"

"That was during the day, and we were with a group." Their
suburb had a wilderness club that arranged for lectures and the occasional trip for its members. A wilderness club in a suburb suggests a paradox, an affectation, something theatrical or bogus. Not

so. Consigned to hundred-foot lots, why wouldn't the residents of suburbs yearn for lectures and films on something remote and spacious? Why would they not want to peer into caves and view the world from mountaintops even if it was only on a six-by-six-foot screen? Liz and Tom enjoyed seeing places too far for possibility, but not too far for imagining. When in winter the little redpolls and snow buntings down from the Arctic tundra appeared at the Graytons' feeder, Liz and Tom welcomed the connection with a far land.

Liz had kept her figure and her husband still enjoyed watching her dress. Self-conscious about the wear and tear of age she tried to distract him: "Didn't you find those butterflies yesterday sad?" She hesitated over her jewelry, wondering what she might risk on a trip into the city.

"What was sad about them? They were exhilarating." A bus had taken them across the river to Canada, to a park on Lake Ontario where monarch butterflies gathered by the thousands before their migration to Mexico. It had been one of those thick autumn days with the sun making a broth of light. The park ended in a spit of sand stretching for a quarter of a mile into the lake. The orange-and-black monarchs were scattered helter-skelter over the sand; pendant on twigs; clinging to blades of grass; perched on stones that appeared strangely soft, sheltered as they were by the wings of the butterflies. The world pulsed. Every few minutes a small progress of the monarchs took flight over the lake, sometimes drifting back with the light wind, sometimes fluttering into the water. A few sailed along until they were out of sight. Liz was surprised at how she was caught up in their successes and failures. She was from a generation brought up to protect, but the one person she had most wanted to shelter, their son, Jimmy, had escaped her care. From time to time they heard from friends that Jimmy had called them, either for money or just to pass the time of day. He kept in touch with these parents of his childhood friends, who were always happy to hear from him and would report, "He sounds just fine."

Liz rescued one of the monarchs from the water, holding it in her hand until the wings dried and the butterfly was airborne. She followed its flight among the reckless multitude until she saw it flutter down into the water again, well beyond her reach.

"It was eerie moving among them," Liz said. "I thought we ought not to have been there. It seemed a private thing, like a family celebration or an alumni reunion."

"I don't think we were any more to them than walking trees."

Liz chose a lipstick. "I'm beginning to feel excited. How long has it been since we've been downtown at night?"

"We were at Bienvenue for the Slaters' anniversary."

"But there were six of us in the car."

"All in our seventies, hardly a formidable group."

"Why were you so anxious to hear the symphony tonight?"

"They're doing Mahler's 'Das Lied von der Erde.' I haven't heard it in years, and the soloists are all excellent."

"It's such a gloomy thing—everything darkness and death." She preferred music with a melody, Strauss or Puccini.

He had first heard the Mahler his senior year at the University of Michigan. A famous orchestra had come to the campus for the May Festival. In those days, Ann Arbor was still a small town with a lilac bush in every back yard; you walked to the auditorium from fragrance to fragrance. The Mahler pointed to innumerable sorrows ahead. In one night, his bright, uncomplicated life muted into a kind of chiaroscuro. He fell into reality.

Before leaving the house, Liz and Tom went through the usual routine of locking up; even in the suburb you couldn't be too careful. At the entrance, before she set the alarm, Liz stopped for a minute to consider the garden. She had swept the terrace clean of the fall's first dried leaves that morning, but the leaves were back, rattling lightly with the evening breeze. It was becoming impossible to keep up with the garden work; little by little the wild grapevines and errant lilies of the valley were taking over. It was the same inside. When she closed the draperies, little puffs of dust started up: the whole house suffered from sins of omission. Their cleaning woman, who had worked for them for thirty years, had arthritis and could barely move. Although they offered her a generous pension in hopes of getting someone younger and stronger, she would not retire. "Whatever would I do with my time?" she asked. Tom and Liz could give her no answer.

Liz asked, "Do you want me to drive?"

Tom's cataracts caused problems at night. It was time to have the cataracts taken care of, but he hated to walk through the doors of a hospital. "They'll get their hands on me and never let me go." He slid into the driver's side. He still felt the way he had at fifteen driving for the first time—an automobile could take you anywhere. Pulling out of the driveway he asked, "Should we take the expressway?"

"I don't know that one way is better than another. When the

Mitchells took the expressway, they were bumped by someone pretending it was an accident, and when they pulled over, they were robbed. Angie Barker stayed off the expressway, and when she stopped for a light a man broke the car window with a brick and stole her purse. Let's split the odds; go down on the expressway and come back the other way."

Their Mercedes, top of the line, was eight years old. He kept it because he didn't like the downsizing of the newer models. For the same reason he engaged suites when they traveled. In all other things he avoided ostentation, but spaciousness had to do with the soul. He was a virtuous man but not an ascetic; he could not have practiced his faith in a cell. He needed around him, at all times, reminders of God's generosity.

Liz sat beside him nervously smoothing her skirt, trying to temper her excitement. She had become a master of relinquishment, giving things up minutes before they were taken away, believing divestment preferable to foreclosure. She had let go of the city, and this returning to it, this getting it back, had the wistfulness of a date with an old lover.

"We used to go to the symphony every week," she said, "and to openings at the Art Institute. Do you remember when I chaired the reception for the Atwater Williams show at the museum?" Williams's paintings were graceless. What you could recognize of the world was askew, faces and bodies distorted into grotesque parodies, flowers witched into monsters, houses like cages or prisons. Liz rejected the curator's suggestion of a few stark blooms and a minimalist refreshment table. Instead she had filled the gallery with rich flowers and heaped the table with silver and cornucopias of fruit. She coaxed the women into wearing velvet and beaded chiffon gowns to the opening. Surrounded by so many splendors, the paintings appeared to be lies. Someone told her afterward that the curator had thought just the opposite.

The expressway that drew them into the city was reassuring. The banks were green with newly planted sod. In this age of cell phones, the emergency phones that had once dotted the expressway with their suggestion of peril were gone. Tom drove in the slow lane, keeping to the speed limit and letting other cars pass. Liz kept her foot near an imaginary brake. They headed west as the sun dropped toward the horizon lighting and gilding the city's skimpy skyline.

"It looks like the promised land," Liz said. She meant it. Against her better judgment she was entertaining a flood of memories. "Mother and I used to shop downtown all the time, both of us in hats and white kid gloves. Mother arranged her shopping list by floors: third floor, linens; fifth, lingerie; seventh, millinery and better dresses; twelfth, handbag repair." Her mother had carried the same purse as long as Liz could recall. In the face of suburban malls, the department store had been demolished, and the downtown had gone with it, although lately new businesses had appeared, surprised and a little tentative, but of course, not the ones they missed.

"There's my old neighborhood," Tom said. He pointed to the steeple of a church visible from the expressway. It marked what had once been a German enclave. He had been born in that neighborhood, but his parents left when he was still in the early grades. For years his family returned to the church on Christmas Eve. The altar was decorated with pine trees and the church smelled like a forest. The pastor of his childhood had been a strong man, but not hard to please; that is, although demanding he was predictable. The church stood empty now.

"Why do the English call the churches they close down 'redundant'?" he asked Liz.

"I think it means superfluous, unnecessary; an awful judgment."

She tended to take things personally.

They exited the expressway and lined up with the other cars waiting to get into the garage. The safest parking spaces, those near the elevator, were taken, and they had a long walk across what seemed a great stone cave. There was a strong odor of exhaust and the echo of voices and engines reverberated around them. Tom took Liz's arm. She felt more fragile to him than he recalled, and he worried that for some reason she was losing weight. In the crowded elevator she stood close to him, and he felt a rush of doubt about his ability to protect her. Then they stepped out into the reassuring familiarity of the street with the auditorium only steps away.

Their seats were good ones, and they felt rewarded for the risk they had taken. The orchestra members were tuning up, adjusting music stands, arranging long black skirts, unbuttoning jackets, turning the pages of their music. A few of the musicians were sitting still with their instruments on their laps, as if they believed the making of music was something out of their hands. Liz wondered at the power of musicians. People said musicians merely performed the composer's work, but suppose they refused, and forever, what a silence that would be. If she and Tom stayed at home, venturing out less and less, their life would be like that silence. She reached over and patted Tom's knee. "I can't believe we're here. I feel like we've sneaked out of the house when no one was looking."

The orchestra was well into the overture to *Fidelio* when Tom realized for the first time in months he was not obsessed with time rushing by. The music created its own time—a kind of gift. Musicians, like astronauts hurtling through space, would be young forever. At intermission the Graytons didn't leave their seats but stood up to stretch, looking around the auditorium for someone they knew. They thought they recognized a familiar face here and there and smiled noncommittally.

Tom looked at the program notes. Floaters, little black dots, like those dots that follow the words when you're singing a song, moved along on the white paper as he read. Mahler had broken with the Vienna Court Opera; his doctors diagnosed heart disease. He lost his beloved daughter, Marie. In his misery the words of an ancient Chinese poet, a drunkard, had inspired him, and Mahler composed this sad music. Musicians, artists, writers couldn't wait to unload their unhappiness on you, and then unburdened they blithely walked away. Tonight Tom was experiencing the Mahler from the other end of the journey. He could recall many moments of joy; only the day before there had been the monarchs levitating over the lake and this morning he had awakened to find the sun imprinting on the walls of the bedroom the intricately cut silhouettes of hundreds of leaves from the tree outside their window. The trick was, as a thing was taken from you, to find something to take its place. As you grew older you had to be resourceful, even inventive, certainly less particular.

That thought led to Jimmy. He had come to terms with his son's life. People said they had lost him to drugs and the Seventies, but Tom looked at it differently. Jimmy had merely taken to heart all the things he and Liz had tried to teach him—the camel and the eye of the needle, the golden rule—never realizing the harm too literal an interpretation could do. Jimmy had dropped out of Yale because he thought it too elitist. He had grown Chinese vegetables in New Jersey, explaining it was a job in which he earned a fair wage and no one was harmed. He harvested sugar cane in Cuba, sending greetings to his parents on a 1950 postcard of the Copacabana night club in Havana—whether as an ironic comment or a belief this was what would interest them, they were never sure. Jimmy drifted west, moving up the Pacific coast, dabbling in carpentry jobs, not from any love of the craft or skill. Tom thought it might be the Christ-like associations.

They supported Jimmy through all of this, sending money for everything from an expensive sleeping bag and a trip through Europe to the down payment on a condo after his marriage, a marriage to a girl from whom he was divorced before Tom and Liz could meet her. They still had the picture Jimmy had sent them of the girl. Her face appeared childishly bright and eager. Tom thought she looked like the girls he remembered in grade school, girls who sat in the front row, their assignment finished before anyone else's, their hands forever raised, eager to impart certain knowledge. The girl would have married Jimmy believing she could mend him.

When Jimmy was thirty-five, Tom and Liz thought it in his best interest to stop supporting him. Jimmy had agreed, explaining he was able to get food stamps, and as for the hepatitis, which had sent him more than once to the hospital—something he said he had not told them to spare them worry—perhaps it was best he stop his medication and give nature a chance, and if he needed a doctor, there were free clinics. They resumed their support, the checks going out each month with the electric and telephone bills.

Tom tried to believe Jimmy's life of no responsibility and no urgency was a pleasant one; the boy was living just as he wished to, while Tom had to admit he and Liz seemed to spend an inordinate amount of time ministering to their possessions. Only this morning he had noted a damp spot in the hall ceiling and guessed before long they would need a new roof. In similar circumstances, Jimmy would just move on.

"You're unusually quiet tonight," Liz said when they were back in the car. "What's going on?" It was their harmless deception to pretend to have no secrets from each other.

"I've been thinking our life hasn't been so bad."

"Wait and see what the next years bring."

"You can't just think of the eventual," he said. "You have to balance it all out."

"So speaks the banker."

They stayed off the expressway on the way home, heading back to the suburb along a street that had once been a major boulevard and was now a tour of all that was wrong with the city: plants closed down, stores boarded up, deserted homes, empty lots with piles of trash. The few intact businesses, check-cashing establishments and all-night drug stores, were encased in steel shutters, while small storefront churches with their signs that both warned and comforted stood unprotected.

Whole blocks were leveled. Tall grasses and weeds gave Liz and Tom the impression they were driving through countryside rather than the heart of the city. But there was nothing pastoral in these stretches of land; rather, they had the appearance of desertion, escape from a natural disaster or some man-made calamity. It was in one of these deserted stretches that Liz said, "You aren't steering the car properly. It keeps pulling to one side."

"I know that."

"What's wrong? What's that noise?"

"We have a flat tire." His elderly car appeared to be as vulnerable as he was.

"Why don't you look for a gas station?" Liz often gave too much advice.

"I have been looking. They all seem to be closed." He tried to keep his voice calm, not wanting to frighten her. He maneuvered the car toward the curb, and then had second thoughts. "I should have left it in the middle of the road where the police would have been sure to see it."

"There haven't been any police cars. Use your cell."

"I left it on the dresser." He struggled with the phone's small print, sometimes having trouble turning it off and on, and he didn't want it to compete with the symphony. Last Sunday it had gone off in the middle of the sermon. "I'll have to change the tire, but I don't like leaving you alone." He told himself it was ridiculous to regard an entire city as a threat. There must be many places where nothing at all happened. The trouble was he wasn't sure he could manage the task.

"I won't have you out on this street by yourself. We'll just sit tight."

"We should never have gone out tonight; it was a crazy idea." He said it because he knew she wouldn't.

"I'm glad we went. This will give us something to talk about."

"We haven't been that hard up, have we?"

Four young black men walked toward the car and, seeing the couple, slowed, peering into the windows. They wore black leather jackets and knitted caps. Only one of them had a shirt on under his jacket; the bare chests of the others were hung with gold chains. The men pounded on the roof and moved on, laughing.

Showcased in the windows of their gaudy car they waited to see what would happen next.

"Looks like we'll be here until the stations open in the morning." Tom tried to make it sound like a lark.

Liz went along. "Remember the summer we rented the cabin up north? Jimmy was nine. It was the cabin where the garter snake came in through a crack in the logs, and you were tossing it out the door when you saw the northern lights. We woke Jimmy up and went outside to watch." To fend off bitterness they made a point of recalling nourishing stories of Jimmy's childhood. This one was a favorite for its memory of the three of them huddled under the same blanket for warmth, the ground on which they sat dampening with the late-August dew, all around them the presence of creatures they could not see, and overhead the restless shifting of colors that suggested caprice, even a prank.

The sky they looked out at from the car windows was unremittingly dark. There were no neon signs, only a meager glow from the streetlights. The chill of the autumn evening penetrated the car. Tom put an arm around Liz. An old car, its paint pocked by splotches of rust, drove past them. The car was crowded with black women wearing white dresses and veils. A keening sound came from the car. The women had a more sacrificial than ceremonial look. "It seems late for church services," Tom said.

"It looks more serious than church. I don't know why we're sitting here being so afraid. This city is as much ours as anyone else's; we've lived here all our lives."

"Not quite in the city, only nearby." Tom felt the city retaliating for their desertion. He told himself people were free to go where they wished. They had never said to Jimmy that he could not go where he wanted to. That you could not take a step without leaving something or someone behind was beside the point.

A young man walked toward their car. They watched him appear and disappear as he moved from one streetlight to the next. His movements were unhurried but deliberate. A black face appeared in the window on Tom's side. It was a boy of eighteen or nineteen. There was a friendly smile on his face.

"You got yourselves some trouble?" With the glass between them, they could barely make out the boy's words.

"Don't open the window," Liz said.

"We can't sit here all night. If he had wanted to rob us he could have used a brick on the glass. The next person who comes along might do just that." Tom rolled down the window.

The young man leaned in and looked closely at the car's leather

interior. "Man this has got to be my most favorite car. I'm Alvin."
He waited for their introductions and then reached in and gravely
shook their hands. "What's happening here?"

"I have a flat tire." Tom was embarrassed not to be out there
changing it, but it had been years since he had changed a flat. He
wasn't even sure where the jack was.

"I can do that for you. No problem."

Tom would not let himself sit there while the tire was being
changed. He patted Liz's arm. "I'll be right outside. Just keep the
car doors locked."

He opened the trunk to find the interior pleasantly familiar.
There was the jack just where it should be and the spare was at
hand. The boy reached for the jack, and Tom released the spare
and lifted it out. He pried the wheel cover off. The boy had found
the wrench and handed it to Tom, who worked the lug nuts loose
on the flat. Alvin slipped the jack in place and began pumping.
Neither one of them spoke, but together they worked as a team,
each task accomplished with the next one at hand.

Tom was thinking of the last time he had changed a tire. Jimmy
had been ten or eleven, anxious to help and furious that he didn't
have the strength to loosen the bolts, struggling with them until
tears started in his eyes. When finally the first bolt gave, Tom could
have kissed it. When they were finished he let Jimmy drive the car
along the country road. He could still see the look on Jimmy's face
when he got his hands on the wheel.

Alvin pulled off the flat and leaned it against the curb. Tom
lifted the spare, buckling a little with its weight. Alvin quickly took
it out of his hands and with a grunt lifted it in place. "You better

get some more air in this tire when you get a chance," the boy said.

When the car was back on the ground, Alvin stood aside and let Tom tighten the lug nuts. Tom appreciated the courtesy, but after he was finished he handed the wrench back to Alvin for a final tightening.

Alvin took off his jacket. "You don't want that that pretty hubcap scratched." He held the jacket up against the wheel and gave the caps a smack.

They looked at one another, pleased. Tom hated to dispel the camaraderie, but it was necessary to pay the young man. "What do I owe you?"

"You don't owe me nothing. It was something special to have my hands on a car like this. I don't guess that's going to happen again."

Tom would insist on giving him money, of course, but there might be something more. "How would you like to drive the car around the block? See that it's OK?"

"You serious?" He didn't wait for an answer but headed for the driver's seat.

Tom explained to a startled Liz.

Alvin said, "What you going to do, Mr. Grayton, you going to climb in the back seat there. If I start running off with this nice lady, you jus' tap me hard on the head with your shoe."

He pulled solemnly away from the curb, both hands gripping the steering wheel, too excited to feign nonchalance. The ride around the dark, dilapidated block was stately. As they turned the corner, the car with the black women in white gowns and veils passed them going the other way. "Who are they?" Tom asked.

"They drive all around praying for the city. They work in the daytime, so they have to do their praying nights."

"Couldn't they pray in their homes or their church?" Liz asked.

"They say the Lord tells them they got to be right on the spot." Alvin was approaching their starting point.

Tom said, "You certainly know how to change a tire. Do you work at a filling station?"

"I work at that all-night drug store you passed about a mile up the street."

"Stock boy?"

"I do the books."

"The books?"

"I took accounting at school, spreadsheets and all that computer stuff. I do his tax returns, too—on the money he tells me about. I don't ask questions."

"Who helps you?"

"There's no one helps me." He sounded impatient.

"We're so grateful," Liz cut in. "We might have been here all night." She gave Tom a meaningful look.

Tom reached for his wallet.

"We're even," Alvin said. "I never thought to sit behind the wheel of a car like this."

Tom leaned over. "Why don't you drive us home? I'll call a taxi to take you back." He worried that the tire might go soft, and now there was no spare. He tried to think if there was a pump in the car or what would happen if they had to wait again for an open station. Even having Alvin in the car made him feel more secure, as if Alvin were a sort of official representative from a foreign country.

He could translate for them.

"How far you live?"

Tom named the suburb.

"That's all right."

As they drove, Tom leaned over the front seat keeping up a conversation, wanting to dispel any suggestion of chauffeur and employee. He relaxed when he saw Alvin's pleasure in handling the car precluded any such idea.

"You drive very well," Liz said. "Where did you learn?"

"You can find yourself a car most anywhere."

Liz pulled nervously at her skirt.

The boy went on. "My sister got herself a car. I painted it for her so she lets me take it out. But you gotta watch where you go; there are some streets in this city where no one safe."

"I learned to drive in the country," Tom said, remembering the long dusty roads, the neat farmhouses, and the comfort of his father sitting beside him. "I taught my own boy there." He regretted his words. Alvin might not have a father to teach him things, yet here he was just out of high school with a job, supporting himself.

"The country," Alvin said. "My grandma's been to Tennessee a couple of times. She's watchin' some property belonged to her daddy down there. If she can find the money for the back taxes, she can have it." It was a subject much discussed in his home, having, as it did, almost nothing of possibility to spoil it.

Alvin drove slowly and with ceremony through the darkened streets. The car felt heavy in his hands, substantial, the older couple light as feathers. He thought, *If I were alone I'd mash down the accelerator*, but he was afraid any jarring of the car might in some way imperil this fragile couple put into his keeping. On her living room wall his grandmother, who had raised him, had a picture of an angel whose wings were spread protectively over a little cluster of children. *I be that angel*, he thought and smiled.

A police car cruised by, and he worried because they were nearly into the suburb, which was sure to have its own police. After they crossed the dividing line, Alvin felt less sure of his passengers. Their invitation to drive them home began to seem odd. He cast sidelong glances at the large homes lining the streets, homes too big for him to think into. His mother, before she went away, had worked for a woman in a suburb like this one, a Mrs. Coster. Mrs. Coster was in her eighties. "She's like a little doll," Alvin's mama had said. "So tiny and skinny, like a twig. She got all these friends who come see her and she say to me, 'Dorene, you make us a nice cup of tea,' and I put the tea in cups thin as eggshells with dainty flowers painted on, and I give her the one with the cracked saucer like she told me. They sip the tea out of the pretty cups, little sips. They read to her because she's got the sugar and her eyes are failing. Her house has more books than a library. You never heard such stuff as they read. I'm standing behind the kitchen door and listening to see what's happening in the story and nothing ever does, but they don't care, they just read and read."

Alvin could see the size and fineness of the suburban lawns, the fullness of the trees that hung over the streets, their crowns like sooty clouds floating in the darkness. He was excited but worried. Suppose they just told him to get out right here and start walking. The danger of the thought made his stomach tighten and dried his throat and mouth. His hands on the wheel were cramped and sweaty. Only once before had he been so afraid—when some men in a car had come racing down their street and shot a boy who lived next door to him. The boy had been sitting on his porch minding his own business. Alvin had heard the shots and ran out in time to watch a red pool slowly flower around the boy's body. Alvin's grandmother had pulled Alvin inside. Someone said it was drugs; others a fight over a girl, but it turned out they had the wrong boy.

"Left at the next street," the man said. "That will be Cambridge, then right on Sussex. It's the third house from the corner, just pull in the driveway."

The man led him into the living room. Alvin looked around. The walls of bookshelves were too much like a schoolroom. Everything was so tidy and so obedient; there appeared no place for him. He might be caught in a web of order from which he would never escape. There was a lack of life here. He sat on the edge of his chair waiting to see what they would do with him.

The couple took off their coats and invited Alvin to do the same. The man made no move to call a taxi, instead he followed the lady into the kitchen where Alvin could hear them talking. When they came out the woman had cookies and milk for the three of them.

"We have a little snack before bed each night," she said. In the warm house Alvin slipped off his jacket. He accepted the milk and cookies. He would have liked pop, but he could not see his way to asking for it. "You have a lot of pretty stuff." He looked around, unable to narrow his comments to one thing. At last he picked up a small bowl on which were painted blown roses. "My grandma has good luck with roses," he said.

"What kind does she grow?" the man asked.

He noticed the woman frowning slightly and he put the bowl down. "Pink, mostly," he said. "She puts her dishwater on them every night. It keeps the bugs down."

"How many children you got?" he asked, seeing so large a house doled out in some sensible way.

They were quiet and he thought he had made a mistake and there was something wrong, but the man said, "We have a son who lives out on the coast."

"Whereabouts?"

"The northwest."

That seemed vague, and Alvin knew what his grandma would say if he took off for some distant place without explaining exactly where so she could get at him any time she wanted to. He began to feel shut in and surrounded in spite of the house's space. "I better be going," he suggested.

"Before I call a taxi," the man said, "I have a question or two."

Alvin felt all his bones come together.

"I don't want to pry, but I wondered if you might be interested in getting a little more schooling?"

"What you mean?" He had worked hard at school. What part of his ignorance was showing?

"I was thinking of a couple of years in accounting at a local community college. With your aptitude for numbers and some training, you could get a job someplace where you wouldn't have to worry about your employer cheating. We'd be glad to help with the tuition."

Alvin tried to guess what was being offered to him, but in that careful room he could not think properly. What if he became as much theirs as that pretty bowl? "Thank you. I'll think on it, but I better be going now."

The man wrote down their phone number and handed it to Alvin.

Alvin folded it carefully and put it in his pocket. He stood up awkwardly and began to tug on his jacket. With a loud thump his gun landed on the floor. He bent down and hastily put it back in his jacket pocket where he kept it handy. He wasn't supposed to take it home from work where he needed it nights when he worked on the books, but the streets weren't safe and he had never forgotten the sight of the boy next door with all that blood.

When he stood back up he saw the expression on their faces. "It's for the store. We been robbed two times this month already and I have to do with the money. I guess you not used to seeing one of these."

The man gave Alvin more than enough for the fare and was firm with the cab driver, who seemed not to want Alvin in his taxi. As soon as the cab was within a couple of miles of his house, Alvin tapped on the window. "You can let me out here, man." The driver, glad not to have to venture farther into the city, took the money Alvin gave him and drove off. Alvin walked toward his street. He had never felt so free. For reassurance he reached under his jacket and felt the gun's cool metal. He was sorry to have scared the old couple. It was really weird how they let him drive that fine automobile. Now that he was free of it, he thought with pleasure of their house and was glad to have seen it; but it wasn't a house for living in. He couldn't imagine plopping down in one of those stiff chairs with a big sandwich dripping mayo the way he liked it. He couldn't see his nephew DeJuan, with his sticky fingers, in a house like that or his sister Tara putting polish on her nails with that scary way she had of balancing the bottle of nail polish on the arm of the chair.

He was sorry the gun upset them. They didn't understand. Probably nobody next door to them ever got themselves killed for no reason at all. He knew the dudes who rapped on their car and their gang, the Lucifers. He thought maybe someday the old couple would be stuck in their car again and someone from the Lucifers would try to rob them. He would come with his gun and save them; then they'd know why he had to carry it.

Tom and Liz were surprised at how pleased they had been to have the boy there. After he was gone, Tom said, "We won't hear from him."

"Probably not," Liz said. Like the willful monarch butterflies drifting over water on their perilous journey, he had escaped their care.

om Grover's school bus was twenty minutes behind schedule, but that was normal for the first day of school, when mothers dragged out their good-byes to little ones, though a few of the mothers looked downright relieved. The long stretches of country between houses were filled in with Christmas tree farms and empty acres of jack pine and pin oak. Much of the stands of poplar had been cut by beavers resident in nearby lakes and streams.

Kids, unhappy about boarding a school bus on an August morning, straggled out of their houses defiantly wearing shorts and flip-flops. Out of habit and temperament, Grover was sympathetic, believing that starting school before summer was over, and not a leaf off a tree, was cheating the kids.

Driving the bus suited Grover, who was of a contemplative nature. Afternoons were busy as the children got rid of their pent-up energy, but in the mornings they climbed onto the bus still groggy with sleep and settled down like pastured sheep, leaving to Grover any piece of the world he wanted.

He pulled the bus up a foot or two from Crystal Davidson, who stood at the road's edge with her seven-year-old daughter, Heidi. Heidi was a second grader this year. Even the year she started kindergarten she had given no trouble, climbing into the bus for the first time like it was a job she was hired for. Grover decided

Crystal's presence beside her daughter this morning was a wish to get out of the house and try out the summer day. You might have thought Crystal was one of the older kids herself, for she was a small thing with long brown hair and a childishly round face full of unanswered questions. Like Heidi she was wearing a T-shirt and cut-offs. It looked more like Heidi holding onto Crystal than the other way around. In the background was the Davidsons' house, a trailer with a half-completed porch jammed rudely against it as if the porch had not wanted to be there.

Driving by in his truck this summer, Grover had noticed Crystal working on her garden. The county was built on sand and Grover had brought in a truckload of manure from a nearby turkey farm to build up his own vegetable garden, but it didn't look like Crystal was going in that direction. Instead she had planted what you could find along any roadway: Queen Anne's lace, butter and eggs, mullion, and field daisies, flowers that didn't ask for much.

The bus door swung open and Heidi got on. Before Grover could stop her, Crystal climbed in after her daughter. He was so surprised it took him a couple of seconds to admonish her. "Crystal, parents aren't allowed on the bus." She paid no attention but just followed Heidi down the aisle and sat in the seat next to her. Grover switched off the ignition and went after them. "Crystal, I'm sorry but you got to get off the bus. It's a matter of policy. Insurance," he said, reaching for a word he thought had some push.

She didn't look at him but just sat there like they were in two different worlds, worlds that had a long way to go before communication was established. He was suffering from lack of sleep and had five more pickups. The kids around Crystal were turning restless, a flock of birds with a strange bird in their midst. He couldn't heave her out bodily, certainly not in front of the kids, who looked embarrassed at being around adults who weren't making things work. He tried once more but there was nothing doing. All that was left to him was to go back to his seat and start up the bus. He had little experience in breaking the law and listened for sirens. In spite of a lifetime of evidence to the contrary, he believed every criminal was caught and punished. Even though it might be hard on him, he thought it should be so.

It was a small town, so he had heard gossip about Crystal and her husband, Jason. It was the old story, marry early and live to regret it. They had been married right out of high school. Grover had been on the job for twenty years, so he had them both right through grade school. High school was another bus. He wouldn't have put them together. Crystal had been a quiet little thing, keeping to herself, always weighed down by an armful of books. Jason made a point of sitting in the seats that were hardest for Glover to see in the rearview mirror. When missiles started flying, they came from Jason's direction. If someone got pushed out the door, Jason was behind him. He wasn't a bad kid, just someone who couldn't let five minutes go by without making something happen.

Grover had never seen Jason pay attention to Crystal unless it was to give her the kind of quick glance you give when you notice something out of place. After their marriage Jason got a job reading meters for the power company. Next thing Grover heard, Jason had been fired. It was hard to see what deviltry he could get up to in a job like that, but then he didn't have Jason's imagination. Now Jason was helping out at the feed store, heaving sacks of turkey feed onto trucks. Friendly enough, Jason always came over to say hello when Grover stopped by for birdseed. The bird feeders were something new for Grover, who was growing to depend on the birds' comings and goings.

Grover saw Crystal from time to time at the Hole in the Wall, where she waited tables. He and Doris always went to the restaurant after church for a big Sunday breakfast, always pleased when they got their favorite table by the window. Elaine worked the griddle, managing pancakes, eggs, fries, and French toast all at the same time. The order slips were strung out like a row of green flags, and he and Doris kept track, telling each other how far their order had advanced. Doris brought along a bottle of their own maple syrup for the little dollar pancakes. She said what the restaurant served never came out of a tree. After Doris died, he sat at the counter. Chatting with Elaine was about all the conversation he got these days.

The bus was right on schedule now, passing the Baylors' farm, where each morning and each afternoon Grover saw the Baylors' two white horses like pictures in a children's book. The animals stood there patiently day after day, as if they were created for nothing else but waiting, which didn't seem so strange to Grover. Five minutes later, Grover pulled into the school driveway. The kindergarten teacher was outside in a summer dress with a big smile like a kid would draw on a face.

As the bus emptied Grover expected Crystal to follow Heidi into the school; instead she stayed in her seat like she was waiting to be dismissed. He marched down the aisle. "Crystal, what are you thinking? You could of got me into a lot of trouble."

"I'm sorry, Mr. Grover, if an alligator had swum by this morning I would've climbed on its back."

"That's not much of a compliment. Anyhow, you want to get off here or you want me to run you home?" In for a dime, in for a dollar.

She looked as if "decision" was a word she had never studied.

"All right then. I guess we're off." He turned on the ignition. Crystal got up and started down the aisle. Grover thought she had changed her mind and was reaching for the lever that opened the door when she settled onto the seat behind him. Little kids who were shy always made for that seat as if it were his lap. He remembered Crystal used to favor it, sitting there reading in the midst of the squirming and yelling.

"You can drop me off at the lake," she said.

"No problem." He was glad to have a destination. She meant Indian Lake, about half way between the school and her house. From there she could walk home. Grover fished Indian lake early in the summer when the bass were just off their nests, and sometimes he went after bluegills with flies. The big ones could be scrappy and were good eating. He would fillet them and take them home to fry up crisp in bacon fat. Doris had been a checker, and when the supermarket was busy she often worked until six o'clock or later. Because he was finished driving the bus by late afternoon, he had done most of the cooking. After Doris passed away, cooking never seemed worth the trouble. He got by on fried eggs or a can of baked beans and a couple of hot dogs. Sometimes the picture on the cover of a frozen dinner would take him in.

It was one of those late-August days when you could fool yourself that summer still had a way to go until you saw the first red leaves on the stressed trees along the road and the flocks of blackbirds strung along the telephone wires, antsy and just waiting for a signal. He didn't know how he would get through the winter. He hadn't been sleeping much. It hadn't mattered in the summer when he didn't have to drive the bus, but he worried about what it was going to be like getting out of bed in the dark with no sleep and miles of icy roads ahead of him. Sleep had always been automatic, like tying his shoelaces, but now his nights were shared with the resurrected who came to him in dreams.

He tried reading through the night, conscientiously, as if there would be a test in the morning. He liked stories about famous men who overcame great odds and mystery stories where you had to keep going to be sure the bad guy would be caught. He read the newspapers cover to cover and the few magazines that came into the house, *National Geographic* and a couple of Doris's women's magazines that he couldn't bear to cancel. He liked *National Geographic* well enough, but he couldn't work up a lot of interest in places he had never been and would never see. He had not traveled much apart from hunting trips to the Upper Peninsula and a trip downstate to see a game in the new Tiger baseball stadium. He and Doris had journeyed to Massachusetts to attend the marriage of their son to a young woman who introduced them to her friends without identifying them as the parents of her husband.

There was TV. You'd have to see it with your own eyes to believe what they put on late at night. They sold things, too, things you'd never want in the light of day, but alone at that hour, it was almost like they were giving you wonderful gifts, and he'd gotten stung a couple of times. There were old movies—Judy Garland and Mickey Rooney as a couple of kids, a sassy Katherine Hepburn getting the best of her leading men. When he couldn't watch anymore, he made himself a peanut butter sandwich and ate it out on the porch steps, listening for the rustle of a leaf that let him know there was a raccoon or a skunk or maybe a deer out there going about its business and he wasn't alone.

He pulled the bus into Indian Lake's public access. If the state hadn't picked up these acres years ago for a tax default, the lake would be ringed round with cottages; instead it was just a lake. A morning mist nestled over the water. Along the shore the trees floated in the white fog. He thought it was too eerie a place to leave someone, but Crystal was already at the door. He watched her move from the road down a cement launch that stretched to the lake allowing you to back your boat into the water. A moment later she was enfolded in the white nothing.

He asked himself what Crystal was doing there. The word had been on the edges of his mind ever since Doris died. He had wanted to be with Doris. It seemed to be where he belonged, but he had been ashamed of his thoughts. Suicide was self-indulgent. It meant you weren't doing your share. Grover considered his next move. It shouldn't be any business of his, but for seven years, morning and afternoon, she had been in his charge. That counted for something. He parked the bus and hurried toward the spot where he had last seen her. Nothing.

"Crystal," he called, trying to keep panic from his voice. He listened for sounds of struggle from the lake and considered removing his shoes, worrying that he had never been a strong swimmer.

"Here." Her closeness startled him. She was sitting on a bench at the edge of the lake. He settled next to her, relieved, but at a loss to explain his presence. He didn't want to put ideas into her head. The mist was lifting, and together they peered down into the landscape beneath the water. There were little ridges of sand and random arrangements of shiny pebbles. A crab like a dead man's hand scuttled purposefully along. A raccoon had left a trail of spent clamshells.

"I thought maybe you might change your mind and want me to drop you off at your house."

"I don't want to go back there."

"What's the trouble?"

"They don't need me there. Jason's got someone who's just waiting to take my place. She's already got one foot in the door."

"What about Heidi?" That seemed foolproof.

"The woman gave Heidi a kitten, and when I made her give it back, Heidi said she hated me."

"What woman is that?"

"Angie Marks. My mom down in Florida had a new hip put in and I had to go down and stay with her for two weeks. Angie was my best friend and she needed the extra money. She agreed to look after Heidi until Jason got home from work and that's all, but she started making meals for Jason and Heidi every night. When I got back all I heard from them was why couldn't we have this kind of chicken with dumplings and that kind of cake with little bits of chocolate in it? They were always holding Angie up against anything I did. I told them when I work around greasy food all afternoon, I don't feel like coming home and cooking up a storm."

Grover remembered Angie Marks as one of those kids who was always changing seats in the bus to get some advantage. When he told her to stay where she was, Angie sulked and gave him a dirty look, but he only said, "Maybe she was just being neighborly."

"I found lipstick on one of the pillows on our bed, and I never wear lipstick. Jason said Heidi was running a fever and Angie stayed over and used the pillow when she slept on the sofa, but I don't know how to stop believing the worst."

"Jason is a little impetuous, but I wouldn't have thought he'd get himself involved with another lady. Maybe you ought to talk things over with your pastor."

"Our pastor's in the midst of getting a divorce."

There were only rags of mist now. You could see the fringe of green hemlock along the shore mirrored on the lake. A loon floated motionless on the water. Loons needed a lot of room to take off, so it was unusual to see them on a lake as small as this. Grover wondered where the mate was. Lately he noticed pairs.

"Can't you just believe Angie did a good job of taking care of Jason and Heidi?"

"I don't want to look the fool. As soon as I find a place to live, I'm taking off. Elaine says I can work dinners. That would give me enough to support me and Heidi. I want my independence."

Grover had his independence, and he didn't think much of it. What he did have was work that got him up every morning. If he didn't get up, how would the kids get to school, learn their lessons, and move out into the world?

"Elaine says getting away from Jason would be the smartest thing I ever did."

"I don't see her as being any expert." Elaine had burned her way through a couple of marriages. The last divorce had gotten itself in the local paper when she tossed her husband's things out on the sidewalk and put a "For Sale" sign on them.

Grover looked over at Crystal. Her straggly brown hair could do with a wash and a haircut. She was painfully skinny. There were two vacant bedrooms in his house. Right away they were moved in. He saw Crystal and Heidi sitting at his dining room table eating away. He'd fish again, not only bluegills but trout. He knew they were still biting. He'd stuff the trout with wild rice and green onions. He'd scrape the barbeque grill clean and make ribs and burgers. Heidi was well behaved and would be no trouble. Sundays after Crystal was through at the restaurant, he'd drive them up to the city for a movie or, if Crystal was tired, they'd turn on the TV and see a movie in the living room, Crystal and Heidi curled up together on the sofa and him in his lounge chair. He'd make popcorn.

He was so used to them being in his house that when Crystal said, "I guess you better take me home," he thought for a minute she meant his place. He teetered. He could offer his place, tell her he'd had his eye on Jason from kindergarten, tell her she was better off without him. When he got home from his morning run, his house wouldn't be empty. Crystal would be there to sit across the table from him and have a cup of coffee before she left for the restaurant. Her thin body would have filled out and her hair would be shiny. Maybe she'd start going out with a nice boy like Mark Jordan, who was home from Reserve duty in Iraq and working in the hardware store. Nothing serious to take her away, but something to keep her happy.

Crystal was saying, "The thing is, Heidi did have a prescription from the doctor for an antibiotic, so maybe Jason was telling the truth."

He got her back onto the bus and said, "You're doing the right thing. You got to cut Jason some slack. You don't want to take Heidi away from her daddy. Give it another chance. Being alone is no bed of roses, I can tell you."

Once when he was just a boy he had found a billfold with nearly two hundred dollars in it. He returned it to its rightful owner, but for a long time afterward he had daydreams about what he might have done with all that money.

Emily was getting supper so I answered the door, turkey feathers in my hair and clinging to the wool of my sweater, turkey manure on my shoes. It was Toivo Hautala, whose dark, death-ridden work had won him a Pulitzer and a National Book Award and was said to have changed American poetry forever. He had been the subject of my MFA thesis: *The Last Word: Hautala and the Image of Death*. Like the wings of a menacing hawk, his work shadowed my own.

Hautala was the reason Emily and I were living in a remote town in northern Minnesota, where I intended, finally, to write the poems that would bring me if not fame at least recognition, and if not that, the sour peace of the resigned. Then there was always the possibility of picking up enough information on the young Hautala for an article or two.

The town we were living in, Millberg, was famous for two things: you hear it mentioned on national weather forecasts—on this first day of June, the people up in Millberg, Minnesota, woke up to five inches of snow, and it was Millberg was where Toivo Hautala grew up. I hoped some of Hautala's inspiration would rub off on me. I was looking for revelation in the exhausted mines and the hills of tailings, the scrub forests, and in the town itself, which in the days of active mining had been moved twice in a frantic search for ore. (Hautala's poem, "Lost Homes.") I had no expectation of meeting Hautala. He left the town when he was sixteen, revisiting it only in his evocative poems. When he wasn't a poet in residence at Princeton or Berkeley, Hautala lived in New York, checking himself into treatment centers, marrying and divorcing and issuing terse bulletins on the ruinous state of American poetry.

Now he stood at our door taking in the feathers. "They told me at the Empty Lake Bar and Grill a poet resided in this house and I came to purge him. This is Hautala country. One poet to every hundred miles. That's the territorial rule."

Hautala was carrying a bottle of sour mash, offering it as if it were a neighborly gift of homemade preserve. I had met him once before. Eight years ago he gave a reading at the college where I was a student. Along with a dozen other admirers I hung around, waiting while he signed his work. Handing him his book, I had the fatuousness to murmur, "I write poems." I hungered for fraternity. Hautala paused, pen in midair, and, giving me a withering look, wrote, "God help you," and signed his name.

He was in his sixties now, his blond beard grizzled, the solid chunkiness ebbing and caved, the swagger a kind of slink. The much-mentioned blue eyes were lumpy with buttery yellow ridges. All this I saw much later. At that moment I was so astonished by his presence in our house, and so desperate for a witness to the phenomenon, I called to Emily.

It had been the chaos of Hautala's life that had made me quit my job. His example suggested a safe life was antithetical to poetry. A mediocre life meant mediocre poems. I took a leave of absence from teaching in a university creative writing program and moved north, leaving behind my colleagues hunched over their computers, their novels building. I had mistakenly imagined this remote town would guarantee incidents, encounters, upshots. We had been in Millberg five months, and until Hautala knocked on our door, the quiescence had been steady.

Emily was the first to rally. She introduced herself to Hautala and apologized for the room's disorder—a pile of third-grade essays, their penciled words hurrying out of the ruled lines, and sheets of orange construction paper on the way to becoming pumpkins. The pumpkins were a change from her school downstate. Holiday myths were discouraged in the city schools, innocence considered life threatening. Halloween was a time to warn children about pins in candy bars and razors in apples.

Emily fetched glasses and ice along with a chaste can of decaffeinated Diet Coke for herself. Hautala stared at Emily, at her red hair and her skim-milk skin and the body whose abundant pleasures she muffled with prim white blouses and over-the-knee skirts, as though with enough provocation the eight-year-old boys in her class might be driven to wild grabbings of buttocks and breasts.

Hautala, without looking my way, slid the sour mash across the table to me and turned permanently to Emily. Access to his bottle in exchange for access to my wife? "You teach school?" he asked, entranced, as though it were a profession he had just discovered, as though Emily with her jack-o'-lanterns, and not Hautala himself, was the most sought after teacher in the country. "Second grade? Third? Wonderful. By sixth grade it's all over. Wet dreams and cigarettes and you're on your way to hell and death. They've built a new school here since my time. It looks like a factory."

"It's really very good. They've gotten all their millages passed." Emily had a hard core of loyalty, which I was counting on now to foil Hautala's clear intentions toward her.

"A room full of sullen Finn kids smelling of *hapanleipa* and praying for a snowfall to bury every school bus in the county."

"*Hapanleipa* is sour bread, right?"

I interrupted Emily, not able to bear the thought that the man I had idolized, a man now sitting in my living room, should be wasting time talking about ethnic food. "What are you doing in Millberg?" I asked.

He responded with reluctance, even irritation. "If you want to know the truth, I came back here to see if there was anything left to squeeze out of Millberg—one more Finn poem or father poem. On a less noble note, I'm keeping out of the way of my ex-wife's process server. What's your excuse, Birdman?"

"Larry. Larry and Emily Brighton." My identity was becoming obscure to me and needed stating. "I came up here to have some time for my poetry. I work on a turkey farm. The pay isn't bad and it's non-academic. I taught at a college downstate, but I found I was writing poems about students writing poems."

Betraying me Emily said, "You should know we chose this town because Larry admires your work so much. He even wrote his thesis on you." I had heard her describe many times the process of reinforcing a student's positive image.

Mercifully he paid no attention to what she said. "A turkey farm? Thousands of plump, pristine white breasts." Hautala had downed two drinks to one of mine, but appeared startlingly sober while I was having trouble focusing but was too nervous to stop drinking. Emily, seeing how things were going, hurried into the kitchen and came back with slices of apple and a bowl of her own healthful trail mix.

"Actually," I said, "there is nothing pristine about turkeys. The man I work for has a couple of thousand. It's my job to inseminate the hens; you can't leave it to the toms. They have to be milked." For the first time I had Hautala's complete attention. I could see the imagery he was developing. I had been working on it myself and had written two turkey poems. I cautioned myself to say nothing more about the turkeys, which were rightfully mine—he had the whole world. I had read somewhere about his recent trip with other writers to Bulgaria. I would have killed for material like that.

"Tell Mr. Hautala about the owl," Emily said. It must have been in just such a tone of voice that she brought out her shyer students.

"Yes, tell me about the owl." Hautala was poking through the trail mix, probing among the dried fruit and seeds as though he was at a loss to understand their purpose. In all the time I spent with him I never saw him actually eat, causing me to speculate that he moved about at night, fangs bared, looking for tender necks. "The owl," he prodded.

I thought of lesser wolves performing acts of obeisance, giving over a kill, even groveling a little. I had planned to write the owl poem on the weekend and already had two good lines. I said, in a barely distinguishable voice, "We had an owl fly into one of the barns the other night. The turkeys panicked and ran into a corner, smothering one another." The bare minimum. I wouldn't give him the details or use my metaphor: a muff of turkeys. Emily looked disappointed with my recitation, probably grading it a C-minus. Hautala pushed away the half-empty bottle and got up. He kissed Emily lightly on the forehead and unexpectedly and, with no opportunity for me to refuse, instructed me to be ready at seven o'clock on Saturday morning. "I'll take you hunting for rabbits. I've got a friend who'll lend us a couple of beagles."

The minute he was out the door, I saw how gauche and gelded I had been, yet I wasn't sure what more I might have done — mentioned my publications? I congratulated myself for not reciting his poems to him — I had many of them by heart.

I lusted for the turmoil, the debacles, the breakups and crackups, the wrecks and confusion of Hautala's life. I regretted coming to the middle of nowhere. I was wasting time working all day with fluttering, gabbling, stupid and stinking turkeys. Apart from a help-wanted notice at the local café and a worn, half-legible sign in the service station window requesting a mechanic (spelled without the "H"), it had been the only job advertised in the depressed town. I could have taught. There was a community college fifty miles north, but that was what I was escaping. I could have gone to another God-forsaken town, but I had wanted Hautala's town. Emily was right; I wanted it to rub off on me. I was sniffing out his secrets.

When Hautala was gone, Emily said, "He could help you with your poems."

"You mean correct them? Grade them?"

"You know what I mean. He knows the editors of all the important magazines."

Out of her own goodness Emily postulates the goodness of others, thereby putting me in the reluctant position of continually having to disillusion her. "He isn't here to help me with my poems; he's here to steal them. He's probably home right now writing turkey poems. That's not all he's here to steal."

"Meaning?"

"Meaning the way he was ogling you."

"Ogling! You make him sound like those little men with big eyes who used to be on the cover of *Esquire*."

"He was hitting on you and he's a lecherous bastard, as any one of his numerous wives and mistresses can testify."

"You were the one who was smitten."

"Smitten?"

"You're a fine poet and you should have let him know that."

"Brought out a scrapbook?"

"Maybe you could write an article about meeting him?"

"Suck up to him and then sell him?" I couldn't answer as scathingly as I wanted to because the same thought had occurred to me: my turkeys in exchange for a saleable piece of Hautala's soul.

The day after Hautala's visit I came home to find the smell of whiskey in the house. "I don't know how you can possibly tell," Emily said. "You reek of ammonia and formaldehyde."

"Turkeys pee, and their eggs are washed in the formaldehyde. Nothing in *my* life remains unexplained. Now tell me why Hautala was here."

"He stopped in this afternoon looking for you."

"He knows I work; he came to see you."

"Don't be jealous. He's really rather pathetic." This was the most frightening thing she could say. For Emily, *pathetic* was a call to arms. Soon she would tell me we must "reach out" to Hautala.

I was indignant. "How can a man who gets ten thousand dollars for a one-hour poetry reading be pathetic?"

"He doesn't have any center to his life. He misses his children and Tamara." Tamara was the well-known model he had been living with. Their arguments were legendary. You saw pictures of them in front of celebrated restaurants glowering at one another in a licentious way.

"He's trying to get your sympathy."

"He has my sympathy."

"That's only for starters."

"It's insulting for you to insinuate I'd fall into his arms. I don't think of him like that. And he doesn't think of me in that way either."

I believe small-town elementary schools with their determined celebration of holidays and legends are the last bastion of innocence. Which of us would not hurry back into that world? When have we felt safer than we did with our heads down on the desk while our teacher read a story to us? Who has forgiven those teachers for making everything afterward seem shoddy and tinged with corruption? What then were my feelings when two days later Emily told me Hautala had come to read to her class? "They loved him."

"He read his depressing, obscene, scatological poems to your third grade!"

"That's not fair." Emily's severest criticism. "You love his poetry. Anyhow, he read Longfellow — the poem about the shadow following the little boy and the one about not wanting to go to bed while it's still daylight and some of Hiawatha. Actually he didn't have to read the poems; he knew them by heart."

I saw the paper I could give at the next Modern Language: "Toivo Hautala and Longfellow—the Hiawatha Link." But I was relieved that he had not brought into the school knowledge that would corrupt, so it was with friendly feelings on Saturday morning when, at the crack of dawn—he said he had stayed up—I climbed into Hautala's truck and settled down between two overwrought beagles. He was driving an ancient pickup. The bed of the truck was rusted and dented, the cab filthy. In the firmament of the dashboard only black holes remained where there had been cigarette lighter, radio, and glove compartment. He was vague about where he had found the truck, and I suspected he was keeping the information to himself for a truck poem.

It was one of those damp and chilly November days that let you know the benign part of fall is over. The trail was only a suggestion of a road. I couldn't guess what clues led Hautala to turn off the highway. The truck cab stank of bourbon, and the beagles, slathering and whining, were climbing over me in their eagerness to get out and do their stuff. "Why the hell are we hunting rabbits?" I asked.

"The blood sport of my youth. My dad used to take me hunting. He would close down the hardware store and off we'd go to kill bunnies."

Of course, his poem "Two in the Dark Woods, Searching," only the poem made it sound like their prey might be moose or lions, certainly not rabbits.

I have always regretted knowing so little about hunting and fishing, so popular with other poets. My father had been a grade-school principal, his avocation was model trains. The outdoors for him was constructed of twigs, dyed sponge, and lakes made of pocket mirrors. I only learned about guns to acquire one more Boy Scout badge.

Hautala appeared nervous, distracted. When he finally stopped the truck, he braked so hard the beagles skidded off the plastic seats and onto the floor. In a minute they were back flinging themselves against the windows and doors, using me as a launching pad, their nails penetrating two layers of my clothing. Hautala didn't move from the truck. For a minute I thought he had changed his mind about hunting. Finally he said, "What the hell. Let the dogs out."

He was crashing through the withered bracken and brush like a bull elephant. The commotion would have emptied any forest of game. I began to suspect hunting was not what we were there for. Hautala's shotgun went off. I heard him curse—a stream of vulgarities, disappointing in how unimaginative they were. At least he was alive. "Stumbled over a tree," he called. "Nearly did myself in."

I thought of T. S. Eliot secure in his publishing office where a tea woman went around with her cart in the afternoons. He had written no poems about hunting and fishing. The beagles yelped from time to time. Hautala was swigging from a flask. He handed it with reluctance to me. I was alarmed to find it nearly empty. On the walk back I would stay well behind Hautala and his rifle. "The trouble with you, Brighton, is that you don't think there's any wisdom behind Emily's innocence."

"I think I know my wife a little better than you do."

His lecherous smile indicated otherwise. "Emily hinted you did a paper on me, which makes you no different than all the nubile virgins in my writing classes, who won't kill themselves like I do, bleeding into my poems; they want to hitch onto my immortality, they want a line or two in the definitive biography.

"The trouble is, Brighton, I'm a weak man—and a generous one. I give the girls what they want. Tamara didn't like that, and who could blame her? The dean didn't like it either, so I'm out of a job. I now appear to be on a blacklist. No job, no poems, no women, no cash. I thought I'd come up here and start over or just stop altogether. Don't misunderstand me. I'm not whining. I wouldn't trade places with you—not for your youth or for Emily— if it meant giving up as much as a line from one of my poems."

"I don't remember offering you my youth or Emily," I said. We could hear the beagles getting closer, their yelps full of hubris. A rabbit appeared in front of us, but Hautala didn't raise his gun. The startled rabbit disappeared. The yapping beagles clawed at us. When they saw their work had been for nothing, they sprawled panting on the ground. "We may as well get out of here," Hautala said. "Nothing's going to happen now." He said it with relief and disappointment. It was like seeing a film in a foreign language; I had watched Hautala carefully, but I had missed something crucial.

Hautala stayed away for a few days, then he was back. While he was making passes at Emily, I comforted myself with the knowledge that it was Toivo Hautala in the room. If only I were patient, I would learn his secret. But any effort to talk with him about his work met with amusement, even contempt. Although he would answer no questions about himself or his own life or work, his curiosity about our lives and work was insatiable.

At first it was flattering to be the focus of so much attention, but after a while I resented my life as a source for Hautala's poems. There would be Brighton poems, but I would not be the one to write them. Emily could not understand my impatience. "He's desperate," she said. "I think we should help him if we can. His work is so important."

"What about my poetry?" I had stopped writing.

"He isn't keeping you from writing."

"I can't get around him. Anyhow, just when I get an idea for a poem, he senses it and steals it."

"You're being paranoid."

Hautala wasn't our whole life. Other things happened. I cleaned the chimney, forgetting to tape shut the fireplace opening first. Emily made ten pints of apple butter from apples grown on untended trees we had discovered in the woods. We went to the township meeting and heard a two-hour discussion on the township's need to spend forty thousand dollars for a holding shed to store bodies during the winter when you couldn't get a shovel in the cemetery's frozen ground. On Friday nights we shopped at the supermarket where everyone in town was getting their six-packs and picking out their weekend DVDs.

In the evenings I exploited the thesaurus while Emily ironed. My printer wasn't working, and when one of my manuscripts was returned, Emily would iron that too—on a low setting, lightly moistening the turned-down corners. When I sent it out again, the manuscript would be fresh and crisp. I thought bitterly that Toivo

Hautala's wives and mistresses never had to iron his poems.

There were visits when Hautala regaled us with stories of growing up in this town among his Finnish relatives, half of them strict Lutherans and half of them Communists, but I had the feeling those anecdotes were meant to divert me. It was Emily in the afternoons who heard what Hautala was really thinking.

"He's staying at the motel," she told me. "He drinks all night and sleeps until after noon. Then he wakes up and sees the gold drapes and the dirty carpets and he has to get out. So he comes here after school is over."

"He must know someone else in town. It's full of Finns."

"Most of the people he knew are dead or have moved away. The ones who are left are scandalized by all his wives and mistresses or angry with him for what he said when he turned down that dinner invitation at the White House.

"His father died when he was fourteen. The family owned the hardware store on Maple. After the father's death, the mother ran the business. Hautala used to work there after school. His mother hated the store, hated having to handle all the heavy, sharp things, and wouldn't learn the differences between the grades of sandpaper. All she wanted was to sell the store and move down to Indiana where her sister lived and there was time for the tomatoes to ripen before the first frost.

"Hautala loved the store. He felt his father was there. He loved selling all the things that kept a house together—nails, hinges, braces. He was devastated when the store was sold."

The poem "The Houses Falling Down." "What does he do when he comes here?"

"He doesn't do anything," Emily said. "Well, just talk."

"You're having the kind of interviews with him writers would die to have."

"They aren't interviews. He just wants to relax. Nothing he says is that important."

"Everything Hautala says is important."

"That's exactly the kind of thinking that bothers him so much. How would you like it if people paid attention to your every word?"

"I'd be ecstatic."

"One day after he had been on drugs, he woke up believing any word he used would immediately disappear from the English language. No one would be able to use it again. He was too terrified to say anything. So he spoke French, because he said the French were so stuffy about their language they deserved to lose words. He was finally hospitalized."

Much to Emily's displeasure I was taking notes.

"Sometimes he stays an hour, sometimes just a few minutes. I really worry about him. I think he's depressed. He talks about death all the time."

I didn't pay much attention to Hautala's depression and talk of death. He had been in and out of treatment centers for years. I believed his depressions were chronic, not acute. Besides, it was only a few days before Thanksgiving, and at work I had all I wanted of death. We shipped hundreds of turkeys this time of year. The barns were covered with blood and feathers. The owner's sisters and nieces came in each day to pluck. A fenced runway led to the grisly operations, and the turkeys lined up on the runway patiently waiting to have their necks chopped.

The first week of the deer-hunting season, Hautala appeared at the turkey farm looking for me. Half a million hunters were fanning out over the state's northern counties. The usually empty streets of the town were crowded with hunters in day-glow orange. There were waiting lines at the gas station. It was smart to stay off the county roads after the bars let out, not only to escape the hunters, but to avoid crashing your car into deer chased from their hiding places.

Hautala was unshaven, a cap shoved down over his forehead, the bill shadowing his face, hiding clues. He immediately took a lively interest in the turkeys. "Why are they waiting in a line?" He watched the turkeys crowd eagerly onto the runway. I explained with reluctance, since I had already started to write a runway poem—"The White Feathered Line." I determined to finish the poem that evening and submit it electronically to some obscure quarterly where it might be printed before Hautala sent his out to *The New Yorker*.

Hautala said, "Beg off and we'll go deer hunting."

Since every man in the turkey operation and a couple of the women had taken off the opening day, I saw no reason why I couldn't have a day of hunting as well. "What about a rifle?" At least we wouldn't need the slathering dogs.

"I'll take care of that. Let's get out of this shit house and join the blood brothers."

The shocks in the pickup were bad, and we bounced along the rucked trails. Hautala pulled up to a shack guarded by the two frenzied hounds. He threaded his way through a wheelless wagon, a bike minus its handlebars, a burnt-out car, and an ancient windowless bus sheltering skinny chickens. He disappeared into the shack, the hounds at his heels.

I knew I should not go into the woods with a drunken, death-obsessed man carrying a rifle. I didn't move. I was waiting for some clue, some quick parting of the curtain to show me how it was done, where the words came from. I wanted to pry the secret from him and then send him off into a mythical forest where old poets were exposed to the elements; so new, younger, wiser, and better poets might have an opportunity. I longed to be rid of this swaggering, sick, superior man who ignored my poems and coveted my wife and dragged me off to blood sports I despised. But I did not want to be rid of him quite yet.

He came back and tossed a rifle my way. "This is Esko's place. He was in school with me." I saw he had brought a bottle of wine as well as the gun. When the truck swerved to the wrong side of the road, I grabbed the steering wheel. Hautala took a long pull from the bottle. "You're one of those people who want to live forever," he said, "which means you don't live at all. I saw the constipated poems you left laying around for me to read. Crafted. That's what the reviewers would call your efforts. Crafted. Put together with hammer and nails, like the bungled birdhouses kids make in manual training—every step along the way perfectly obvious."

We were lurching down a two-track in some remote part of the woods. I had been a fool to give him the chance to read my poems, to pronounce, judge, finish them off. He wasn't through.

"Do you have any idea how many poets there are? How many chapbooks and broadsides? Do you know what your chances for immortality are?"

Hautala stopped the truck and climbed out and I followed him, fascinated by the thought that the first thing I might kill would be Hautala. We loaded our rifles and started walking. The woods were white oak and jack pine: trees crabbed with disease and reluctance. He kept talking, throwing words over his shoulder at me, nothing I hadn't told myself on sleepless nights, but this was early afternoon and someone who knew what he was talking about was saying it. I locked my rifle and kept it pointed down, terrified I would trip over something and my rifle would go off by accident and kill Hautala because I wanted it to.

As if he could read my thoughts, he swung around. "If it's immortality you want, here's your chance. Kill me. I mean it. We'll work it out so it looks like an accident. Your name will go down in all the biographies about me. There'll be interviews and curiosity about your poems. Guaranteed publication. A whole book of poems on your suffering over my death. Who would suspect you? What motive could you possibly have? There's no history. No one but you, and I know how much you hate my guts.

"To tell you the truth, I came up here to Millberg with the idea of doing myself in. The perfect symmetry—die where I was born. But I don't have the guts to do it myself. The insurance policy wouldn't pay out. If it looks like an accident, there will be plenty for my kids. You wouldn't want all those kiddies of mine to starve?"

"You belong back in the hospital," I shouted at him. I headed toward the road. I didn't care how long or how far I had to walk; I just wanted to get out of there.

"I'll give you a motive," he called after me. "I slept with Emily." I swung around. "You're a lying bastard!" I knew he was goading me. I didn't believe him, but I wanted to kill him for using Emily's name. When he saw my anger wasn't going to be enough, he threw his rifle down and, leaning against a tree, began to cry. When I walked over and put my hand on his shoulder, he swung at me, knocking out a front tooth.

"There's no murder in you," he yelled. "You'll never write a decent poem."

We rode back to town in silence, Hautala for the first time intent on his driving. I was preoccupied with the iron taste of blood in my mouth. He took off the next day. Nothing I could learn about Hautala—not the boozing, the wives, the suicide gestures—none of that would teach me anything about his poetry. It was all camouflage, gaudy disguises to divert everyone while the poems were building.

Emily was busy cutting Pilgrims or Puritans—I can never tell the difference—out of black construction paper. At the farm a long line of turkeys waited on the runway. Winter would come to this remote northern town. Wordless snow would fall.

ICY MIRACLES

Martha shifts the car lights from bright to lose some of the snow swirls. Squirrel Road is slick with ice. In her headlights the tree trunks are black patent leather. This December morning Martha feels a kinship with her daughter, Janice, who like herself is keeping an eye on ice. While Martha drives through the early morning hours, Janice, two thousand miles away, is up in a plane tracking icebergs in Baffin Bay. Janice joined the navy and went to weather school. Now she flies all over spotting icebergs in Antarctica. Martha decided she wanted her own adventure. When she saw an ad in the *Beacon* for someone to deliver the newspaper to homes in her rural county, she applied for the job.

Her husband Donald had been against it. "You must be out of your head. You have to get up at four in the morning."

"I don't sleep half the time anyhow." Each year there were more nagging ghosts freighting her dreams, pushing her into the asylum of wakefulness.

"I don't want you to do it; it's too dangerous. You know what the winters are like."

"You didn't tell Janice she couldn't go up in a plane and fly over icebergs."

"I would have told her if I had thought she would have listened to me."

"Well, I'm not going to listen to you either." At fifty-six Martha was hired for the first job she had held since she had clerked in the local feed store right out of high school.

Delivering papers doesn't pay much, but there is a feeling of closeness to Janice, a sharing of her danger. In her last letter Janice described an iceberg that had calved off of a huge glacier. She called the icebergs by their numbers. This disappoints Martha, who thinks they should have names like hurricanes do—cold glacial names like Serna and Isolda.

There is no need to worry about her other child, Jerry, who works at the gas station in town. Martha loves to take the car in to have the oil changed or the tires rotated. She sits there in the shelter of the service station, smelling the oil and rubber smells, studying the showcase with its dusty display of wiper blades and candy bars in faded wrappers. The old calendars on the wall give her back time. She likes to listen to her son talk with the other men about hunting or the high school football team, making jokes and winking at her to be sure she's in on the laugh.

There is still no hint of dawn as Martha passes sparse houses shut into themselves, their windows darkened, the dogs still asleep, the yawning mailboxes waiting for the morning paper. She doesn't know what's in the paper she's delivering. She doesn't know what kind of news she's bringing to the people on her route, people for whom she feels a responsibility. A man might read of the death of an old girlfriend or the election to county office of a man whom he knew for a cheat. Lives will be changed, hopes raised or diminished.

Her day begins in a world not yet created; she's on her own. She eases down the brake to see if the car will skid. It fishtails and straightens. Ahead is the cedar swamp, where a small herd of deer winter. Twice now she has seen a doe and a yearling standing at the edge of the road, tentative visitors from some more benign world.

Her headlights reveal a blue pickup parked at the edge of the swamp, its motor running, the white exhaust billowing out. She slows, ready to help if someone is having trouble and doesn't have a cell. She knows everyone for miles around and has no fear. As she draws closer, Martha sees the sides of the truck's bed are decorated with dancing flames. The truck belongs to Rich Stemple. She has seen it often enough. Rich used to work at the gas station with her son, Jerry. Rich was always bragging about his hunting prowess. You couldn't sit in the station five minutes before he was telling you about the buck he shot that scored two hundred points. He was fired for skimming the station's money.

Her son, Jerry, had been the one to make the discovery. Like Martha, Jerry tends to keep an eye on the way people behave. It isn't that he's the type to bear tales. He just likes things orderly: right separated out from wrong. Rich paid back the money and nothing more was done.

She isn't thinking of that now; she is thinking that Rich might be having trouble with his truck. It is a fault in her to be helpful, even when help isn't needed. She recognizes her failing but has trouble holding back for fear of letting the world fall to pieces. She pulls up beside the truck and, seeing Rich in the cab, is about to hail him when she notices the beam of a flashlight zigzagging through the trees. As the light approaches the road, Rich honks his horn twice and the beam is extinguished.

There can be only one thing a man would be doing at four o'-clock on a winter's morning in a cedar swamp with a flashlight. Shining deer. Poaching. There are restaurants downstate eager for venison and no questions asked. Rich climbs down from the cab of his pickup and starts toward her, walking with a kind of jaunty lurch.

He stands outside her car, trying out a smile. "Mrs. Rickards, when I heard you were delivering the *Beacon*, I figured we might run into you. How you doing?"

She knows exactly what she ought to say: "Fine. Just saw your truck and wanted to be sure you weren't in any trouble." Instead, perversely, danger in every word, she asks, "Rich, what brings you out here at this hour?"

"Well, you probably figured that out. I always thought you were one smart lady, just like your boy, Jerry. He never misses a trick. We can cut you off a nice tender haunch right here if you want it."

"No, thanks. I've got to be moving along."

"Well, say hello to Mr. Rickards for me. I always admired how you two stuck it out so far from anyone. Nearest house to you must be a mile and a half away." His smile widens, revealing gaps where there should be upper back teeth. "Give my hello to Jerry." Rich saunters back to his truck. At the same time a shadow vaults into the seat on the passenger side. As Rich pulls away, she spots a black tarpaulin pulled over a couple of large lumps in the back of the pickup. Deer carcasses. She feels something as looming and dangerous as anything Janice might discover in her cold seas.

The icy roads that appeared treacherous seem less so now. Danger is relative. She completes her route and turns into the two-track that leads home.

Martha heads into the kitchen where Donald is switching on the coffee maker. "How was the hill on Maple Road?"

"The boys are out there sanding it." Donald takes Maple into town, where he works as the county assessor.

"Guess what," she says. "I saw Rich Stemple's truck parked next to the cedar swamp down by the North Branch. He and someone else were poaching deer."

"I hope you drove right by."

It's not that Donald would condone something like that. He has always demanded of her and the children, and most of all of himself, a high level of what he calls "decency." At the same time, he allows his neighbors to do whatever stupid thing they wish.

"They're breaking the law."

"Then let the sheriff get them."

There's a January thaw, three days of bright sun melts the snow and ice to slush. People grin at one another, then, lest they be mistaken for fools, they say, "Well, we know the bad stuff's coming."

Secretly they are hoping for roses to push up.

In Antarctica the icebergs are melting. Janice writes, "The melt pool is the bluest thing you ever saw." Martha can't imagine a winter blue. All of her blues are summer: chicory and larkspur and indigo buntings.

It's late January and Martha and Donald watch the weather on the local TV station before going to bed. There will be a heavy fog the next morning. Martha is out of bed and ready a half an hour early. Donald is up too. She knows being dressed makes him feel he is watching over her. "Keep your brights off," he says.

The fog is worse than she expected. The delivery van from the city is late. When she gets out on the road the fog is a teasing white wall that refuses to recede until she is nearly upon it. The road, the houses, and the trees are gone. The earth has been wiped clean. She drives by memory.

Rich's truck is parked in the same place. It seems risky to be shooting in this fog, but it's a perfect cover. A figure emerges and stands absolutely still. She drives on.

A mile beyond the swamp Martha parks and, taking out her cell, calls the sheriff. The phone rings several times before the deputy, Morgan Haver, answers, his voice business-like to make up for the wait. He was probably dozing.

"Morgan?" she says and thinks that even then it is not too late to hang up. "It's Martha Rickards. Rich Stemple and someone else are out by the swamp poaching deer."

"They see you?"

"Yes."

"Well, Robertson's car is close. I'll send him right over, but he might be too late. I appreciate you sticking your neck out."

Back home she says to Donald, "You better give yourself a little extra time. I couldn't see two feet in front of me." They sit with their mugs of coffee in front of the TV to watch the crawl of school cancellation notices spool out under the news.

Now is the time to tell him. "I saw Rich Stemple's truck again. Why should he get away with that? I called the sheriff."

"Rich will put two and two together. He isn't the kind of man who is going to sit still for someone giving him trouble. After Jerry turned him in for stealing, he sawed off Jerry's mailbox and those two nice spruce Jerry and Emily planted at the end of their driveway."

"You never told me."

"I didn't want to worry you."

"How am I supposed to figure out the world if I only know half of what goes on?"

"You let me figure it out for you."

"You don't know *my* half."

They both laugh. This has been going on for thirty years.

The phone rings. Morgan says, "We got Rich cold. Had a doe and a yearling. A yearling, for God's sake. And in the shack outside his trailer he had a buck butchered and ready for shipping. Robertson said he just happened to be driving by, but you know Rich didn't go for that. You two better stay out of his way for a while."

A week later Rich and another man are arraigned. They plead guilty and receive a sentence of twenty-five days in jail, twenty-one hundred dollars in fines, court costs, and a year's probation. Their guns are confiscated. Both men are banned from hunting for three years.

"You tell Rich he can't hunt," Donald says, "and you might as well shoot him."

When Rich's twenty-five days (less seven days for good behavior) are over and he's out of jail, Donald insists on driving with Martha for the first couple of weeks. She is glad to have him along. They drink coffee together from a Thermos, discuss their children, and listen to the news on the hour and half hour. Once they hear a spot on icebergs. They learn an iceberg carries a load of debris, fragments of glacial rock, which it gradually strews onto the floor of the sea. Sometimes Donald falls asleep in the car, which is the most reassuring thing he can do. When two weeks go by and nothing happens he agrees to let her drive alone.

She hears Rich Stemple's wife has left him, taking their two sons. Once when Rich was still working at the gas station he showed her a picture of the boys. "They look a little skinned there," Rich said. "I just give them haircuts when that picture was taken."

Spring comes one bird at a time. An oriole builds a nest at the top of an oak with the raveled hemp fibers she and Donald put out. The confusing spring warblers appear and disappear so fast Martha and Donald don't have time to find them in the bird book.

In August there's a notice in the *Beacon*: foreclosure. Default having been made in the conditions of a certain mortgage made by Rich Stemple. There will a sale at ten o'clock in the forenoon on the steps of the courthouse to the highest bidder. Unreasonably, she sees herself at the courthouse bidding on Rich Stemple's trailer and then giving it back to him. A ridiculous fantasy. She hasn't the money and it's none of her business. Coming home from a township meeting, Donald and Martha find a tree across their road. Martha is alarmed, but the gnawed and pointed stump tells them it's the work of a beaver.

October is mild. Being able to walk outside without a coat is like forgiveness. Janice writes she was blue-nosed, explaining it's part of an initiation ceremony for someone making their first flight over the North Pole. She says the crew of the plane made a list of what they wanted for Christmas and dropped it over the pole.

On the fifth of November there is a snowstorm, one of the earliest ever. By the fifteenth there is plenty of snow on the ground for tracking. The deer hunters swarm through the town. The parking lot at the Ernie's Bar is filled. The buck pole is up on Main

Street. In the morning a string of carcasses will be suspended from the pole in what always looks to Martha like a chorus line of death. Martha has been thinking of Donald's remark, "If Rich Stemple can't hunt, you might as well shoot him." She doesn't know how to get Rich's wife and sons and his trailer back, but she will do something about the hunting. Without saying anything to Donald, Martha drives to the next county and applies for a deer license. She has never fired a gun.

On the first day of hunting season she hurries through her delivery route and is back to watch Donald put his hunting gear together. Opening day has fallen on a Saturday, so Donald is free to hunt with Jerry, who comes by in his truck to pick up his father. They will be at their deer blind by daylight.

After they leave Martha takes Donald's second best rifle. She gets in his truck and drives as fast as she can to a place on Covert Road where she has learned Rich Stemple is living. It's one of those homes that begins with a basement and never gets any farther. To Martha such houses reek of ruined dreams. A smokestack sticks up, and an enclosed entry way leads down a stairway like a groundhog's burrow to windowless rooms below.

She knocks and after a long wait Rich opens the door in a wool shirt and long johns. Martha blushes. He stares angrily at her. "You checking up for the sheriff? I'm not hunting if that's what you're here for."

"I've got an offer. I have a license and a rifle in the truck. I don't know how to shoot and I wouldn't want to, but you could come with me and show me where to go and do the shooting yourself. If you get a deer, we'll put my tag on it and you can have it. There's no law against giving a deer away, and I'll never tell that you did the shooting." She has rehearsed the speech for days but she still has trouble getting it out.

His laugh is nasty. "You think you can trick me. The minute I pick up that gun the sheriff will pop out from behind a tree and take me in." But there is longing on his face.

"I guess you've had some bad luck since I turned you in."

"Hell, yes, I have. You really messed me up. So why should I believe what you're saying? Why should you do me a favor?"

"To tell the truth, I'm doing it for myself. Donald would be furious if he knew what I was up to."

For the first time Rich appears to believe something she has said. "Let me get some clothes on." He shuts the door in her face.

It's cold standing there. A reluctant light that looks as though it were being wrung out of the earth begins to leak across the horizon. The door swings open and Rich emerges with a hunter's orange jacket and a cap with earflaps. His face is eager, the defeated look she saw when he first opened the door is gone. Still, he pauses to glance uneasily around. "I must be losing it," he says. "This better not be a trick, or I swear it'll be the end of you."

It occurs to her she will be alone in the woods with Rich and a rifle. She gets behind the wheel. "Where do you want to go?"

He appears embarrassed. "Drive over to Bear Creek Road where they clear-cut about ten years ago. To tell you the truth I fixed up a spot. I knew I wouldn't be hunting, but what the hell, there's always miracles. I'll tell you what I did." From the relief and joy on his face, she sees he is a man who hasn't had anyone to talk to. "There's a deer trail with rubs and scrapes all over the place. It leads right up to a fence where the wire's been cut. The deer went along that way and then made their way through the hole in the fence. But you can't get downwind of them there. No place for a clear shot. What I did was pile up a lot of brush next to the opening so they'd look for another spot. Then upwind I made a new opening." He looks at Martha and, seeing she's not suitably impressed, he explains, "Deer, they follow a fence."

Martha parks the truck and they get out. The new growth is a perfect height for deer to browse. Rich cautions, "Stick close to me. With that brown jacket, someone could take you for a deer." On the other side of the fence Rich pauses at heart-shaped tracks in the snow. "A buck. Bucks drag their feet." He motions silently to a log stretched across the ground. They brush off the covering of snow and settle down. First Rich glances around, then he reaches for the rifle. After inspecting it carefully, he gives her a look that suggests she might have done better for him. He loads the rifle with the ammunition she has brought.

The dampness that rises from the creek creeps into her bones. Snow begins to fall, lightly fingering everything. Rich is silent, listening. With no wind the snow accumulates. Trees, logs, branches, dried weeds are all gradually erased. The snow paints out their feet and shoulders and the tops of their heads. This disappearing act gives Martha an eerie feeling. She doesn't want to vanish from the world in the company of Rich Stemple. Inside her mittens she doubles her fingers into a fist to warm them. Even this slight motion gets a glance of reproach from Rich. They sit silent, growing whiter and whiter, transfigured by the snow.

Soundlessly a buck appears about thirty feet away, decked out in antlers that look to Martha like fanciful bric-a-brac. She thinks at first the buck must be some conjuring trick of Rich's. He has willed the bewitched deer there. She is thrilled. Then she is alarmed. This is the worst part. It's all she can do to keep silent. He moves so quickly Martha doesn't see the rifle swing up. She hears the shot and sees the buck fall.

"Goddamn!" Rich says. There are tears running down his cheeks. The buck lies on the ground, his legs scrabbling at the air. He makes a sound like a bellows working. Then he lays silent and still. Rich walks over to him. A bright red stain is spreading on the snow. Unlike Martha, Rich has thought to bring a knife.

"I'm not going to stay for this." She hands him the deer tag. "I'll wait in the truck." He hardly hears her.

She turns on the heater, and then, because she needs to have whatever she is thinking interrupted, the radio. Someone is giving the weather. During hunting season they give it often. They begin with the national weather. A storm is gathering off Greenland. Martha thinks of Janice up in a plane. Unable to guess the consequences of such a prayer, she is shy about asking God to change the weather, but assigns him to keep an eye on Janice.

Rich comes out of the woods carrying the rifle. Before advancing toward the truck, he looks warily in both directions and then quickly puts the rifle in the truck and goes back for the deer. He slides the carcass over the fresh snow, leaving a streak of red. Enlisting her reluctant help, he hoists the deer into the bed of the truck.

Rich grins. "Well, I guess we both got something on each other."

She doesn't like this bond.

Mischievously he taunts her, "You're breaking the law. You're aiding and abetting me or whatever they call it. You going to turn yourself in?"

"Don't worry. I'll figure out a way to punish myself, I always do." Janice had written that it was too cold in Antarctica for bacteria to breed. Things there didn't decay. Martha imagines Antarctica in its pristine whiteness, immaculate and incorrupt.

He grins. "You had it to do over again, I'll bet you wouldn't have called the sheriff on me."

She makes her voice as hard and cold as a chip of ice. "Oh, yes, I would."

KEEPING YOUR PLACE

Amid the seeming confusion of our mysterious world, individuals are so nicely adjusted to a system and the systems to one another and to a whole, that by stepping aside for a moment, man exposes himself to a fearful risk of losing his place forever.

NATHANIEL HAWTHORNE, WAKEFIELD

Anne pushed open the door and away went a mouse, leaving the cabin sadly empty. The welcoming familiarity of everything was a reproach, for she had agreed to tear down the family cabin for the government's better purposes. She waded into the receding tides of accumulated life. This was her last visit to the cabin, and Anne Hennert was there to carry away the remnants. She felt in all its accumulated years the cabin's authority and wondered who would watch over the family when it was gone.

On her drive up to northern Wisconsin from Chicago, the car radio talked to her of nothing but Nixon's resignation. The president would be in the White House packing his clothes, or would Pat see to that? The government was taking *his* house, too. Not far from the cabin she had come upon a bulldozer like a large yellow toy. Over a hundred miles of the La Croix had been declared a National Wild and Scenic River. The cabins that bordered the river were being destroyed for the greater good. The cabin built by her father after his return from WWI was marked for extinction. For years the river had appeared a complaisant friend to her family, while all the while it lay waiting, and now it was going to have its way while the family would be bereft.

Her stay at the cabin would be a lonely one, for her children were scattered. But when have children in one way or another not returned home? She carried provisions into the cabin, as she had done hundreds of times, and put them on known shelves. The kitchen had both an electric and a wood stove, so you were free to choose your era. There were beer and wine ads on the assorted glasses, as if the family had spent the last half-century carousing. Stuck on the wall, a Land of Lakes butter carton with its Indian maiden seen against an idyllic land of water and trees served as a miniature landscape. The bookshelves displayed years of summer reading: *The Trail of the Lonesome Pine, Pollyanna Grows Up, When Knighthood was in Flower*, romantic books that in their persistent innocence, accused. A lean-to was built onto the kitchen and was home to fishing poles, nets, wading boots, and tackle boxes. It had a sink and wooden board for gutting fish and scraping scales. A faint whiff of fish lingered over it all, as if some returning fisherman had just slapped down the day's catch.

The freezer was in the garage. For many summers a milk snake had crawled into the space beneath the freezer and, rubbing against it, left behind a transparent ribbon of discarded skin. There was a cardboard box on one of the garage shelves where in the winter a dozen flying squirrels holed up in a tangle of tails. While you stood there looking at it, the box wiggled as the napping squirrels changed position. When the time came, not only people would be displaced.

In the living room of the cabin was a photograph of Anne's parents, Charles and Carol Hennert, taken shortly after her father built the cabin. The photograph had presence and permanence, qualities missing in recent family photographs. The chairs in the photo on which the Hennerts sat could still be found on one of the porches.

Upstairs the bedrooms were named: Mom and Dad's Room where her mother and father had slept, and then it was Anne and Kent's. Tonight Anne would sleep there alone. Her daughter Laura's room had not been used since Laura's marriage. Anne's youngest daughter, Sheila, preferred the screened sleeping porch. At twenty-two Sheila was in the Peace Corps in Mali. Her letters were full of virtuous intent. Sheila planned to bring a school to the girls of Mali, who spent hours pounding millet for porridge. She sent requests asking for money to sink a new well that would cut down on the miles the women had to walk for water. She begged the family doctor for the samples left by pharmaceutical reps.

Mark's room had a deserted look. Their son was in Canada and wouldn't be coming home. He had written, "Could you save some of my fishing gear for me and Dad's collection of dry flies? I name them when I can't sleep."

Once Anne unpacked, she felt a need to leave the cabin, which had taken on an accusatory atmosphere. On a whim she went to pick blackberries for her dinner. Lately her dinners were drab affairs meant for survival rather than pleasure, so why not a little treat and accomplishment in the getting? She followed a worn path into the woods. Raccoon scat dimpled with seeds told her others had been at the berries before her. As she picked, the afternoon sun stopped meddling with the birch and pines and the path darkened. The berries had taken her to a place in the woods she didn't want to be, a place where the hawk pounced and the fox ran down the hare. These woods were full of small murders; it was Milton's regions of sorrow, where she had been living ever since her husband's death eight months ago.

Kent died in November, the month of the dead. The Native Americans were cooking up corn soup and fry bread for their Ghost Suppers. It was All Souls' Day in the Catholic church, *Dies Irae, dies illa,* day of wrath, dreadful day. In Mexico they were picnicking in the graveyards, where children were eating sugar coffins and chocolate skeletons. Her husband's death left her struggling with problems of relativity. An object existing by itself can't be defined. There must be a second object against which to measure it. Without Kent, she didn't know where she was.

Kent had died of a subarachnoid hemorrhage caused by an aneurysm. The fatal aneurysm occurred in one of the branches of the circle of Willis, a vascular complex at the base of the brain first described by the seventeenth-century English physician Thomas Willis. After Kent's death, Anne learned all she could about what caused his death. If she could just discover enough, Kent's death might be undone. Thomas Willis, she learned, was addicted to "the opening of heads" in order to discover the secret places of man's mind. In his explorations he could not satisfy himself that the soul was entirely located in the brain. Therefore, he came to the conclusion that man was "a double-soul'd animal" with a material soul in the brain and a separate ephemeral soul. This was a concept that Anne could embrace, for her brain and her instincts had drifted apart.

The congregation had been kind, letting her stay on in the parish house for a month, though there was no gifting of chicken casseroles and chocolate cake as there would have been were she a widower. Women were expected to look after themselves. She took to reading the whiney psalms, "I am poured out like water" and "we are killed all day long," and kept her sorrow to herself. It was no accident that mutes had once been hired to march in funeral processions.

Returning to the cabin in darkness, Anne reached for the switch on the outdoor flood to find it covered with duct tape and remembered that in the spring the phoebe had built a nest on the floodlight and they were avoiding scrambled eggs. Someone said every act results in positive good or positive evil. You could be cautioned into paralysis. In the kitchen a cloud of fruit flies lifted from a bruised peach as though her presence had ended a spell. Last summer there had been a plague of fruit flies in Chicago. Kent discovered them in the communion wine. Anne put the peach in the oven and left the door open. In the morning the peach would be covered with fruit flies. She would close the door and turn on the broiler. Or perhaps not.

When her daughter Laura called that evening with her request, Anne was relieved of worrying about how she would fill the emptiness of the cabin. "Can you keep the girls for the week?" Laura asked. "I'm auditioning for the position of second violin with the absolutely perfect quartet for me. Dietrich is traveling with the symphony on their summer tour, and I have the girls on my hands twenty-four hours a day. They don't complain, but if I try to practice, I feel them in the other room growing larger and larger. For little girls they're such a presence."

Anne was being asked for help, and she would help, knowing from long experience that when Laura's voice edged up an octave, desperation was not far away. She had heard the same note when Laura hadn't been invited to a friend's birthday party or lacked a date for a prom. But this request involved the lives of others.

Two years ago Laura attended a master class for violinists given by Dietrich Midner, the concertmaster for the symphony in the city where Laura had returned for her master's degree with the idea of supporting herself by teaching violin until she could find an opening in a string quartet. Dietrich agreed to take her on as a private pupil. A year later they were married, and at twenty-five Laura was stepmother to Dietrich's two girls, whose mother had died three years earlier from acute leukemia.

Anne had met the girls and, seeing how needy they were, she worried that Laura had taken on a task that would consume her, or worse, that she would not take on the task. Music had brought Laura and Dietrich together, but Anne was suspicious of music, something that grabbed you by the throat and took you where it wanted. Now music was sending the girls into her own home.

She still had the night to get through. The bedroom's trapped air was suffocating, and she opened all the windows. At once the sexual smell of the river filled the room. There was a tear in the screen, and she repaired it with a swatch of duct tape. After Kent's death she had stopped sleeping, reproaching herself for not having been sufficiently watchful.

As she lay awake she imagined birds and animals with insomnia, snakes tossing and turning in the middle of the bundle keeping the other snakes awake; the owl with the sun in its open eyes. She had read of a disease, Fatal Familial Insomnia. The onset was usually in the middle years. At first the insomnia was occasional, but then the patient ceased to sleep all together. Dementia ensues. In a year the patient is dead.

Daylight finally came, and like the early rising monks of St. Bernard who hoped to arrive in their chapel before God, she wanted to be first on the scene. Pulling on her jeans and an old sweater that had belonged to Kent, she ventured out to see what was on offer. Because it was late in the summer, there was no birdsong to fill the interstices of silence. The poisonous mushrooms, *Amanitas*, were fruiting out in beguilingly bright colors of orange and lemon. They tipped roguishly this way and that, belying their deadliness. She pried some fat puffballs from the ground to take home and fry for dinner, but she left the purple-and-white *Clavaria* that grew like clusters of coral. *Clavaria* was eaten with mixed results: some people enjoyed them, some died.

Around a bend a bearded tom and his flock of hens, gorgeous in iridescent plumage shading, from rusty copper to bronze with highlights of green and purple, feasted on an early drop of acorns. One of Mark's endless childhood questions had been "Mom, if turkeys can fly fifty-five miles an hour and run just twenty miles an hour why don't they always fly?" At the time she hadn't known the answer, but it had to do with the energy it took to lift the large body of a turkey into the air. The task was not as daunting as starting the task. It was time to return to the cabin and begin packing.

She heard brakes squeal and opened the kitchen door just as John McCraig raised his hand to knock. John had come into their lives when she and her mother had moved into the cabin during the Depression. Her father remained in Chicago trying to resurrect the bank. Anne was nine and felt unprotected, for she sensed her mother's qualms at having to manage on her own in what her mother believed to be a menacing country full of treacherous mischief. John had been there to trap the raccoon that came down the chimney, clear out the bat nest under the eaves, prime the well, and when Anne tripped on a slippery boulder, he brought ice for her sprain and bound up her leg.

John had been more than handyman that year; he had been husband and father. He had been a part of Anne's children's lives as well. It was John who had taught Mark to fish. Kent loved fishing, but he hadn't the patience to teach and he liked to fish alone. John knew the deadheads and the holes. He knew if it should be a spinner or a minnow, and if you wanted trout, he knew the little feeder streams and the names of the hatches. He hummed a little tune before each cast as an obsession or a charm. John made Mark clean his own fish and release what they wouldn't eat. And there was the year when he had taken in their daughter, Sheila, to live with him. It was impossible to think of the cabin without thinking of John.

Anne hardly recognized him. His clothes were familiar, the same green checked shirt, the khakis with ragged cuffs and worn knees, and the brown leather high-tops, but he had a crumbled look as if a giant fist had squeezed him. Every one of his eighty-two years was there. She tried to hide her shock with a warm hug. As he took her in his arms, she was reassured by the familiar smell of mosquito repellant and pipe tobacco. She hadn't seen John since Kent died and she couldn't help crying. Her mourning wasn't complete until she shared it with John. Not needing an invitation, he sat down at the kitchen table, familiar land. Anne settled across from him.

"I was real sorry not to get down for Kent's funeral. I was up in Duluth having a new knee."

"You never told us."

"It wasn't a big thing. How are you doing?"

"As you see." She wiped her eyes with her fists like a child.

He gave her shoulder a dog pat. "I thought I'd never get over Helen's death. I was ready to go myself. Then something happens, like I was outside early one morning, and on nearly every spray of goldenrod I found a bumblebee hugging a bit of blossom waiting for the sun to warm it. You wouldn't want to miss something like that. You just have to wait for those little things to drag you back into the race. And you've got the kids. How are they?"

He was telling her she was lucky. She had the children. John and Helen's only child, Sam, had been killed fighting in WWII. "Laura's fine." And since she had always told John the truth, "Well, it's been a little hard for her taking on Dietrich's two girls. She's had to cut back on her music, but Sheila is great. She's thriving in Mali, practically running the place."

"She sends me a card every now and again. How about Mark?"

Anne dreaded the question. In talking with John, she and Kent had been purposely vague, saying something about Mark "seeing the world." Now she tried to make her voice non-committal. "Mark's in Canada."

"What's he doing in Canada?"

For a moment Anne thought of making up some story about Mark being in school there, but John deserved the truth. "Mark's in Canada avoiding the draft."

"How the hell did you let him get away with that?"

"I had nothing to say about it." She would never admit her passive complicity to John. She had to have him on her side.

"What about Kent?"

"Mark wouldn't listen to him."

He took pity on her. "Sorry. I didn't mean to lose my temper, but I just never got over Sam. You were pretty fond of him yourself."

"I might have married him."

He surprised her by saying, "Oh, I knew all about that. I saw our car parked off in the woods near your cabin when you sneaked up from college to spend the weekend with Sam just before he left for the war. I could have stopped you and Sam, but I didn't. I'm glad Sam had that." The anger disappeared and he gave her one of his wicked grins. "After that I always thought of you as family and your kids, too. Maybe that's why I feel so strongly about what Mark's done."

To change the subject she said, "How long will you be staying in your cabin?" The McCraig cabin was a mile upstream, and his cabin, like theirs, was scheduled to be torn down. John had built it the year before he helped her father build his. The Hennert cabin had been John's first job. After that he had made a good living building fishing cabins and small summer getaways for people up from Chicago and Milwaukee.

"I'm not selling to the government no matter what. I hope that's how you feel. If there are enough of us, we might have a chance to stop them. Your Dad was so proud of bringing you up here to a place he built himself. He'd turn over in his grave if he knew you were giving it up. The government is just a bunch of Communists, Annie, coming up here and tearing down our cabins."

"They want to preserve the river, John, keep it wild. Everything is being built over. We need some wild places, even if people do no more than just know they're there."

"I'm not arguing that. But let them find a place that doesn't already belong to someone."

She felt her betrayal. "I've already signed the papers. The children aren't interested in the cabin. Mark might have been, but now that doesn't matter. With Kent gone, it's too much for me. Anyhow, we don't really have a choice, do we?"

"You bet we have a choice. They're going to have to come for me with a gun, and I'll tell you what, if there's any destroying of the cabin, I'll do it myself. In the meantime, I'm thinking of giving them a little hell."

"What kind of hell?"

"Sand in the bulldozers' gas tanks. Tie myself to the cabin when they come to tear it down."

"John, that's nonsense. I know you too well."

"You tell me another way to keep the government from taking my land."

She looked at him and he read her mind. "You mean how can I criticize Mark for defying the government? It doesn't equate. Over there the government is protecting the land from someone who wants to take it. Here the government is taking land from someone who wants to keep it."

"Let's change the subject. While you're here, would you have a minute to help me pick out what I ought to save for Mark from the fishing gear?"

She saw him struggle and reluctantly give in. Carefully he tested the rods, weighing them in his hand and giving them a couple of trial swipes. He selected a bass rod and a trout rod and some other paraphernalia—a vest with hidden surprises in its many pockets and a couple of landing nets, one of which had a tear.

"I'll take it home and mend it," he said. He took up the landing net and after a conciliatory hug drove off, his familiar truck spitting sand as it rounded the curve.

Laura arrived in the early afternoon with the furtive, guilty air of a mother leaving her child on the monastery doorstep. The two girls, Clara, nine, and Maria, seven, climbed out of the back seat, swathed in manners. They submitted their small hands to be shaken by Anne as if they were compliant virgins offered up to a rite to which they assented, even knowing it meant their deaths. Though the girls were clean, they had a pulled-together look that suggested they were too much in charge of their own grooming. Clara's was a nun's appearance, her shoulder-length hair sculpted back from her forehead with a black band, her dress too long and with no waist. Maria's dress of taffeta was more appropriate to a party than it was in the woods of northern Wisconsin. Her untidy blond hair fell over her eyes and got in her mouth when she spoke. The girls appeared vaguely foreign, and indeed they were, for they had come to this country from Germany with Dietrich and their mother. They had to learn a new language, and then their mother became ill, their father occupied, and the two girls left with no intermediary or familiar words to help them move from their old to their new world.

Laura saw Anne's appraisal of the girls. "We had to rush so I could get up here and back to the city tonight." Her impatience overrode any consideration of how Anne might feel about so abrupt an escape.

Inside the cabin the girls stood at the ready waiting for orders. They had long ago, and in the face of many disappointments, abandoned their own fancies. Laura suggested, "Why don't you go outside and look around. There are all kinds of things to see." When the girls drew together at so expansive a challenge, Laura said, "Then take your things upstairs and pick out a bedroom. You can have my old room if you like. It has a poster of Heifetz."

Anne wondered at so meager an inducement, but Clara and Maria picked up their small bags and trudged dutifully up the stairway, one more journey they didn't want to make.

Laura waited until the girls were out of sight and hearing before she said, "I'm all wrong for them. They're so needy. They don't hate me; they don't consider me the evil stepmother, but I'm not their mother either. They keep waiting for me to tell them to take their next breath. And Dietrich is gone so often. Of course I understand what his responsibilities with the symphony are, but they're his children."

Anne said, "They are your children now as well."

"Yes, yes, of course, but this fabulous opportunity has come along with the string quartet. They lost their second violinist when she had a baby and couldn't keep up with the practice schedule. They're just getting started so they don't have a lot of tours signed up, just festivals and the campus circuit. I'd be right in the city. They have a wealthy patron and they've had excellent reviews in the local paper." She could have been describing a new lover. "They play intimate settings. They don't have that heavy style that quartets playing large concert halls have. I've heard they're very democratic; everyone gets their say on interpretation. I'm playing a Mozart quartet with them for the audition, and you can't hide anything with Mozart, so I have to be perfect. If I could just have this one week to myself, I know I can do it."

Finally she stopped. Anne said, "I'm looking forward to it, dear." That was not entirely true, for she had seen how the girls banded together. "What do they like to eat? What's their bedtime?" Surely they came with instructions.

"Oh, they eat hardly anything, so it doesn't matter what you give them, and since it's not school, they can stay up. I let them get really tired so they sleep all night; otherwise they prowl. But they're very well behaved. Of course she probably wouldn't do it anyhow, but don't let Maria run around too much so that she falls. If she gets a bruise she's terrified that she's going to die. Her mother had them all over her body with the leukemia."

Laura began to explore the cabin, noting all the absences. "It must be hard for you packing up everything. I used to love this place so much. Of course I was at music camp a lot during the summers, but it was always so peaceful when I got back to the cabin. Mark and Sheila and I used to go off for picnics and hikes, and on hot days we'd sit on the boulders and let the river wash over us. I wish I could stay, I really do. It would be perfect if you were in the city taking care of the girls, and I was up here at the cabin practicing." She paused for a moment as if she actually were considering how that might be effected. "But I didn't bring my violin."

When Laura said good-bye to them, the girls accepted Laura's good-bye kisses as if they were gifts meant for someone else. As she drove away, the girls stood beside Anne to watch but did not wave in response to Laura's disembodied hand signaling from the car window. They had run out of farewells. Anne was certain that whatever activity she suggested the girls would resist, and if she were to ask what they would like to do, they would respond, "I don't care." She would have to rely on their German engrams and give an order, one that suggested work, a double assault on Teutonic tendencies.

"I'd like to take some of these small white pine seedlings back to the city with me," she told them. She had some idea of planting them in pots on her condo terrace, a bit of continuity. "You'll need to change your clothes. It's messy work."

She found some old shorts and T-shirts. "These belonged to your mother," she said; but when she saw the look on their faces she amended, "to Laura." They put them on as if the clothes would scorch them. Clara and Maria were supplied with trowels and pots and Anne gave a demonstration. "You have to be sure to get as much root as possible so that the little trees survive. Then give them a drink of water."

The ground was damp, the sandy soil accessible, the seedlings only inches high. It seemed so simple. Clara was working away, but Maria was crying. "The trees don't want to go."

Anne relented. "Never mind. We'll go for a walk before dinner," and, not taking any chances, added, "follow me." She headed for the river. It was where she had been taken when she had been Clara's age and, like Clara, wanted to be someplace else. The girls held hands and stayed several paces behind Anne, making it impossible for her to carry on a conversation with them, but to each other they whispered like lovers.

At the sight of water the girls bent down and scrubbed the sandy soil from their hands, reducing the river to a washbasin. This cleansing seemed to relieve them, and they accompanied her more readily along the path that followed the river.

Maria pointed to a turtle sunning itself on a log.

"A box turtle," Anne told her.

"Does it bite?" Maria asked.

"No," Anne said, pleased to diminish one worry. "It can squeeze itself all the way into its shell so it doesn't have to bite. Snapping turtles can't do that, so they have to be more aggressive to protect themselves."

The girls listened attentively to her explanation, and she remembered hearing that Germans faced with two doors, one marked "paradise" and the other "lecture on paradise," always chose the latter. She would give them lectures; wasn't she a professor?

At dinner it was instructive to see with what ingenuity they did not eat. They were like determined prisoners who from some hidden principle refused food. The food was still there, but rearranged, the ham hidden under bits of bread and the potato salad squashed into a paste and spread tastefully about their plates.

After dinner Anne found small notebooks and pencils for the girls, who dutifully tore away sheets of grocery lists and gin rummy scores and wrote their names on the first clean page. When they set off into the woods they kept close to her like students eager to find favor with the teacher. She held out a handful of dried crisp lichen to them and had them dip the lichen into water. "Lichens," she told them "have been around for thousands of years. Indians soaked dried lichen in water to make an instant soup, and they tucked it around their babies' bottoms as diapers." This caused embarrassed giggles.

It was Maria who found the little grouping of Indian pipes. "Are they ghosts?"

"No, but I understand why you'd think so. They're plants without chlorophyll."

The girls looked at her, pencils poised.

She spelled the word. Maria printed, Clara wrote in cursive. Anne explained, "It's what makes plants green."

Maria continued to study the fleshy white pipes, not believing Anne's explanation. "I think they got sick and died," she said. "And what killed them is catching, and the trees are going to die and their leaves will be all white."

Death had been closer to the child's experience than science and had won out. "That would make a lovely story, Maria." Anne insisted on it being fiction but acknowledged the power of the image. Maria would not be the first to translate sorrow into fiction.

Anne showed them the square holes made by pileated woodpeckers and the heart-shaped tracks of deer. When Clara found the feather of a jay, Anne spoke of how birds molt. Clara stuck the bright blue feather in her hair, which was another kind of lesson. After their walk she offered a canoe trip down the river, but the girls moved together, and Clara said, "No, thank you" with such urgency Anne did not coax them. She told them, "We used to see if we could throw stones all the way across the river," and demonstrated, purposely falling short. She picked up a couple of small rocks and put them in the girls' hands. They threw them with reluctance, as if they were hurting the river.

As it grew dark the girls hurried toward the cabin. Anne asked, "Shall I read to you?" *The Secret Garden* still remained on the shelf. She read the first paragraph before remembering the part the death of Mary Lennox's parents played in the book. She paused, but the girls wanted her to keep reading. They knew the book nearly word for word and anticipated the happy ending.

When she closed the book they went up to bed with no word of protest, reconciled to being as unhappy upstairs as downstairs. Later, when she checked to be sure they were all right, she found the two girls asleep in Clara's bed. Anne knew the easy thing would be to leave them in their reluctance and sorrow, but after breakfast the next morning she confronted them. "You're probably angry that you're here, aren't you?"

Their silence told the story. But then how could they express anger at someone who had power over them?

"Laura loves you, but she needs a little time to herself to practice. She was always happy here when she was your age, and she thought you would like the cabin, too. I know this has been a hard time for you—your mother's death and moving to a new city and making new friends."

Clara said, "We don't need friends."

"Everyone needs friends."

"Well, we don't. We can play by ourselves, you don't have to bother with us."

She would take the hint, but she would watch. They sat in the screen porch and drew pictures of fierce wild animals with sharp teeth and claws. They rescued some old curtains Anne had put into the trash and asked for a scissors and glue, which they carried upstairs, immuring themselves in their bedroom. When Anne looked in, she saw they had a small box they were decorating with a square cut from the curtain. When they saw her, they tucked the box out of sight, leaving her curious.

Dinner was a silent affair, and Anne told them a story of a couple who, not wanting to be seen as silent during their dinner in a restaurant, told each other in the most animated fashion the story of the three bears.

"I know the story," Maria said. "Shall I tell it?"

"Let's tell it to one another," Anne said.

At first Clara didn't join in, but then she leaned toward Anne and Maria and said, "You'll never guess what was on the table — porridge!"

Very excited, Maria said, "There were three dishes!"

"Yes," Anne said, "and can you believe it, the porridge was very hot!"

The girls were giggling. When they finished with the story, they asked permission to sit outside on the steps. Anne was thrilled with their voluntary stepping outside of the cabin. "What will you do?" she asked, but they had no answer, so she didn't know whether it was the beginning of bravery or a step toward escape.

While they were outside she went up to their room and searched for the small box they had concealed. She found it under Laura's pillow. For a moment she paused. It was obviously a private thing, and Anne had never read her children's journals or letters. But the two girls were so elusive, so resistant, and there were days to go. Inside the box she found fine white ash and slivers of some a hard substance.

"That's mine!" Clara stood at the doorway. Her anger heated the room.

Startled, the box slipped out of Anna's hand and fell, spreading the contents on the floor. Clara ran at her furious, hitting her, the blows surprisingly hard. When the child's fury was exhausted, Clara bent down to scoop up the ash. Anne did not need to be told what it was. She got a soft brush and a sheet of paper. Together they retrieved what they could, but some of the ash remained ground into the widening cracks age had inflicted on the wood flooring. Clara was crying.

When she had the box safely in her hands, she said, "I'm sorry I hit you."

"I deserved it. I had no right to pry into something of yours. It's just that I want you to be happy here, and you and Maria seem so miserable. I thought if I learned more about you, I would know what to do." After a moment she asked, "How did you get that?"

"After Momma's funeral, and everybody went home, Papa and Maria and I went out to our back yard where Momma had a garden she planted and took care of. She sent away to Germany for flower seeds and made a rock garden of tiny plants, alpines she called them, because they grew in the mountains near her home. They stay small so the snow and cold doesn't have so much to kill. Papa sprinkled the ashes there. He said they would enrich, that's the word he used, enrich the garden and the flowers would grow better, and that way Momma was still helping the garden. But Maria and I wanted some of her, so when Papa was on the phone we went outside and scraped up all the little bits we could find and saved them in the box. Now there won't be so much left. But don't tell Maria."

Anne put her arms around the child and was alarmed at how slight she was. There didn't seem room enough in the flimsy body to contain so large a measure of grief. Clara allowed herself to be held, and afterward they went down the stairway hand in hand to find Maria coming in search of them.

Anne dug out the picture albums she had packed, and with Maria on one side and Clara on the other she turned the pages, hoping to capture the girls in the net of family memories but apart from some attention to the pictures of their German shepherds, "Why did you have such big dogs?" only absences caught their interest. "Where are your grandfather, mother, husband, daughter, and son now?" they asked with a hint of accusation, as if she had been careless.

When she saw how their interest lay in what was gone, Anne said, "Tell me about your mother."

"She was teaching me to cook," Clara said. "We would roll out the strudel on the kitchen table until it was so thin you could read a newspaper through it."

"She let me put the apple slices on it," Maria said. "She made dresses for my doll, Liebchen."

Things that require time. Worse, Laura took manual training instead of cooking class, and she had never held a needle in her life. "What do you and Maria do with Laura?"

"We keep out of the way," Maria said.

Clara wanted to be fair. "She has to practice a lot."

"What do you think of her playing the violin so much?"

"Papa likes it," Clara said. "Sometimes he plays duets with her. I wish she would teach me."

"Have you asked her?"

"No, she wouldn't have time."

Anne imagined the conversation she would have with Laura. "You took them on when you married. You have as much responsibility to them as you have to Dietrich or your music." If Laura demurred, she would be relentless, "Yes, your music." And she would pass on Clara's wish. She imagined Laura with Clara standing by her side. Music instead of strudel. And Maria? "Do you want to play the violin, too?" she asked.

"No, it takes all day. I want to do what Daddy does, just wave your arms around."

It grew dark. The three of them sat on the porch, reluctant to go upstairs and end the day. As they sat there, sparks like gold confetti began to flash among the grasses.

Clara hesitated as if it were too improbable to have a name and then asked, "What is it?"

"Fireflies," Anne told her, pleased to be furnished with something to amuse the girls. She remembered their interest in learning and added, "There's a river near Bangkok where there are so many thousands of fireflies that at night fishermen are guided home by their light." She thought of the bombers that took off from their bases in Thailand for air strikes in Vietnam and imagined them navigating home by the fragile flares.

"Why do the fireflies do that?" Clara asked.

"The male flashes and the female signals back, and then they meet."

"What will happen when Laura and Papa have babies?" Clara asked. The leap was breathtaking.

"I'm not sure they will," Anne said, thinking of the disdain in Laura's voice as she described the second violinist's choice of her baby over the quartet. "But, if they did, then you would have a brother or sister."

"They would still keep us?" Maria wanted to know.

"Yes, of course. I'm sure you're the most important thing in your father's life and always will be." They appeared reassured.

"Can you catch fireflies?" Maria asked.

At first Anne wanted to discourage them, not liking the idea of constraint for something so ephemeral, but then she thought of the bits of ash and bone scrubbed into the wood of the cabin, and it seemed a fair trade. "They can't live in captivity for more than a few days, so you must be sure to release them before you go home." She poked holes in the jar's cover and added some leaves, and then together they tiptoed around in the damp grasses capturing the little lights. The girls went to bed with the jar of fireflies on their dresser, content to sleep, each in her own bed.

When Laura drove up at the end of the week, the retrieval of the girls appeared an afterthought. Her mind was on her first performance with the quartet. But Anne saw how the girls put themselves in Laura's way. Something had given them the courage to be noticed. Clara told about the fireflies, showing Laura the empty jar. Maria insisted Laura come and look at the Indian pipes.

"Well, you two have settled in," Laura said. "It's a pity the cabin is going to be torn down."

The girls gave Anne accusing looks. She should have prepared them. She seduced them into the heart of the cabin, and now the cabin was going to be taken away. Why wouldn't they feel betrayed? "We'll find another cabin like this one to rent," she said, but they looked away embarrassed for her and fell into the silence of their first days.

When she was alone for a minute with her daughter, Anne said, "Clara wants to learn the violin."

"That's just a phase. She has no idea of what's involved, of the sacrifices."

"I didn't say that to you when you asked for lessons."

"Touché. I'll get her a teacher."

"You used to give lessons."

"I have no desire to go back to that. Anyhow, she wouldn't want to spend that much time with me. I don't think she even likes me."

"You're going to be living with Clara for years; you can't be her mother; why not give her the violin? Maybe she won't stick with it, but if she does, she won't forget where the gift came from."

Before they left the girls shook hands with Anne and thanked her nicely. Anne wanted to put her arms around them, but they had not forgiven her for allowing the cabin to be torn down and kept their distance. When it was time to get into the car, the girls hesitated. Laura said, "Clara, sit in front and check the map for me." Maria objected and was placated with a promise that she would have a turn. Laura appeared pleased to be in demand.

In the cabin Anne was disconcerted over how little of the girls remained behind. Their towels and washcloths were neatly folded. They had made their beds. Their closet and dresser drawers overflowed with emptiness but stuck in the mirror was the jay's blue feather, which Anne took not as something rejected, but as a gift, and she put it with the things she had come there to take away.

Anne was nine during the Great Depression. When she first heard the term, a bank holiday, she had an image of her grandfather's bank with its marble pillars picking up its skirts and dancing down the street. Before she and her mother left Chicago for their enforced summer at the cabin, her father had a serious talk with Anne. There was a note of wonder in his voice, as if what he was about to relate was hardly credulous, so Anne didn't take him seriously.

"Your grandfather's bank has had to close down, Anne. I'm afraid we lost a lot of money. Things are sure to get better, but right now the best thing is for you and your mother to stay at the cabin."

With a child's pitilessness she refused to acknowledge the plea in his voice, angry that he should be asking something of her when it ought to be the other way around. "You promised I could go to camp this year. They've got horses at the camp." Her copy of *Black Beauty* was falling apart from love. The little china horses she collected were named Lizzie, Ginger, Marylegs, and Sir Oliver after the horses in the book.

"That's a very expensive camp. We can't afford it."

"Grandpa would give me the money." She was not ashamed to play one off against the other.

"Your grandfather doesn't have the money. Anyhow, you are not to bother your grandfather. He's not well."

"What's the matter with him?"

Charles was pleased to see at last on his daughter's face genuine concern for someone else. "Your grandfather has had a little stroke. I'm going to stay here with your grandmother and keep an eye on things. I have to see that people get their money back."

"Did you and Grandpa take their money?"

This suggestion wounded her father with its echoes of the depositors' wrath. That Charles and his father had lost everything was considered by the depositors just punishment. "Of course not, Anne. What a terrible thing to say." He tried another tack. "John's son, Sam, will be there. He must be your age."

"Sam's two years older and he's a boy. Anyhow, John lets him do anything he wants and I can't."

"Mr. McCraig to you, and he certainly doesn't let Sam do anything he wants. Sam has lived up there all his life, so naturally there are things about the woods he knows that you don't. This summer will be a good time for you to learn, and he'll be glad to teach you."

Anne compressed her lips into a slammed door and resolved to have nothing to do with Sam.

It was Carol's first time to drive from Chicago to northern Wisconsin without Charles, and in her reluctance she made wrong turns. With the car windows open the hot, dusty air rushed in, with the windows shut, Carol and Anne suffocated, but the car itself was a bulwark. It was a large Lincoln sedan with gray velour upholstery and down cushions. On the windows were silk shades. Charles had moved the car each night so the sheriff couldn't find it. Their oriental rugs, Carol's silver dresser set, her diamond engagement ring, and Charles's Purdey hunting rifle had all been surrendered. Carol's worst moment came when she asked Anne why she no longer wore her add-a-pearl necklace with a pearl for each birthday. Anne whispered, "I hid it so the sheriff couldn't take it."

They came at last to the country of feed stores and bait shops. The drive down the last mile of sandy trail to the cabin brought them to the place neither one of them wanted to be. When Carol wrenched opened the cabin door, they were attacked by a revenge of hot air furious at months of being cooped up. The slashed curtains and nibbled cushions suggested chipmunks had been trapped inside. Now Carol and Anne would exchange places with the prisoners.

From upstairs in her bedroom, where she had gone to nourish her misery, Anne called, "Mom, it stinks in here from a dead bird." There was a note of pious satisfaction in her voice.

Carol called up the stairway, "Wrap the bird in newspaper and get rid of it."

"I don't want to touch it. It's got bugs in it."

"Use the dustpan."

The small gruesome activity appeared to satisfy Anne, who marched down the stairway displaying the dead bird to Carol in a way that suggested it represented everything Anne felt about being there.

Before Carol had come up to the cabin for the first time, Charles had told her beguiling stories of the woods and the river. On her first visit Carol was faced with the reality of black flies and an outdoor toilet. The cabin had come between Carol and Charles early in their relationship. They had planned to marry as soon as he was out of the army, and then she had received a letter from somewhere in France. The letter began in a chatty way with news. Two hundred Sioux Indians had arrived to join in the fighting. Charles's division had adopted a little French war orphan, Marie Louise. The Quartermaster Corps was passing out free seeds: peas, beans, and cucumbers. Charles was using his trench pick to break the ground and his helmet as a sprinkling can.

And then the reason for the letter. "I've been thinking a lot these last months," he wrote Carol. "You know how anxious I am to make you my wife; I wanted to get married before I shipped out, but I'm not sure I'm in any shape to be a husband right away. Before I bury myself in Dad's bank and settle down, I'd like to go up north to a spot on the river where I used to camp. If I'm not thinking about you, which is what I do most of the time, I'm thinking about the north woods. At night in the trenches I close my eyes and see myself in a canoe on a sunny day when you can look clear down to weeds waving in the current. Nothing hidden. My grandmother left me a little money, and I've been thinking of spending it on a cabin. I know someone up there, John McCraig, who would help me build it. It wouldn't take much money and then it could be our getaway for the rest of our lives. Write me and let me know what you think and be honest."

Their marriage was delayed a year.

Although the cabin now had conveniences, Carol continued to resist visits. It was like childhood days at summer camp where for a few weeks you lived in a cabin, and then, after you packed your things to go home you looked around and nothing remained to say you had been there.

Charles came on his own for hunting and fishing trips. Seeing Carol and Anne off that morning he had not been able to hide his envy at their good luck while he had to remain in town to care for his father and sort out the catastrophe of the bank's closing. His attitude suggested Carol and Anne were embarking on a kind of lark or idyllic vacation. That angered Carol, who mourned the loss of their home. She was a woman who might have painted a picture or written a book. She had ideas that did not fit into social conversation. She put her creativity into the house, whose every room was that picture and that book. She didn't blame Charles, but she was angry with him for not admitting how much she was losing when their home was taken from her. When Carol drove away with Anne, she and Charles were barely speaking.

Taking possession of the cabin, she unpacked the Staffordshire china, putting a dozen double-handled bouillon soups in a cupboard that had held ammunition and gun-cleaning supplies. The pearl-handled dessert knives and forks went into a drawer that had been home to hammers, screwdrivers, awls, and chisels.

Anne, who watched with dread this evidence of settling in, demanded, "Why did you bring so much stuff?"

"I told you that Dad will be selling the house."

When Carol saw the expression on Anne's face, she stopped what she was doing and said in a voice suggesting the promise of untold pleasures and a reckless denial of mosquitoes, "Let's have a picnic down on the landing." A circumspect woman, she had been driven to a rash act by her daughter.

She rubbed Anne with citronella, gathered up paper plates, ham sandwiches, and a box of Nabiscos, and marched down to the river, with Anne trailing her as if she were being led into an ambush. The early June evening was full of daylight, the sun's reflection on the water a second afternoon.

The melting snows had filled the river, and the gorged waters rushed past them with casual indifference. The landing on which Carol settled was nothing more than rough boards. She would no more dip a languid hand in this river than thrust it into an alligator's mouth.

Anne said, "I'll get slivers from the boards."

"Sit on a couple of paper napkins."

"When are we going home?"

"The cabin isn't winterized, so we'll have to go back in the fall."

"I memorized the way we came. I could hitchhike back if I wanted to."

Carol said nothing, reluctant to remove her daughter's hope of escape. She had her own daydream. Perhaps when she and Anne were well away from the cabin, a fire would burn it down.

Anne pointed to a small brown animal undulating through the water in graceful circles. She whispered, "It looks just like Grandma's fur piece." The mink, apparently fearless, even aggressive, moved closer to the dock, its triangular head above water, its beady black eyes regarding the interlopers. It dove and swam away. They were silent for a moment, missing it.

The sun moved behind the stiff fringe of red pine and tamarack. A chill crept up from the river and touched them with cold fingers. A series of yapping barks came from somewhere in the woods.

"What's *that*?" Anne asked.

"I think they're coyotes. Coyotes don't attack people." Carol tried to make her voice convincing.

"I wonder what Dad's doing?" Anne brought her father into their small group as protection.

"Time for bed. It's been a long day." Carol attempted to sound authoritative but doubted that anyone could be in charge in so unstructured a place.

"It's still daylight," but Anne allowed herself to be shepherded into the cabin, watching with relief as Carol bolted the door against the approaching woods.

The routine of washing and getting into their nightgowns helped them through the next half hour. Anne paused at the entrance to her mother's room. "I could sleep with you." Carol's quick agreement seemed to worry her daughter, as if their roles might be reversed. In the night they heard the coyotes again. Nothing in Anne and Carol's past comportment suggested that they might draw close to each other so they stared alone into the darkness assessing.

They were eating breakfast when John McCraig and his eleven-year-old son, Sam, appeared at the door. John had helped Charles build the cabin. Carol knew him only as someone stopping by to repair a leak in the roof or summon Charles for a fishing trip. He was to be the one she would turn to in emergencies. Charles had said, "I know I don't have anything to worry about with John to keep an eye on you."

His greeting was formal, almost distant. Carol guessed he was a man who had gone through life embarrassed and resentful of his good looks, a target for girls at school, but clearly not a man to make the most of his attraction.

"Sam brought something over to show your girl."

Sam was holding a small cage. He removed what looked like a

stuffed toy. Instinctively Anne reached for it.

Sam warned, "Be careful it doesn't get away. It's a flying squirrel."

"Flying?" Anne let the tiny animal lay quiet in her hands, terrified but trusting.

"It's got this membrane that stretches out on each side so it can glide from branch to branch."

"Its eyes are so big."

"It's nocturnal. That means it's out at night, so it needs eyes that see in the dark." Sam was a natural teacher; both insistent and patient, certain there was an explanation for everything. He had overheard his parents talking about the Hennerts' troubles, and he looked at Anne in much the tender way he looked at the squirrel. Tentatively he invited, "You want to go fishing?" It was the best thing he could offer.

"I don't know how."

"That's OK. I'll teach you. We've got stuff in the truck." He placed the squirrel back in its cage and asked, "Do you mind if I leave the cage here, Mrs. Hennert? The squirrel won't get out."

"That's fine, Sam."

Carol stood at the window watching Anne adding skips to her steps to keep up with Sam's strides. "Good Lord," Carol thought, "she's in love and she's only nine years old." She turned back to John. "It's nice of your son to take an interest in Anne."

"I was surprised myself. Apart from school he isn't around girls much. He's like me, happiest outdoors. I wouldn't survive a week in that bank of your husband's."

"We're not sure the bank will survive."

"Charles wrote me. I'm sorry. Our little bank up here closed but I didn't have much in it. Anything Helen and I have is invested in my truck and tools. Money comes from what I can do with my hands." He had the confidence of a man whose work is there for anyone to see and judge.

Carol looked at his hands, a builder's hands, and then blushed as if she had done something indecent.

"I'll let you get on with settling in. Sam can walk home." He handed her a piece of paper with his phone number neatly printed as if it were a measurement. "Call me anytime. Helen would have had you and your girl over for supper on your first night, but her mother's just had an operation and Helen's in Milwaukee taking care of her. Sam and I are batching it. My son will catch some fish for your supper, though. You can count on that."

Carol, believing her instincts might be full of danger, worried that she tended to speak before she thought. Nevertheless she said, "Come and have the fish with us. Anne would enjoy Sam's company and I'd welcome talking with someone older than nine."

"That's very kind of you. It would make for a pleasant change." He spoke with an elaborate courtesy, as if there in the woods of northern Wisconsin everyone was a character in some nineteenth-century English novel, as if formality were a defense against the wilderness.

After John left, Carol began to take possession, cleaning, rearranging, recklessly spending a half hour grouping books by fiction and nonfiction as if it were necessary to keep track of what was real and what imagined, for though she knew it was foolish she couldn't get rid of the idea that the cabin had a mind of its own and she was there on sufferance. At any moment the cabin, recognizing the antipathy she felt for it, might rise up and evict her. Its resistance was apparent in the way the drawers stuck and then spilled everything when she pulled hard, how the pilot light in the water heater had gone out, even the pump that sucked in the water from the river skipped beats like an unwilling heart. She made a list of things for John to do. In a desk drawer she found, among decks of soiled playing cards and expired fishing licenses, a diary Charles had kept of the cabin's construction. John's name was mentioned several times. If he helped to build the cabin, he must have influence over it.

JUNE 12, 1919

Turned down an invitation from John and Helen to stay at their place while John and I build the cabin. Don't know what they'd make of my nightmares. I've pitched the tent at the edge of the river where the sound of the water over the boulders is restful, but the early spring mists creep in, laying a wet hand on the canvas and even my bedclothes. Woke up last night crying out and there were reciprocal howls from a pack of coyotes across the river. Later a porcupine woke me up gnawing at the posts that anchor the tent. Saw bear tracks around the tent this morning, bear probably lured by the smell of food. Don't mind all that. Just as soon not to be alone in the night.

I didn't have it any worse than anyone else, but for several weeks my detail scouted the battlefield identifying dead bodies or parts of bodies, a torso or a head. Once I found a pair of clasped hands as if the soldier had been killed at his prayers. Stands to reason the

army frequently rotated the detail. After a month I was transferred
to communications.

JUNE 14, 1919

Up with the sun notching logs with John. I kept at it until dark,
long after John took off for his own cabin. Before he left he said,
"You're going to kill yourself with work before this cabin gets built."
I try to read at night but the oil lamp's not bright enough to see by,
so instead, I think. Not a good idea. We're going to have to find a
couple of men to help us wrestle the logs into place.

JUNE 16, 1919

There was no wind last night but there was a loud rattling of dead
leaves on the forest floor. When I shined my flashlight on the leaves,
I discovered the noise came from emerging earthworms.

JUNE 20, 1919

I moved around the stakes to outline the perimeters of the cabin,
testing the view and auditioning the light. Would a morning sun
be better in the bedroom to encourage you to get out of bed and get
started or would the sun be better streaming into the windows of
the living room in the late afternoons? I'd like a view of the dead
tree across the river, the one where the eagle perches because there
are no leaves to cut off its view.

John disagrees with me about where I want the cabin. He's ar-
guing for a location on a rise, protected by trees and well away from
the river. "It's going to be too damp," he warned, "and the river acts
like a chute for the wind. You might as well live in a canoe."

I finally made my decision and pounded in the stakes for the final time. Tonight I moved the tent inside the vacant perimeter, and what do you know, I slept.

The diary with Charles's love for the cabin made her jealous and shamed her for not giving the place the credit it was due. When John and Sam came for dinner, Carol mentioned the diary to John.

"I never knew a man more eager to get a building around him."

The four of them sat at the table like a family. Anne appeared to have a personal relationship with each piece of fish. "I caught this one myself, and the one you're eating, Mom, Sam caught. He said it was one of the largest he'd seen this year. Mine is more the regular size. The one on Mr. McCraig's plate I caught on a leech. I put the leech on the hook myself. Leeches are really squishy and they suck your blood, but Sam said you can't be a fisherman unless you can handle them."

There was no stopping her. "I'll bet you don't know the difference between ruffed grouse and sharp-tailed grouse or what's red pine and what's white. Sam showed me a beaver dam, and he took away some sticks, and then we waited and in a little while a beaver swam out and slapped the water with its tail, and its tail is like this." Anne demonstrated. "A muskrat's tail is like that." She turned her hand. "Sam knows the clouds, and he said it's going to rain tonight because the clouds are mare's tails."

Sam was clearly embarrassed. Carol and John avoided each other's eyes. Anne wasn't finished.

"And he knows a lot of things in the woods you can eat beside these."

On their plates were boiled and buttered early milkweed pods that Anne and Sam, like simplers, had gathered in the woods. At first Carol had hesitated but John reassured her. "They taste like a mix of green beans and asparagus. Perfectly safe. Sam reads books about Indians and pioneers. He comes home with all kinds of things, and we're still alive."

After dinner Sam headed into the woods with a glass jar followed by Anne, who was lured by the potential of the jar's emptiness. Sam had not invited her, but he slowed his pace so she could keep up.

Carol and John settled on the screen porch. Carol was used to men who worked in offices doing things you could not see or understand. Here was a man who built, right before your eyes, the house that would shelter you.

Politely he asked, "It must be a change for you, living up here in the cabin."

"I hate it." She had not been that direct with anyone else, not Charles.

"You're probably spoiled. Anyone with any sense would love it." It was going to be a two-way street.

In minutes they had traveled far. "I'm not like Anne. I don't much care what's out there. I care about what I left behind—the city, my house. I'd rather have a painting of a landscape than a landscape. All this seems waiting for someone to come along and do something with it. I keep looking over my shoulder. Anne crawled in bed with me last night, and I was relieved to have her there. I shouldn't have to rely on my daughter for courage; I should be the one protecting her."

He put a comforting hand on her shoulder.

She had honestly tried to put him off, showing him a side of herself that would be unattractive to him, but the light weight of his hand on her was fatal. June bugs flung themselves relentlessly against the screen, vibrating their wings in a frenzy of frustration at being kept out. Like a revenant a pale green Luna moth manifested itself, looked in at them, and then disappeared. From somewhere in the imminent darkness she heard Anne's call, "Don't go so fast. I can't see you."

Sam must have waited, for they arrived together. Anne was holding a jar that imprisoned an emerald-green creature as perfect as a jewel.

"It's a tree frog. Sam says I can keep him."

After John and Sam left, Anne, drugged with fresh air and exhausted from her long walk, had no complaint about bed, insisting on the sleeping porch. "Sam says it's healthier to sleep outdoors."

Carol waited until Anne was asleep before she stole out to the landing and the indifferent river. Masses of clouds swept the sky. A wind with a chill to it caught at her skirt and her hair. Dead leaves, leftover from the fall, swirled through the air to settle in new places. She thought of herself as exiled to an inhospitable place, like a Russian émigré living in sufferance in France. Everything was unfamiliar and took extra trouble and a different language. She didn't know the vernacular. She missed her home. She missed Charles and blamed him for leaving her on her own where she was floundering.

A streak of lightning sliced the sky. It was so close she could smell the sharp odor. A warning. A gust of wind shooting the tunnel of the river sent up an unearthly howl. Sheets of rain came at her. She ran for the cabin, seeing it for the first time as a refuge. Lightning struck a nearby tree. A little later a branch brought down by the wind landed with a thud on the roof. Carol had resisted the cabin, but when, like the ship, it stood fast, she relented.

In the morning John came over to see if there was any damage. "Thought I'd better check." After that he came nearly every day. There was always something to do: Carol was particular and John conscientious. He was a teacher like his son. When the kitchen lights went out he introduced her to the fuse box, and under his tutelage she discovered the workings of the pilot light and the shutoff valve for the water.

At home she called repairmen and left everything to them. It had never occurred to her that she might have a part in the process, that a home's many visceral secrets could be learned and any waywardness mastered. She gained confidence under John's earnest teaching and chatted easily with him about stopper seals and adapter plugs. This new knowledge cheered her. If the small world of the cabin could be mended, why not the universe. And there was a part she could play. She had discovered an aesthetic in the mundane.

If John arrived in the morning, she made coffee; and, when he finished his repair and his instruction, they sat at the kitchen table or on the steps of the back porch not too close to each other, their relationship crafted of diffidence and distance. Parallel to their caution was a sensitivity that made being together in the most ordinary circumstances exquisite. The simple request, "Can you steady the ladder, Carol," was full of suggestion, her hands only inches from him.

One afternoon John came into the kitchen after repairing a patch on the roof. "I was hurrying to get the job done," he said, "but the rain beat me to it." Carol handed him a dry T-shirt of Charles's. John broke some unspoken rule, stripping off his wet shirt in front of her. She and Charles undressed privately, and she was not prepared for the shock of John's bare chest, secretly pale against the tan of his arms and throat. She stood there unprotected. He saw at once what he had done and wavered, but the two of them were like soldiers whose years of training kept them, as they faced almost certain death, from deserting. Hastily he put on his the shirt.

The screen door slammed as Anne hurried into the room saying, "I'm thirsty." Turning away from John, Carol poured a glass of lemonade over shards of ice.

The next day John dropped by to explain, "My neighbors are putting on an addition. I'm going to be working pretty steadily on it. I've written down their number in case you have an emergency, but I'm sure you can handle what comes up."

She was on her own. That was what learning led to.

"Helen called. She's coming back next week. I hope you and Annie will come over for dinner." He was allowed a fond name for her daughter.

"We would love to. Don't worry about us. We'll be fine." She smiled to let him know they were friends. "I'm looking forward to fixing the place up. Anne and I are driving up to Duluth to get some new curtains."

He looked relieved. "That's the spirit."

Although there was no ostensible reason in the world to do it, they shook hands, two explorers who have come upon each other safe in dangerous country.

ere is Anne Hennert in her senior year at the University of
Michigan using her birthday money to buy a ticket for the
Greyhound bus that will take her by a meandering route to
her assignation with Sam. She likes the word "assignation" with
its whiff of sophistication and experience, qualities she has yet to
attain.

In Ann Arbor she leaves behind a university playing at war. The
students who have enlisted in the ROTC attend class in their uni-
forms so that the university seems always on parade. On an optimistic note a Japanese language department has been set up to
train soldiers to rule a defeated Japan. Lawyers in their thirties and
forties, drafted into the Judge Advocate School, play volleyball in
the law quad to firm up flabby stomachs. Anne herself has had a
hand in what the world will become. She arranged for Eli Culbertson to address the Post-War Council of which she is president. A
mild, courteous man, Culbertson gave an optimistic lecture on
world government. However, in Anne's Russian classes all is not
well. There is war between one of her Russian instructors, whose
Cossack son was killed by the Bolsheviks, and another instructor
who teaches the students Red Army songs.

In the *Michigan Daily* editorials urge students to make sacrifices for the war, but formal dances are held on Friday and Saturday nights at the Union. At Anne's sorority house you are expected

to wear silk stockings and high heels for dinner.

Sam is in the real war. He is leaving for overseas in a week and Anne's secret traveling is to spend the weekend with him at the one place where they know they are welcome but will remain undiscovered: her family's summer cabin in the woods of northern Wisconsin. Sam picks Anne up at the bus station in Duluth. He has been at a training camp in Lincoln, Nebraska, so it's the first time Anne has seen him in uniform. The university is only a Hollywood costume drama.

Sam enlisted in the spring after graduating from Northern Michigan College with a double major in the lit school and the school of forestry. After the war he wants to spend his life employed by the government he is about to save, tending their many wildernesses, reading books, and as his life fills up, he will write his own book.

For this weekend with Anne he has borrowed his dad's truck, explaining to his parents that he wants to camp out somewhere by himself. His parents, John and Helen, are a little hurt, but their son has given them a week of his leave and his need for trips into the wilderness is nothing new to them. It was John who gave Sam his first trout rod and his first hunting rifle.

Sam's father, John, is as patriotic as the next person, but he doesn't know how he can give his son to the war. He has no dream in which Sam does not figure. He and Helen scrimped to supplement Sam's scholarship, and when Sam stood at the podium, valedictorian of his college graduating class, John wept.

"We make war that we may live in peace," Sam had said.

"I don't know how you think up a sentence like that."

"I didn't," he told his father, "someone said it over a thousand years ago."

John would take nothing away from Sam. "Well, it was your idea to say it now." When Sam wanted a weekend on his own, John would not deny him.

Anne and Sam park the truck a mile or so from the cabin on a trail where Sam says no one ever goes. It's late September but a gentle Indian summer warms them. Anne reaches up to catch hold of leaves as they tumble down, but however hard she tries the leaves elude her.

Sam explains, "Your reaching for a leaf creates a draft of air that takes the leaf in another direction."

"You're not going to be in your pedantic mode all weekend?"

"No." He drops what he's carrying and holds her so tightly that when she is lying next to him on the leaves he can see on her breast the imprint of the tiny eagles from his brass buttons.

Sam's father is the caretaker for the cabin, and Sam has made a copy of his father's key. He opens the door to a room filled with vases of autumn wildflowers: goldenrod, asters, pearly everlastings, and sneezeweed.

"You've made me a bower!" The familiarity of everything overcomes Anne. There on the chairs are her mother's needlepoint cushions that she has seen evolve stitch by stitch, each pillow with a different species of duck that can be found on the river.

Her father's telescope is trained in their direction.

When John begins to undress her, she leads him upstairs.

The sun lowers, cooling the sleeping porch. The bed swings on its chains and she recalls childhood nights when storms came up and the bed rocked with the wind.

They play at keeping house. Anne opens a box of macaroni and cheese and a can of peas. She lights candles and sets the table with silverware in the order her mother taught her. Sam makes a fire and opens the bottle of Chianti purchased in Duluth and snug in its straw upholstery.

They are at opposite purposes. "I don't understand why we can't get married," Anne says. "The government can hurry things up if you're going overseas." They sit in front of the fire toasting marshmallows and vying with each other to see who can slip off the most charred skin from a single marshmallow. This is an old competition.

"It wouldn't be fair to you," Sam says. "What if I don't come back?" He is embarrassed to be using the hackneyed excuse, for he expects to come back. He sees himself after the war, seasoned, a little pessimistic, even in despair over what he has experienced, but better suited for the life he plans. He doesn't have a great deal to write about now, but when he returns he will write about what he learned on the battlefield. Much as he loves Anne, and he does love her, only then will he be ready to marry. If by some misfortune Anne no longer cares for him, well, he will write about that.

"You're not twenty yet," Sam says.

"Juliet was fourteen."

"Look how that ended."

Anne believes if she marries Sam, nothing will happen to him, as if so holy a compact would protect him from the dangers of war. She has considered getting pregnant. Sam would be sure to marry her, but he is taking precautions. Anne did all she could do to sustain herself in the long moments it took to effect the precautions, which at first seemed like some sort of hygienic exercise involving a third person until he invited her to help.

Anne cries and Sam cries, too, for the serious turn their lives have taken. From supporting players they have become principals. The lives of others are drab and without meaning or consequence while their own lives are caught up in love and war, the great themes of literature. They have become important.

There is an old windup Victrola and they dance by the light of the fire to "Stardust" and "It's Been a Long, Long Time." They play records that belonged to Anne's grandparents, "Tea for Two" and "My Blue Heaven." As they change the old records, the labels' gold dust rubs off on their hands.

It's after midnight and they are on the sleeping porch when they catch sight of fingers of light clawing at the dark. Red, green, yellow pulsating streaks sweep across the sky. They have seen northern lights but not when they have been together like this. They run outside naked, shivering and laughing, exposing themselves to solar winds, and ten thousand volts of electric currents and the great magnetic pull of the earth that promises to keep them grounded.

Next morning Sam goes out with his fly rod to catch their breakfast. After the close world he and Anne made for themselves, the morning around him is spacious and the cold air startles him into awareness. There was a light frost and the tips of the grasses are white. The algae in the water have died off with the cold weather and the boulders lie visible beneath the showcase of clear water. A pair of migrating wood ducks with painted clown faces let the river's current carry them along with a fecklessness that Sam envies.

The bluegills are shy of his artificial fly and there are long waits between catches, which he doesn't mind. He thinks of the men in his company whom he will soon be joining. His closest friend is Tom Medler. Medler is a veterinary from a small farming community near Saginaw, Michigan. He has endless stories about assisting at the births of calves; some of the stories involve deliveries with ropes and are alarming. Sam confided to Medler his plan to meet Anne, and Medler warned him not to make any commitments. "Next thing you know you'll be all tied up," and Sam shivered thinking of Medler's ropes. There is Jimmy Southerman, whose father was regular army and who has lived all over Central America and can curse in Spanish. There is Vito Morrini, whose family has a fancy food store and whose father sends boxes of cookies and jars of exotic jams and jellies like guava and passion fruit exported from countries that are now killing fields. Sam hadn't missed the men while he was with Anne, but on his own he wonders what they are doing and what stories they will bring back and how much he can tell them of his weekend with Anne. Not much. The fishing and the northern lights.

Coming from a small town in the middle of the woods, he has known, apart from summer visitors like Anne's family, only people like himself. The students at his Upper Peninsula university were familiars. It is the army that has given him a glimpse of how wide the world is and how foolish it would be to settle down without experiencing it. He tells himself the great adventures of his life are ahead of him. In a few weeks he will ship out. The Fifth is advancing in Italy. France and Brussels have been liberated. They are marching into Germany. He could be sent anywhere. It has taken a war to shake him loose from his small universe, but he means to keep going. He hopes he isn't too late.

He believes he understands the dangers ahead of him. He has read the battle scenes in *War and Peace* and *All Quiet on the Western Front*. He has read between the lines of newspaper reports. Thousands of men are dying every week. The best you can hope for if you are among the chosen is a quick, clean death, but it's foolish to dwell on death with the perfect September morning all about him. He hoists his string of bluegills, still flapping, onto the landing, and one by one he slams them against the planking and fillets them wondering if Anne knows how to cook them like his mother does, fried crisp in bacon fat.

He postpones going back into the cabin, thinking there must be one other thing in this brief solitary freedom, and there is. Across the river, just out of sight, something is moving along the shore causing the alder bushes to bend. A black bear pads out into the water. It is large, at least three hundred pounds and maybe more, probably a male. It has the rare white markings on its chest. The bear makes a swipe at a fish, missing it. It stands there in the river oblivious of Sam. After another fruitless swipe it turns to a patch of horsetails along the shore, pulling them up and swallowing them, the ends hanging from its mouth like a scanty beard. The bear is gorging on food to provide for its long winter sleep. In the spring the ravenous bear will emerge from some hollow tree or cave, its skin hanging in loose folds. Berries and ground squirrels will not be enough. It will go on the prowl picking up the scent of a newborn faun or bear cub, perhaps its own. Sam grabs the fish and hurries toward the cabin.

Anne watches Sam head for the river with something that is not quite relief, but a welcome chance for the ordinary. She washes her hair and puts it up in rollers she finds in her mother's dresser and then continues the exploration of the dresser. There are snapshots that have not made it into family albums. She discovers a bleached picture of herself and Sam on the landing squinting into the sun. She is standing as close to Sam as he will let her. She is nine and Sam is eleven. It was taken the summer she and her mother moved up to the cabin after her father's bank failed and they lost their suburban Chicago home. It's the summer she fell in love with Sam. After that she lived for visits to the cabin, refusing to go to camp or lounge around the county club swimming pool. She has dated other boys but she measures them all against Sam.

Anne unfolds her mother's old blue cardigan and puts it around her shoulders. The wool is matted from countless washings. Her mother knows how she feels about Sam and warned her, "It's a great mistake to settle on one boy so early in your life. You have no one to compare Sam with, and the person you are now may not be the person you will be in a few years. You're still changing and your needs will change as well. Give yourself a little time and a little variety."

"Did you change?" Anne asked.

"Yes, I changed." It did not occur to Anne to ask if the change was before or after the marriage to Anne's father.

She wanders down into the kitchen, where she feels strangely alone. If she marries Sam, it will be like this. She will set the breakfast table as she is doing now, as her mother does. After breakfast Sam will take off for some kind of work. And then what will she do? There will be housework and eventually there will be children to care for, but the children will grow up as she has grown up. It would be nice to write novels, but she hasn't really written anything and when she applied to the creative writing course at the university she was not accepted. Up to now her life has been family and Sam. She reviews what her mother and her mother's friends do. None of them have jobs. Several of them volunteer. Her mother plans house tours and auctions to raise funds for the symphony.

She imagines herself on the phone calling other volunteers as she has seen her mother do, or stuffing envelopes, or working with a catering firm for a reception. She becomes a little angry with Sam for going off to his job and leaving her each morning to these dull tasks, so that when he comes into the cabin exhilarated from his fishing she argues with him over frying the bluegills, insisting on butter instead of bacon fat, which she says will ruin the delicate flavor of the fish. Sam says he knows more about the way bluegills taste than she does because he had been catching and eating them all his life. They finish their breakfast in silence and again she thinks of her parents and how sometimes they have silent meals like this.

They are afraid the silence will kill them but don't know how to climb out of it. He tells her about the bear and she listens politely. She goes upstairs and brings down the picture she has found of them as children and he smiles. They decide to leave the next day a little earlier than they planned to be sure to give her enough time to catch the bus. At last he reaches for his unfailing resource. "Let's go down the river."

They drag the canoe from under the porch where it has been stored for the winter and throw in cushions and paddles. They have made this trip together a hundred times. "Watch it, water's low," he calls out. They ease their way around the boulders. They know the deadheads, the trees the loggers left behind, menaces just below the surface to trap a canoe. A family of otters, a mother, father, and three young ones frisk around the canoe. Twice they see deer melting into the woods. Around a bend and far down the river they spot Sam's father. John's canoe is anchored. He's after bass, casting across the river to a bed of weeds.

Sam digs in his paddle. They have just passed the entrance to Lost Creek, a feeder stream where Sam has often fished for trout. Sam and Anne back paddle the canoe into the stream, hoisting it up onto the shore, and fall on the ground smothering their laughter. They are together again, mischievous children who have outwitted a parent. To give John time to move on, they hike along the stream until they come to its source, a small lake where they wander along the shore among reeds and grasses. Green kernels float on the surface of the water.

"Wild rice," Sam says.

"Let's take it home and cook it."

"It has to be aged and parched first, besides, it belongs to the Indians. They have a concession; it's about all that's left to them."

Up in a tree is a deer blind built by John and used by John and Sam during the hunting season. It's an easy climb and they sit in the flimsy shelter looking out at the lake and the woods, pleased with themselves and as much in possession as children in a tree house. This was once Indian country. In another war the Chippewa obtained guns from the French traders and in bloody battles drove the Sioux from their homelands. From this tree the hawk hunts, and beneath the tree the fox snatches the grouse, but none of this concerns them.

The next day Sam turns the key in the lock. They drive away, Anne's head on Sam's shoulder. They're wondering if what they are leaving behind in the cabin is something they escaped or something they abandoned.

Kent and Anne drove to the cabin in separate cars. Anne had to be back at the university where she taught, while Kent would be staying on, having taken a leave of absence from his Episcopal parish. Their German shepherd, Max, rode with Kent. Anne loved him, too, but Kent needed him. The children were spending a long weekend with their grandmother. They had no trouble accepting their father's extended leave. At eighteen Mark half-hoped his father would take up a less embarrassing profession.

Kent arrived at the cabin first. When he opened the car door, Max clambered across him and escaped. The dog was in an ecstasy of renewal, stopping his inventory of familiar smells only long enough to lap water from the river. Kent dropped his gear in the cabin and followed the dog into the woods, a man on a treasure hunt, recalling how Luther said God wrote the Gospel not in the Bible alone but also on trees and flowers.

Last fall's skittish leaves were pinned down by thrusting blades of new grass. On the trees the diminutive leaves were comprehensible in a way they wouldn't be when by the millions they shook out to their full size. Hurrying to beat the imminent shade, a tapestry of trout lilies and spring beauties flourished. Kent knew he was walking in a nursery; most of the fawns born in these woods would be born in the next few days. He considered Mahler's Third Symphony, the awakening of Pan and the coming of summer. He voted not for the marches with the brasses and drums, but the third movement with the off-stage horn solo. "Here it comes."

In his feeble state the energy of spring's progression overwhelmed Kent, and he thought with relief that of all the wonders of nature, the greatest wonder of all was that he had nothing to do with it. There were times when he believed in the Deus Absconditus of lazy theologians, the God who put everything in motion like an intricate clockwork and then turned to other things, settling down perhaps, to a good book. At other times he saw God attentive to an enormous list. Simone Weil, whom he believed something of a scold, though harder on herself than others, announced, "It is not my business to think about God. It is for God to think about me." But that was what Kent was here for. He was here to think about God, for he had become that theological cliché, the doubting clergyman. In the newspaper that morning there was an article about a doctor in Texas who had invented an artificial heart that could save a life. Perhaps some obscure clergyman somewhere was working on an artificial faith that would save a soul.

Max, whose hearing was better than Kent's, turned and bounded back to the cabin to welcome Anne. When Max was through with her, she put her arms around Kent and gave him the careful embrace given to the very old or very ill. In their kitchen back in the city she had watched with him late at night, when glasses of milk and peanut butter sandwiches were shared as solemnly as the Eucharist.

Kent's convictions were in a compartment he could no longer

access; his doubts pulled from their locked files and scattered about. How could he tell Anne the sacrifices she had made all these years, raising their family in a cramped, graceless house and under the critical eyes of a congregation and having to attend countless church meetings and social gatherings; how could he tell her where his doubts were leading? Would they have to start over with no house and with Kent fifty years old and unqualified for a job, perhaps dependent on her salary as an English professor?

And what about the children? What of the special "clergy" rate for their school and camps and the country club where they swam in the summers and met their friends? He could never afford those luxuries on the small salary he would probably draw in what his parishioners often reminded him was the Real World.

On a positive note the children might be relieved at no longer having to serve as examples. Eighteen-year-old Laura, on an application for a summer job, had listed him as an administrator.

How would he explain his leaving the church without imperiling his children's faith? At their age, how could he discuss with them the questions that now beset him on the more obscure points in theology? He imagined their responses. His youngest daughter, Sheila, seventeen, would keen with him, while Laura was merciless in the face of failure. Mark was planning to be an astronaut and would retreat into his world of space; his son might find God before he did. Anne, who was generous and a great believer in order, would forgive him and make a list. Even now as they entered the cabin she was pointing out the rotten boards on the porch.

"As long as you're here, you might get some lumber and replace them."

He brightened a little at the thought of accomplishment. There would be plenty to occupy his time. He and the house would heal together. He might build his way to God.

Anne put the pasta on to boil and Kent tossed the salad. They sipped at glasses of Montrachet while they worked. The Montrachet had been part of a case given each Christmas to Kent by a wealthy parishioner who knew Kent appreciated good wine. That, too, might come to an end.

Anne said, "When you get back you'll need to have a word with Mark. He's slacking on his homework. You can give Sheila some support, too. She's signed up to tutor inner-city kids."

He didn't want all his precious minutes assigned, leaving him no time for seeking. He pictured his mind as a vast landing field cleared as for an emergency, awaiting the imminent touching down of a deciding thought.

When he was silent Anne said, "You aren't still thinking of World Effort?"

"No, no. Nothing like that." He actually owned a medical diagnosis. Manic depressive. The depressive part was acceptable. Anyone could understand why a person might be quietly unhappy. It was the manic part of his illness that put people off since it involved them. He had even dragged in the church.

After long months of counseling a parishioner in extremis and observing the increasingly terrifying effects of her suffering with cancer, Kent had awakened one morning to find his faith misplaced. After her death, the husband of the parishioner had come in heartbroken and wanting solace. Instead of speaking to him of the consolation of God's love and the promise of resurrection, or suggesting as the more masochistically spiritual might that suffering tells us we exist, Kent turned to reason to explain, first to the husband, and then to himself. Reason had led him astray.

Then it had come to him as a revelation that cancer—indeed all diseases—could be cured if the world willed it. Hadn't St. Augustine said that evil resulted from the misuse of free will? Instead of using free will as an excuse for God's tolerance of suffering, free will ought to become man's salvation. Suppose all over the world everyone sold their jewelry—all of it—and gave the money to research. With so much money they would certainly find cures. Look at the diseases that had already been conquered. Millions died from malaria and poisoned water, both things now easily mended.

Kent was quickened by purpose. Why stop with disease. Poverty might be vanquished as well. Bank accounts everywhere would be expropriated. It wasn't God's fault at all. That there was still misery in the world was our fault. Evil is that which has been left undone. The solution was there; we had only to make the effort. He read Tolstoy. He took as his example the Apostles, who held all things in common. He reached into Judaism, whose tenets remind us that we are here to finish God's work of creation. And he had been the one chosen to make it all happen! To gain time he stopped sleeping.

He named his plan World Effort and had a letterhead printed. He wrote friends about a fund he established. He withdrew his and Anne's savings. He talked with Anne about selling her few pieces of jewelry. He approached his parents about their investments and made an impassioned speech to the church finance board about using the church endowment fund. He preached a sermon describing someone attempting to enter heaven and having first to make their way through a blockade of every unneeded purchase they had ever made.

Anne pleaded with Kent, the bishop insisted, and a psychiatrist answered with his prescription pad. "It's all right to have those thoughts," he assured Kent after several interviews. "But you must not act on them." World Effort was dissolved and Kent was left with his acceptable depression and a feeling of emptiness he was waiting for God to fill. When Kent asked the bishop for a leave of absence, it was readily granted.

After dinner he and Anne went out to the landing and let the river do their thinking for them. Kent was brushing Max, letting the prevailing westerlies carry away the combings. The combings would end up as building material. One summer he turned over an upside-down plant saucer to find six pink baby mice snuggled into in a nest of dog hair. Birds used it, too. He had discovered Max's fur in a robin's nest. The nest was constructed of grasses, strips of birch bark, and small twigs cemented by a layer of mud. By sitting on the damp mud and turning around and around, the robin had a made-to-measure home. On top of the mud were soft grasses and the hair from the German shepherd. It bore a resemblance to the perfect world Kent had meant to construct.

On the other bank of the river was a clearing, and now he and Anne heard the familiar hiccoughed peep of a woodcock. The bird, a long sharp bill attached to a small round body, began its courting dance, a kind of swaying shuffle. It was persistent and optimistic in his clumsiness. When the woodcock flew off, they returned to the cabin blessed.

In the morning they went out in the woods to hunt morels, carrying string bags so the spores from the gathered mushrooms would fall onto the ground and reproduce. The morels with their labyrinth-like channels looked like secrets and smelled like caves. Anne searched near spruce stumps and elms, Kent under oak leaf pads, roofs to a thousand tiny lives. He didn't hide his own hunting grounds, but Anne, who always found the most morels, was competitive, and never gave away her favorite haunts.

Kent thought about concealment and power, remembering the sect of Judaism that believes there are only thirty-six righteous people in the world and no one knows who they are. Without those thirty-six, it was said the world could not exist. The Sufis, too, believed only a very few were in direct contact with God. So much exclusion, nearly all the world hived off and useless and himself with it.

Before she left, Anne reminded Kent that John McCraig was nearby. John was the caretaker of the cabin and of the family as well. "I wrote to John," she said, "I asked him to look in on you." It had been a relief to tell her cares to John.

"Don't worry, Annie," John assured her, "they're catching some nice bass a couple of miles downstream. Once I get him out on the river he'll be fine."

Kent was not happy to be in John's care. He had always been a little jealous of John. If there was a crisis at the cabin, it was John, not Kent, who was the first person summoned. John would not think well of his weakness. He tended to solve problems quickly, which to Kent seemed like jumping into a river when you didn't know the depth.

Anne offered to take Max home with her. "You'll be fishing."

Max was in disgrace. The evening before they had been out for a walk when they saw a young doe. Max took off after the deer. They ran after the dog, alternately entreating and scolding. An hour later Max trotted up the path with a dog's smile, tongue lolling, blood on his chest, not *his* blood. They looked everywhere for the doe but never found it.

Kent did not want to be entirely bereft. "He can stay in the cabin when I'm fishing."

He watched her car leave, walking around the bend in the road to get a last view. Tentatively he tasted his isolation. Max was companionable but had no words. He remembered his first visit to the cabin. He and Anne were engaged and he was there to be looked over.

Anne's father, Charles, knowing Kent had just been ordained, held off on drinks.

Anne said, "Kent loves whiskey sours. He was a gunner in the navy for three years."

When they sat down to dinner her mother said, "Kent, would you say grace?"

Kent knew the request was well meant but he hadn't liked being singled out as the holy one. "Oh, I'm not on duty. I'll leave it to one of you."

Grace had never been said at the cabin. When the pause grew awkward, her father, who hated a fuss, said, "Better eat before everything gets cold." The moment passed into cabin history, Charles's words becoming the cabin's official grace, repeated by a generation of hungry and impatient children.

Every winter he and Charles had come up to the cabin for deer-hunting week. Kent didn't care much for hunting, but Charles looked forward to the trips, rather pleased to have his clergyman son-in-law in an apprentice role. Stopping in town with Charles for supplies, they would see a chorus line of bucks dressed out and strung up on the buck pole like macabre dancers. In the evenings the bar would be full of hunters, jubilant as boys let out of school. The parking lots edged in with bulwarks of snow. John would have plowed the trail into the cabin for them and turned on the heater. Kent and Charles built a fire and watched the snow come down. You wanted the snow to stop, perversely; you wanted to see how far it would go. Snow was rarely mentioned in Scripture. The mountains that skip like rams and the little hills like lambs were in dry and dusty country. Kent imagined Adam and Eve shivering in their nakedness. What if Abraham had wandered northward or Moses had led the children of Israel through snowdrifts on their flight from Egypt? How they would have chided Moses then, how they would have murmured against him.

Whatever the weather, when morning came he and Charles were out with the first light. When they had just a sprinkling of snow, tracking was good; when the snow was heavy the deer stayed in the cedar swamps. He and Charles each went their own way, the signal of a success two shots followed by another shot. The companion hunter would come to help with the dressing out and the dragging of the carcass back to the cabin. Over the years Charles had had brought down most of the deer.

That was fine with Kent. He was happy enough to wander in the unfamiliar world layered over the familiar. He discovered the home addresses of the birds he had watched all summer. The wonder was, with so many thousands of birds, there were so few nests to be seen among the bare branches. By the end of summer the ramshackle affairs had fallen to pieces. He approved of the biodegradability, for how would trees look if they were littered with the accumulation of year upon year of tattered birds' nests?

He was usually the first to head for the warmth of the cabin, but one year when he got back he found an irritated Charles miffed that age had shortened his day. After that, Kent had seen to it that he, rather than Charles, was the first one back.

There were no newspapers and Charles wasn't much for reading books, so their evenings were spent playing cards or backgammon, Charles monitoring his natural competitiveness. One night Charles asked, "Do you find your profession embarrassing?"

"What ever do you mean?"

"I mean all the contact you have with the Almighty."

"You make it sound like I'm pestering God."

"No, no, I don't mean that at-all. It's just that you're so much more in touch than we are."

"A lot of that is just going through the motions, Charles."

Charles was shocked. "You mean you don't believe in what you're doing."

Kent knew Charles for a scrupulous man, a man who ran his bank hands-on, regarding his duty as sacred as any priest's; there would be no moment when he just went through the motions. Kent defended himself. "Only a saint could be ardent every second." He hesitated, not wanting to trifle with the man's faith. "Like everyone, I have doubts from time to time. I mean you must have questions about the banking system. There were problems in the thirties."

"All that was corrected long ago." Charles explained at length to Kent how the government had reorganized and guaranteed and regulated. Kent had no similar guarantee to offer in return. Nothing more was said of that night's conversation, Charles either forgetting it or embarrassed for Kent that his profession had not thought to develop an inviolable system. Charles disliked the possibility of bungling.

When Charles was dying, he had asked to see Kent alone. Kent sat with Charles in his sick room with all the sad paraphernalia the dying need to accompany their last journey. Kent anticipated some conversation about mortality, but Charles had only wanted to reminisce about their hunting trips.

It was at the end of the reminiscences that Charles said, "I think about all that snow. I feel now I'm walking into a snowstorm, not a bad one, just a lot of soft snow so I can't see where I'm going."

Kent put the dog inside, spoke a few words of explanation to him, and headed for the river. From the river he would learn persistence. There was mystery and comfort in something that didn't end. It was a parallel life.

Last fall he had seen a cloud-shaped mass, nearly five feet across, vibrating over the water. It dipped over the stream, rose, and dipped again. As he got closer, he could see the cloud was made up of shiny green fragments, thousands of migrating dragonflies—green darners. The cloud bannered out and then disappeared. It was a vision, like something saints saw, and in the telling had to suffer the disbelief of others.

As he slipped into the river feeling the cool water through his waders, he thought of John the Baptist in his raiment of camel's hair with a leather girdle about his loins, no many-pocketed vest or landing net streaming out. John ate the locusts instead of using them as bait. Kent pictured it all. Then cometh Jesus to enter the stream and John forbids him, pleading that he, John, is not worthy to baptize Him. It's a hot day, a scorcher, and the Jordan River is cool and clear, and the little grasses along the bank are green, a miracle in that dry land. Jesus persists and John reluctantly agrees. When Jesus gets out of the water, the heavens open and the Spirit of God descends like a dove, and God's voice says, "This is my Son." And it all happens in a river.

Last summer he and Anne and the children had sat outside stupefied by the pulsing hues of the northern lights. The night darkened and it appeared the show was over, but still they stayed, and after a bit the sky broke out again in reaches of color suggesting revelation might come at any time. So he waited.

John McCraig and his wife, Helen, had planned a trip out west through the Black Hills and into Wyoming. It would have been their first real vacation in years. Spring and summer was usually when John was busiest with construction, but Helen had been asking for this trip for a long time. Planning got them through a punishing winter. Helen looked up the addresses of the chambers of commerce of every state they would drive through and sent for travel brochures that arrived in their mailbox like personal invitations. The local librarian helped her find books to read up on Buffalo Bill Cody, and Annie Oakley, who loved to embroider like Helen did. They read about General Custer with his long red-gold hair and how when he rode out on his way to the Battle of the Big Horn the band at the fort played "The Girl I Left Behind Me" and the children drummed on pots. John and Helen admired Sitting Bull and grieved when he had to take his tribe north across the border to the Grandmother's Country, and then later when, on a cold winter day after the Indian chief refused the government's order to become a farmer, a *sunk*, a dog tied to a tree with a rope, Sitting Bull was killed by Indian police working for the United States government.

Two weeks before they were to leave, Annie Hennert called him. "Kent is going to stay at the cabin for a month. I'm coming up to get him settled but he wants to be by himself. He's had an emotional breakdown, John. Knowing you would be nearby is the only reason I agreed to leaving him alone up there. I don't want to dramatize things, but on his own I'm afraid he might do something drastic. I know I can depend on you to keep an eye on him." John had helped Anne's grandfather build the cabin after WWI, and he had been the caretaker of the cabin ever since, an unofficial caretaker of the family as well, looking after Anne's mother and Anne when they spent a summer at the cabin.

Anne hadn't asked if he had plans of his own, but why didn't he tell her? When he tried to explain to Helen, she said, "I understand. Family responsibilities come first." It was the only sarcastic thing he ever recalled her saying. It was not just the end of their trip; he saw he had been diminished in her eyes. She didn't like him at the Hennerts' beck and call. She didn't like their life dwindled to accommodate the Hennerts. She didn't like his becoming a *sunka*.

By the next spring Helen was ill, and the end of that summer she died. John never forgave himself and more than once had dreams in which he traveled through the west with Helen's casket bumping along in the back of his truck.

The summer after Helen's death he came upon Anne and Kent's daughter, Sheila, in town. She was sitting on the bench that Ritchie's hardware had placed there for the convenience of travelers waiting for the bus north to Duluth. The Ritchie slogan, "Everything you need and more," had worn away in bits and pieces where over the years people had leaned against the back of the bench.

John had completed his errands, he was between jobs, and an early morning storm had made the river too murky for fishing. He had plenty of time on his hands and no eagerness to return to his empty cabin. Unlike the Egyptians, who were buried with all their household goods, Helen left everything behind, each thing a reminder.

He parked the truck and settled down next to Sheila, pushing aside her suitcase. "It's too early for you to be going back to the university. Where are you off to?"

Sheila wouldn't meet his eyes. "I'm going up to town for the day. I've got some shopping to do for Mom." There was no mention of the suitcase.

Her voice was shaky and her face red and blotched. She was eclipsed in one of her brother Mark's shirts, the sleeves rolled up and the tail hanging out covering her shorts. Her sandals and bare toes were dusty, so she must have walked all the way into town from the cabin. She was nineteen, but with her long blond hair and oversized shirt she looked younger and unbearably vulnerable. John had known her since she was three months old. Sheila, and her endearing enthusiasms and impulsive, well-meaning missteps always aroused his tender feelings. Of Annie and Kent's three children, Sheila was the one to fall out of a canoe or a tree or get lost in the woods. The family still talked about the time a four-year-old Sheila was stuck in the clothes chute in their city home. Like a captive wild bird she needed constant tending. It was impossible for him to drive away and leave her. These were dangerous times.

"Tell you what," he said, "I've been meaning to get up to Duluth to look at snow blowers. Not much variety here, and if I wait for winter, they'll all be gone. I'll drive you."

"Oh, no. I'll just wait for the bus. I don't want to give you any trouble."

"No trouble at all. Glad to have the company." Before she could reply he had her suitcase and was headed for his truck. She followed along like a dog dragged into a kennel.

He cleared the front seat of rolls of blueprints for the construction of a cabin he was bidding on, and waited while she climbed in beside him. He had never been one to sashay around a subject, considering it not only a waste of time but also a kind of deceit. It was only an hour and a half to Duluth and he got to work. "I guess you better tell me what's going on, Sheila."

"You have to promise not to tell."

He saw that she was desperate to confide in someone, so he had bargaining power. "You know I'm not a man who goes around telling stories. Let me hear what you have to say and then we'll see."

"I'm pregnant."

Out of the corner of his eye he could see tears falling on her hands, which were crunched, into fists. John pulled the truck over onto the shoulder. There was nothing around them but pine slashed through with the white trunks of birch. A restless jay moved from branch to branch, its call more of a screech than a song.

"Do your folks know?"

"I left them a note they won't find until tonight. I put it with the vodka. They always have a drink before dinner."

He imagined Annie and Kent settled companionably in the

screened porch of the cabin taking their first swallow of the iced drinks and opening the note with no idea of how it would change their lives.

"Who's the father? Who did this to you?" He would throttle the boy with his bare hands.

"John, no one did anything to me. It was something I did with someone, and as much my responsibility as his."

"Are you eloping? Is that where you're off to?"

"No. That's an incredibly romantic idea. I never want to see him again. It was just a one-time thing. We both had too much to drink."

"What kind of college lets kids your age get drunk?" Not having gone to college himself, John had always thought of universities as places where, through some process unknown to him, a student turned into a man fit to live in the world. He hadn't thought much about what happened to women.

"It wasn't anyone's fault but my own, but I'm beginning to show and I have to get out of here. I've got the name of a place."

"You're getting rid of the baby?" Sheila was the one to come home with an abandoned fledgling tenderly cupped in her hands, even overturned beetles were righted, and once when Kent accidently ran over the tail of a garter snake Sheila had nurtured the snake, feeding it leeches and digging earthworms for it.

"No. I'm going to a place downstate for girls who get in trouble. I know about it because a girl in Dad's congregation went there. You stay and then they find a home for the baby."

He was trying to keep up with her but she was going too fast. "Sheila, you belong with your family. I know your mother and father as well as anyone could. They'd stick by you."

"The congregation watching my belly grow? Everyone saying, 'Isn't that just like a minister's daughter?' You know about Dad's nervous breakdown a couple of years ago. He was up here with you. The congregation took him back, but there's still a lot of gossip, and I'm not going to add to it."

"Your mom could stay with you up here. It's the middle of nowhere. When the time comes you can have the baby in the hospital in Duluth."

"I wish, but Mom has her work at the college. She's been prepping for her new course all summer and she's so excited about it. Besides, Dad doesn't do well without her, and how would he explain her absence to everyone at church? More gossip. Anyhow I couldn't stand having her around me all the time looking distraught."

A deer wandered out of the woods and begin to graze a patch of grass along the roadside. They looked at each other, smiling, a secret with no consequences. John, who was not given to impetuous acts, said, "Stay with me." Someone in his house.

For a moment the surprise of his suggestion made the possibility credible, but Sheila tested it. "It would be months. You couldn't want me hanging around."

"It's just what the cabin needs." He didn't mention himself. "Your Mom and Dad would know where you were. They could come up in the holidays. You can't want to be cooped up with strangers."

"I wasn't really looking forward to it. I was afraid it might be like something out of Dickens, you know, sort of an orphanage with everyone in aprons and porridge for dinner, and I'm not good about rules."

He let that pass. "You'd be doing me a favor. I'd enjoy the company and you've always loved it up here."

She grasped at the possibilities. "I could help around the house and cook your meals. I'm a vegan, would that be a problem?"

"Not as long as you don't expect me to be one; to tell you the truth I don't even know what that is." If they could just narrow it down to that one problem. He started the engine and the deer disappeared into the woods. "We'll go and have a talk with your folks." He wanted to get it all settled, afraid she would change her mind. "You're not alone in this now, Sheila." She sat very still beside him, as if the least movement would end the tenuous contrivance they had put together.

At first Anne insisted on staying with Sheila, sending Sheila once more down the road with her suitcase, but this time in plain sight of her family. Anne backed down.

There had been an awkward scene between John and Kent.

"John, I can't tell you how grateful Anne and I are for your offer to care for Sheila. No one would take better care of her. I know this will be an added burden, I mean she has her food tastes, which she certainly didn't get from us, so what I'm saying is that I want to make some kind of financial arrangement with you."

"You mean you want to pay me for taking care of Sheila, like I was running some kind of boarding house?" He had thought at last he was a member of the family and instead he was still someone to be hired.

"No, I don't mean that at all, John." Kent was contrite.

"That's all right," John said. "If I run short, I'll send along a bill."

Labor Day Sheila stood beside John and said good-bye to her parents and her brother and sister. Everyone waved and smiled, but there was a sense of disarrangement, as if the pieces of a puzzle had been jammed together, a hasty answer to a difficult problem. They waited until the car was out of sight for several minutes then Sheila climbed into John's truck and drove with him back to his cabin. John let her in, feeling he had captured an aberrant butterfly that had drifted from its known path.

November storms rushed in from the prairie. The day before the start of hunting season Sheila went out to trample out the hoofprints in the snow near the cabin so hunters couldn't use them to track deer that had become familiars.

"The hunters will only go someplace else," John told her.

"Well, they won't be killing our deer."

Our deer. John liked that.

On opening day he stayed home. It was the first season he had missed since he was a boy of twelve, but he couldn't face how Sheila might look when he went out the door with his deer rifle. He thought of the deer blind he had built long ago near Lost Creek. He had used a good grade of pine and it held up well. He sat up there like a king surveying his domain. Today someone else might be up there.

The snows were persistent, rounding the hills, blurring the shapes of the bushes, and making the woodpile vanish. Sheila said, "Nothing belongs to us anymore."

Late one night she called out to him, and he found her at the living-room window wrapped in her flannel robe. "I heard thunder, and when I looked out there was lightning. Thunder and lightning in the middle of a snow storm."

John started to explain about energy and moisture, but Sheila interrupted him. "No, don't explain it away."

He made tea for himself and heated the last of the soy milk for Sheila. She put out cookies she had made with applesauce and raisins. He reminded himself, as he did several times each day, that this would not last, that by early spring he would once again be alone in the cabin. He was trying to prepare himself, as if a man about to undergo an amputation could anticipate the new lightness of his body.

"We'll tell Mark about it," she said, "he loves things that happen in the sky."

The whole Hennert family was coming up for Thanksgiving. They kept in close touch with Sheila. Every day brought a letter or a phone call from one of them. Kent let Sheila know that he had explained to their close friends in the congregation what Sheila was doing up there and they were taking it well. There had been two deaths of parishioners' children from drug overdoses. In contrast, having a baby out of wedlock seemed a healthy thing to happen to a child. He begged her to come home to them, but Sheila wouldn't budge.

John said, "I ordered a twenty-pound turkey for your folks. That should be plenty for the five of you."

"Not five, six. You're coming for Thanksgiving, aren't you, John?"

"No, I don't think so. It's the first time you've had a chance to be with your family. I'll drop by after dinner."

"You have to be there, or I won't go."

"We'll see," he said, sure that in the excitement of a reunion and all the preparation for dinner he wouldn't be missed. The truth was, the family hadn't had much to say to him. The letters went to Sheila, and when he answered the phone there was only a perfunctory exchange of greetings and then Annie or Kent asked for Sheila. Before they left at the end of the summer, Annie had taken John aside and said, "We owe so much to you, John. Without you, Sheila might be alone in a strange place." Mention was no longer made of their gratitude for his caring for Sheila. Perhaps they were envious of him, wanting to be the one to cosset their daughter, a little hurt that she had chosen to be with John.

The outdoor floodlight was on. Looking through snowflakes they saw three flying squirrels at the bird feeder. They watched the squirrels hide coyly on the far side of a tree and then bungee jump to the feeder and back. Sheila had been horrified when John told her the buttoned-eyed, pocket-sized animals had been known to eat birds nearly as large as they were.

"My son, Sam, gave a flying squirrel to your mother when she was a little girl," he said. Sam and Annie had been in love. Then Sam had been killed in WWII. Sometimes he let himself think that if Sam hadn't died, Sheila might be his grandchild.

Before they said good night, they made plans to travel up to Duluth the next morning to visit the Harvest Foods store. Sheila was out of tofu and soy milk. He looked forward to the trip, the two of them cozy in the truck, the heater warming them and outside the world snowed into emptiness.

At breakfast, listening to the weather report on Duluth's KDAL, they learned roads were closed. Sheila had brown rice and carrots for lunch, and for dinner made do with brown rice and tomato soup diluted with water.

"At least you could put a little milk in that soup," he told her. He worried about the baby growing inside of her with no milk or meat to make its body strong. He had pointed out how foxes ate voles and the coyotes brought down deer. "Animals eat animals."

"I'm not an animal, John. That's the whole point. The human race is supposed to make progress."

John kept his thoughts about that to himself.

By lunchtime of the second day the carrots were gone and there were no soup cans on the shelves. He took a bass out of the freezer. "It's a fish, Sheila. You used to go fishing with Mark and me. It was already there in the freezer. It's not like I'm going out there and killing it."

She shook her head. "John, I care just as much for this baby as you do, probably more, and it's not going to be born with a body that's made of God's dead creatures."

He was furious. He grabbed his down jacket and pulled on his boots.

"What are you doing?" He was glad to see he had frightened her and waited for her to admit she was being foolish, but she just watched in silence as he pocketed the keys for the truck and opened the door to a swirl of wind and snow. He had to shovel the drift in front of the garage before he could back onto what had been a sandy trail and was now a foot of snow. He threw the shovel into the bed of the truck. Sheila had the door to the cabin open and was calling to him. He put the truck into four-wheel drive.

Luckily the snow was light and he got through, even the open stretches where the wind had created a new geography. When he turned from the trail onto the highway to Duluth, he was dismayed to see no tracks on the snow-covered road. He didn't want to be the only one on the surface of the earth.

It didn't take him many miles to consider what would become of Sheila if he got himself killed. In this storm the trip would take several hours, and then he would return on roads that would be worse than this. He looked for a place to turn around, but there was only the highway and on either side, the woods with snow-covered trees like white pillars, gateposts to nothingness. At last he came to the trail that led into Lost Creek. Unless you were familiar with the trail, you would never know it was there under the snow, but John fished the creek regularly in the summer. He swung off the highway and felt the solidity of the trail under the snow. After a few feet he backed onto the highway, but the wheels spun on the snow the truck had packed down. He got out and shoveled until he came to the asphalt. His arms ached, the snow weighed down on his eyelashes so that he could hardly see. His heart pounded and he thought about Ed Merkin, who had died shoveling his front walk.

He got the truck going and headed for the cabin. Halfway back he saw a yellow aura through the snow. A plow was moving along toward him. He stopped to let the hurricane of snow it was making pass by, then he made his way back, encouraged that he wasn't the only one out there.

On the porch he stamped his feet and gave himself a good shaking to get rid of the snow, but she didn't wait. She threw herself against him so that the snow fell on her. Even through his heavy jacket he could feel the bump of her stomach. This was her baby and she must be allowed to care for it as she liked.

She fried the thawed bass in olive oil. "I know it should be bacon fat," she said, "but I just couldn't."

"It tastes fine. You don't have to eat it if you don't want to. It's up to you."

He watched her force down small bites. Later he heard her throwing up.

After that he didn't say anything, and she ate the brown rice and some trail mix John remembered he had stored in one of the pockets of his fishing vest. Two days later an unseasonable warm spell turned the roads first into impassable slush, and then into an accessible stretch north. She drove to Duluth with him, and for the first time he went with her into the food store. With its nuts and whole grains it appeared a place where you'd shop for feed for wild birds or rabbits, but he kept his thoughts to himself, only insisting that they get plenty of everything against the winter.

When Thanksgiving came, John was sorry he let himself be coaxed into joining the family for dinner. They all talked at once, catching up with Mark and Laura, who had been away at their universities, and answering Sheila's questions about what was going on at home. John couldn't find a place to jump in. He missed Helen. She loved to cook, and Thanksgiving had given her a chance to shine. The stringy undercooked sweet potatoes were nothing like the tender syrupy ones with pecans that Helen made, and the gravy had come out of a can. Annie wasn't much interested in cooking, reluctant to isolate herself in the kitchen away from the rest of the family.

The worst moment came during a dessert of store-bought pumpkin pies. They began talking about what Sheila planned to do with the baby. Annie was for keeping the baby, saying she would take a leave of absence to care for it so Sheila could finish school, but Sheila saw the child as a gift, something she could bestow on a couple who longed for and couldn't have a child. "I feel like God," she said, eliciting a raised eyebrow from her clergyman father.

Sheila had often described to John the ideal couple to have her baby. Some days it was a farm couple with storybook animals and a screen door that was always slamming as children ran in and out of a big kitchen, some days it was a pair of professors who read Shakespeare to the child as a bedtime story. John listened to her describe all the things she was not, trying to convince herself, against her own desires, that she wasn't entitled to the baby, that she wouldn't be the best mother. Once he said, "Sheila, the best mother is the one who loves the baby best. Why can't that be you?"

"I'm too scared. I'd make mistakes and there aren't any do-overs with kids. Someday, not now."

That exchange had brought on an afternoon of tears, and he hadn't mentioned her keeping the baby again, but if it were just a matter of time, of her being ready eventually, he had an idea.

At the Thanksgiving dinner, Kent spoke of a family in his congregation that was desperate for a child, but they agreed it would be awkward to have the child where Sheila would have to be in such close touch, difficult for the child and the adoptive parents, too. John didn't want to hear that. Though he hadn't said a word to Sheila, he was planning on offering to raise the child himself until Sheila was older, through college and more settled. He could get a woman in a couple of hours a day at first. He thought Sheila would be pleased to have the child where she could see it whenever she wished. They could share the baby. He always thought of the baby as a boy, another son, and imagined teaching him how to fish and hunt, though, maybe not the hunting because of how Sheila felt.

He had become so used to the fantasy of a little boy running around his cabin that it was hard to admit the impossibility of the idea. Sheila would have the baby and some stranger would take it. She would go back to the university and his cabin would be empty again. Still, his dream was so vivid he couldn't help saying, "I'd be glad to take the baby." And he had laughed with the rest of them at the foolishness of the idea.

verything fell to pieces Mark's senior year at the university. He had given up his childhood dream of becoming an astronaut, but like his father, who had been an Episcopalian priest, he still had his eyes on the heavens. He and his father differed about God. When Mark insisted on scientific proof, his father countered, saying that the science Mark studied was founded on postulates, things taken for granted and never proved. "There's no morality in science," his father said. "When it comes down to decisions, you're on your own. You better have a backup."

"Is that what you consider religion," Mark asked, "a backup?" He knew that was unfair. Often when he awakened in the night he heard his father downstairs prowling. A couple of years ago he had taken a leave of absence from the church. Had his father given up *his* childhood dream as well?

Mark had majored in astronomy with the idea of going on to graduate school and eventually getting a job with NASA. He got through geophysics, feeling the shifting of the great tectonic plates beneath him, but statistical and quantum mechanics defeated him. He hadn't counted on the all the numbers, believing planets and stars moved freely. He graduated with decent grades, but his advisor in the astronomy department discouraged him from going on. With the large number of applicants for graduate school, many of them with an eye on keeping out of the Vietnam War, Mark was unlikely to be accepted. Then the letter had come from the draft board ordering him to report for his physical.

He had gone to antiwar rallies and teach-ins, but it troubled him that some of the dissenters had guns and bombs, so that you had to choose which war to go to. At home his father spoke solemnly of war's destruction, but he also spoke of duty. His mother had a peace sign on her car and once, much to his embarrassment, accompanied him to a demonstration. If he could have made it to graduate school, he wouldn't have given the war that much thought, but now he marshaled reasons for opposing it. Ho Chi Minh was a Vietnamese nationalist first, a Communist second. He had freed his country from France's colonialism only to see Americans arrive. There was My Lai. Something else. Hadn't many of the immigrants, including his own great grandfather, come to America to escape serving in the armies and the wars of their own countries? America had embraced those defectors. Jim Morrison sang to him of love and death, Edwin Star sang, "War is stupid." He confided his plans to the girl he was dating, and she regarded him with the kind of rapt deference due to someone who not only has turned against society but also can explain why.

It might have been different if it had been a matter of choice, but he would not be forced. Maybe his decision had something to do with his father's insistence on seeing all sides of everything until you drowned in possibilities.

Remembering that during the Civil War John Muir retreated to the wilds of Canada to avoid a draft, Mark told his family he was going up to their summer cabin in Wisconsin for a week's fishing, and headed north. His roommate had sent him letters from Toronto's Yorktown extolling love-ins at Queen's Park and folk festivals with Buffy Sainte-Marie and Joni Mitchell, but Mark didn't want the hippy drug scene. He crossed the border at International Falls and entered the vast wilderness of northern Ontario, hitchhiking and, when he had to, walking.

It was mid-summer and the black flies were all around him like hostile air. When he caught sight of a small isolated lake off the road, he stripped and submerged himself in the water to get some relief from the flies. Across the lake from him was a moose in the water, up to its shoulders for the same the purpose. Mark was afraid he'd spook the moose but the beast didn't move. Until that moment he had felt alone. Now in his pursuit of survival he had joined the animal kingdom.

Two days later on the eastern shore of a remote Ontario lake he got a job with a hunting and fishing resort catering to people who flew up from the States. Mark was hired to teach little kids to fish in the resort's stocked pond. He was tender with the children, even assuring a young boy that fish felt no pain, when in Mark's ichthyology class he had dissected with a scientist's pitilessness the nerves and brains of fish.

In teaching the children, he remembered how forbearing his first fishing instructor, John McCraig, had been with him. He was a builder who had helped his grandfather raise their cabin after WWI. John lived near the cabin and was both friend and caretaker. When Mark's father was preoccupied, John was there. From the start, John insisted on a canon of rules and principles. Unlike the children Mark was amusing, John never took Mark to a place where he was guaranteed a fish. If he went without a fish, that, too, became a lesson. Mark tried not to think about John, who he was sure would not forgive him for coming to Canada. While his parents tangled love with forgiveness, John would have no trouble keeping the two separate.

When he had been at the resort for several weeks, Mark took a day off and went fishing. It was early May and there was still a filigree of ice around the shore. The first hawks and eagles were back, free to come and go from the country Mark might never see again. He landed a couple of good-sized bass and one large pike, and took pleasure releasing them, leaving them free to go where they wanted.

The owner, a man in his sixties who had bought the resort ten years ago to get away from a bitter divorce and a boring job, was fishing nearby watching Mark. He took Mark away from the children and hired him on at the resort as a fishing guide, never asking for his ID. He knew where Mark had come from and why. After Mark worked at the resort for a summer, the owner said he'd write a letter to Mark's address in the States officially offering him a job. Mark could go back to the States and bring the letter with him when he recrossed the border to Canada. Eventually he would get landed status and could then apply for Canadian citizenship. Mark couldn't bring himself to give up the citizenship of the country where he was an outlaw.

Sometimes the men he guided asked why he had come north. When he was not forthcoming, most of them guessed and were sympathetic, but one told him he had a son serving in Vietnam and asked for another guide.

In November men flew up from the States to hunt moose. By the end of December, the snows shut down the roads. There was a brief thaw in January, but the next day a hard freeze sent cold air over the melted water, forming diamond dust, millions of tiny crystals exploding in the clear air surrounding Mark like shining bits of mercy. His family did not cut him off. Letters were frequent, though he seldom responded. Then his mother called to tell him of his father's death from a heart attack. It had been over a year since he had heard her voice, which was usually so assured. He was stricken by its bewilderment. A week later a letter arrived from his dad, which Mark took as an affirmation of immortality rather than a comment on the Canadian postal service.

He didn't risk going home for the funeral. How could he stand up in front of his father's congregation? It wasn't until he heard their cabin was to be destroyed to turn a hundred miles of the La Croix into a wild river that he considered risking a return. He would go there and be a witness, something his father talked about in sermons, something to do with being counted.

He couldn't figure out how to cross the border, and then the pilot of the resort plane used to ferry guests to the more obscure lakes for fishing announced he was flying into International Falls. He had to pick up someone from the States and yes, Mark could ride along. The border patrol at the small airport knew the plane, so the check in was perfunctory. Mark slipped away like an orphan and hitched a ride on a truck.

Two days later he was inventorying the familiar trail that led to the cabin, checking off the canes of blackberries, the wild asters, the mullein's velvet leaves with its pillar of fading yellow flowers and not a word of reproach from any of it. When he saw his mother's car parked beside the cabin he hesitated. He hadn't counted on her being there, but of course she would be gathering up the detritus of all their summers. Having her there might even be better than being alone in the cabin, where he was sure to be overwhelmed with all the years. There was no time to fortify his defenses, which didn't matter because she always saw through him. He watched her filling a box with books. "Are you going to take Fennimore Cooper?" he asked. Natty Bumppo and *The Last of the Mohicans* had been a part of childhood rainy days.

He had a hard time escaping from her embrace. "Hey, I'm not going anywhere." The irony of his remark was lost on neither of them.

"How did you get here?"

He told her about the plane and the ride he hitched from Duluth. "Truck driver had been going for eighteen hours. Turned the wheel over to me and fell asleep."

"But you've never driven a truck."

"Wheels and an engine. No problem." He didn't mention that it was his first experience shifting gears.

"What if they find you?" Anne gave the windows a suspicious look.

"Mom, they stopped looking for me a long time ago. No one knows I'm here."

"You must be starved." You couldn't endlessly hug and kiss a twenty-two-year-old son, but you could feed him.

He let himself be led into the kitchen. The last time he had been seated at the table, his father had consoled him over his failure to get into graduate school and talked to him about his upcoming service. Though he had heard his father preach on how man must discover the moral equivalent of war, his father was telling Mark that some of his happiest times had been in the navy in WWII. There were tales about larger-than-life characters his father claimed he would never have known had it not been for the war, as if the war's purpose had been to introduce to him an endless number of interesting people. His father had seen action, but he told no stories of battles and death, or what was worse in Mark's eyes, boredom—days and months and years stolen.

His mother gave him scrambled eggs and bacon and toast she had buttered herself as if he were convalescent. Though he would have preferred coffee, the meal was accompanied by a large glass of milk. The family legend was that cartons of milk disappeared as if by magic when Mark was around. Now there would be new family legends about him.

His mother blurted out the question as if she had been waiting for a long time to ask it. "Was there anything I did or said, I mean like the time I went to the demonstration, that encouraged you?"

His mother had gently opposed the Vietnam War, sitting around chummily with Mark's friends as they talked about evading the draft. She had magneted onto the fridge pictures of Mark at his university sit-in. He absolved her, "Don't feel guilty. I made the decision on my own."

"Mark, isn't there any way for you to come back?"

"I wouldn't be able to get a job without a social security number, and they check against a list." She was making him guilty and he asked in anger, "How far away would I seem if I were in prison?"

When he saw her face he relented, "That was unfair. Let's leave it. How are you?" He had been gone only a little over a year, so how could she have aged so much?

"I'm fine," she said pursuing her habit of never allowing her children to see weakness. "It's been a little hard deciding what to pack. I'm afraid what I leave behind is just what I'll want."

He didn't mean to accuse, but still he asked, "How can you let the state do this to the cabin?"

"It's not the state, Mark, it's the federal government."

"I was speaking generically."

"You make the government sound like it's some hostile entity. We're the government."

"Mom, that's a pretty naïve way of looking at the government. Are you telling me the people who have cabins on the river are thrilled to have the government come along and tear them down?"

"They're getting fair compensation, and to tell you the truth, Mark, I couldn't have managed this place financially unless I sold my condo and moved here."

"You always loved it at the cabin."

"Not in the middle of winter shut off from my friends, trapped by snow and ice."

Mark had a different memory of winter days. On Thanksgiving and Christmas the family drove through the season's first heavy snowfall, mushing into the cabin on snowshoes. His father built a mighty fire to warm the room. In the mornings Mark sneaked out of bed and ran to the window to see how much snow had fallen overnight, hoping that there would be so much he would never have to go back to the city. One winter coyotes ran down a weakened deer and then feasted on it. A fox carried off a haunch and crows came. At the end of two days nothing was left but bones and four hooves. He remembered both his horror and wonder at the cruelty and efficiency of the world.

"If you want to talk to someone who feels like you do about what's happening, you should talk with John McCraig. He's devastated about losing his cabin."

"I'm not sure he would want to talk to me."

"You two used to be inseparable."

"Did you tell him I was in Canada?"

"Yes."

He longed for John's forgiveness, but his mother's one-word answer told the story. He remembered when John took him into town for a Memorial Day observance. He was nine years old and afraid he wouldn't measure up to the solemnity of the occasion. He stood at attention next to John while the commander of the town's veterans' post read the names of local servicemen who had died in WWII and in the Korean War. Mark was embarrassed to be holding an ice cream cone, which didn't seem to be sufficiently respectful, but John had bought it for him so he couldn't just drop it, and anyhow he wasn't finished with it. He hadn't been able to keep from stealing a glance at John's face when his son's name was called out: Samuel Lockhart McCraig. John stared straight ahead, the expression on his face fierce as though he might attack the commander for speaking Sam's name aloud. Afterward a couple of men came up and patted John on the shoulder.

Mark thought he ought to say something. "I guess you miss your son."

"He gave his life for his country, Mark, you can't do better than that."

John bought him a small flag, and driving back to the cabin Mark held the flag out the car window to see it whip back and forth in the wind. John looked over at him. He didn't say anything, but Mark could see he was being disrespectful of the flag and quickly retrieved it. Because it had a lot of sadness in it, Mark felt guilty about enjoying the afternoon. But he had his favorite hot dogs and pop and the ice cream cone and there was the band and the marching and he liked being with John, who didn't treat him as if he were a baby like his parents did. When he asked why Sam had fought in the war, John hadn't told him he would understand when he grew up, but took the trouble to explain about Germany and Hitler and the Nazis and Poland and how Russia had fought with Germany and then with us. John told him about different battles and how many thousands and thousands of soldiers got killed in those battles. John had it all by heart, all the numbers. The numbers had stuck with Mark.

"Should I go and see John?" he asked his mother, dreading the possibility

"Wait a bit." As if he could go next week or the week after.

"I can't risk staying more than a few days."

"You said they wouldn't be looking for you."

"My being here will get around."

He was the man in the family now. "While I'm here, I can help you sort things out." He looked around. "What's going to happen to all of this?" He couldn't see anything they could do without.

"I'm leaving it. It's been here forever."

Mark saw that as a reason to keep it. "Don't you have room for some of the stuff?"

"You forget. There's just my condo."

Something else he had not been there to help with. Being with her was becoming a reproach.

"John helped pick out some of your fishing gear. I'll take it back with me. It'll be waiting when you get home." He looked away but she persisted. "Mark, there's been talk in Congress of an amnesty. Maybe the president will do something."

"He's got his own amnesty program. He pardoned Nixon."

"It doesn't help to be bitter. Nixon's gone. The war is ending. No one is thinking of it anymore. There's a recession. Kissinger's sorting things out in the Middle East. The country has moved on."

Another parade he wouldn't be marching in. "How long are you going to be here?"

"A couple of weeks."

"I can stay a few more days. No one from town comes down here?"

"No. I haven't seen anyone, only John. I don't want you to take any chances, but it would help if you stayed as long as you could. There's a lot to do." He winced at the blatant appeal.

"You can start with the books. I've picked out all the ones I want. Take a look and see if there's anything you might like."

His mother would find no end of tasks.

Over the years he had left a trail of books like so many abandoned loves. He rescued *Cochise*. He remembered crying when the dying warrior had asked his braves to carry him up the hillside where he could watch the sunrise. Mark had thought war a noble thing then. Here was *Valiant, Dog of the Timberline* and *The Black Stallion*, books of animal courage. Here from his freshman year at the university was *The Red Badge of Courage*. In the book, after Henry tells his mother he is going off to war, the mother weeps but speaks of duty, "You must never do any shirking, child, on my account."

He worked all afternoon, suffering his mother's excuses to be in and out of the living room as she repeatedly reassured herself he was still there. When he finished the job, he awarded himself a visit to the river, relieved by the indifference of something that was busy with its own affairs. The leaves on the alder bushes were faded and dusty looking. The tamaracks were beginning to yellow. A kingfisher moved on. A painted turtle slipped off a log into the water. Little absences. The water was low leaving a row of sedges exposed. The bass would be waiting in the deep pockets behind the deadheads. Boulders had elbowed their way to the surface. Only someone who knew the river well could navigate it, a challenge he meant to meet after dinner. A canoe rounded the bend, slipping like an otter around the boulders. It was John. Mark stood his ground.

John let the canoe move another few feet before stopping it, apparently as reluctant as Mark for a meeting. He guided the canoe to the landing, and with one hand stilled the canoe by holding on to an upright that supported the deck. He didn't offer his other hand.

"Mark."

"John, how are you?" At eighty his white hair was thinning and he had lost weight, but the shock of the blue eyes in the tanned face was the same. Mark tried to draw on the thing that had always bound them. "I might go out later. What kind of bait are you using?"

"Bait, hell. What gave you the idea that you're better than someone else?"

"You know I don't think that."

"Then why did you run away to Canada?"

"It's not complicated. I just don't want a chunk taken out of my life for a war I don't believe in."

"What about the guy who took your place and got killed? What about the chunk that was taken out of his life?"

Mark's defenses fell away. What were they doing talking about chunks of life as if life were a piece of meat under the cleaver of a butcher? There were articles, books, and speeches explaining why the war was wrong. Why hadn't he paid more attention to them so he could explain things to John as John had once explained things to him: the war his son had fought in, how the caddis nymph built its little house with bits of stone, and why sometimes Mark's father seemed so distant that Mark worried that his father didn't much like him?

John had reassured him, "Your dad is one of those men who have to figure everything out, Mark. Sometimes that much thinking gets to you, worries you, makes you sad. Nothing to do with you, Mark. Your dad loves you."

Mark said, "I can't explain it, John. I guess we just have to agree to disagree."

"Like some debating society? What have you done with your life? Everything was handed to you. My son worked his way through college and volunteered for the army."

"I remember going with you to that Memorial Day celebration when they read out your son's name." Didn't all the days he and John spent together count for something. "That was a different war."

"We're the same country."

"We're not fighting Hitler now."

"We're fighting Communism aren't we?"

"It's too complicated to explain."

"You mean to talk your way out of it. I'm not stupid, Mark, and nothing is too complicated to explain. I don't know how long you're figuring to stay, but if you're here tomorrow, I'll call the sheriff." With that he pushed the canoe into the river, working the paddle as if he couldn't get away from Mark fast enough, as if his need for distance was so strong it would make the boulders disappear.

Mark clawed his way back to the diminished world John had left him. He had always believed John, and he believed him now when he said he would turn him in. He didn't mention the conversation to his mother, but after dinner he went upstairs and got his things ready. He'd get up before his mother did and make some sandwiches. He didn't know how he'd say good-bye to her.

After dinner he and his mother sat on the screen porch. The sun had slipped behind the trees but its unspent light touched everything. A whippoorwill called and Mark and his mother exchanged looks. It had been his father's favorite bird. As he started to explain to her why he must leave in the morning, they heard a truck pull up.

John strode toward them, pulled open the screen door, and tossed a newspaper onto Mark's lap. Mark winced at what was coming. He didn't want a fight in front of his mother. He didn't want a fight at all. That was the whole idea.

John said to his mother, "When Mark and I had our little talk this afternoon, I wasn't taking you into account, Annie. You could use Mark's help for a few days getting this place ready to leave."

He turned to Mark. "Looks like the president's getting mushy."

Mark picked up the paper. Ford had talked to the Veterans of Foreign Wars' convention. "I'm throwing the weight of my presidency into the scales of justice on the side of leniency." Ford spoke of the eventual reentry of those who had gone to Canada, an earned reentry.

Mark stayed another three days but he fished alone.

A car screeched to a stop, and a moment later the screen door banged shut. Anne's daughter, Sheila, hung on to her as if she were keeping Anne from falling to her death.

"You're in Mali!"

Sheila was vivid, her skin bronze, her blond hair ablaze from the African sun's bleaching, her dress rich with tribal colors and patterns. "They needed someone to give recruiting talks for the Peace Corps. When I got your letter about our cabin being torn down, I volunteered. I've got a month before I have to go back." Anne's youngest daughter had joined the Peace Corps with an eagerness that suggested it had been devised just for her. In the past she had blundered into opportunities of benevolence, often with disastrous results. Her acts of helpfulness and mercy were a cause for concern. She watched a local boy rob their cabin and then gave him time to escape. "His father beats him and his mother drinks," she explained. She devised a warming center for the homeless in her father's church. Before it could be opened, the heater she improvised shorted and caused a small fire.

Sheila lugged in her duffle bag. "I brought you something." There appeared to be no clothes in the duffle. She produced a mask of woven reeds, the eyes circles of white shells, the hair a ruff of orange fibers. "The men put them on and dance around with sticks to frighten the women. Of course the women don't give a damn. Where will we put it? Up here on the wall?"

"Sweetheart, I'm afraid it will have to go back to Chicago with me. It will be cheerful company in my condo." The family had always lived in borrowed houses. Their only real home was this summer cabin. When Anne's husband died, the parish insisted there was no hurry for her to leave the rectory, but the new priest was on the way and she got out.

Sheila looked around at the cabin's empty bookshelves and the ghostly spaces on the wall where family pictures had hung. "You mean you really have to give up the cabin. You're giving up half our lives. I came back to say you can't."

"I don't have a choice. The river is being returned to its natural state. Our cabin's just one of a lot of cabins that are being torn down." These last weeks Anne had been choosing what she would take back to her small Chicago condo, her days spent in relinquishment, each object sacrificed a betrayal. The destruction of the cabin would release the family's summer memories to wander the world like revenants. She had walked among the trees and along the river, gauging the practicality of packing it all up. There wasn't a leaf she could do without.

Sheila said, "Well of course the river should be shared with everyone. Only that shouldn't mean tearing down the cabin. I'll figure something out; right now I'm starved. I've been traveling for days, and there was nothing I could eat on the plane or in the airports."

Anne marveled at how Sheila found time for her own needs while she changed the world for the better. "What about being a vegan in Mali?"

"It was horrible. I had to watch while they slit the throat of a goat and let the blood drain in a bowl. They roasted the goat for a sacrifice and everyone had to eat part of it, and I was expected to eat it, too, or it would have been disrespectful. I had to explain that I was unclean, you know, menstruating, and couldn't take part in the sacrifice and I had to keep that up all the time I was there. The men thought I ought to be confined to the hut where the women stay when they're having their period, and the women were so impressed with how long it went on they wanted some of my blood as a kind of charm because they have to keep having babies. Anyhow, I lived on onion balls and millet mush, but I didn't want a woman to have to spend all day pounding millet for me so I ground my own and it took hours." She held out her calloused hands and pushed up her sleeves to show her muscular forearms.

Sheila pulled out of the fridge every green thing she could see. She grabbed at the corn on the kitchen counter and began shucking it. Anne put on water to boil. They smiled at each other.

"The corn is from John McCraig," Anne said. "He'll be so pleased to see you. He's having a hard time facing the loss of his own cabin. He's had all sorts of wild protest schemes."

"I'll join him. We'll be parade of two and march to the state capitol."

"You'll do nothing of the kind. I've finally talked sense into him."

They sat at the kitchen table. Sheila slathered honey onto the corn and ate four ears. She brought her brother and sister to the table. "Remember how Mark and I used to compete to see who could eat the most corn? Laura was always on a diet. What are her little stepgirls like?"

Anne told her how Laura had come to the cabin with the two girls, Clara and Maria. "I took care of them so Laura could be on her own for a week to practice her violin. She's auditioning for a quartet."

"What's the matter with her? Why doesn't she just stay home and love the girls?"

"That's not fair, Sheila. Laura's entitled to love her music, too. It's just going to take time to find the right balance."

"If they were mine, I'd never let them out of my sight."

A few years ago Sheila had found herself pregnant. She had the baby and then let it go out of unselfishness, eager to make someone a gift of the child she felt she wasn't ready to raise. All the children in Mali couldn't make up for that. "Your brother Mark was here from his exile in Canada." Another lost child.

"I'm going to find a protest against the stupid war to march in. I worked out a way to end it and sent it to President Ford, but I haven't heard back. Will Mark ever come home?"

"There's talk of amnesty."

"But there won't be any cabin for him. He has to be outdoors or he suffocates. Me too. To tell you the truth, I think I'm ready to leave Africa. I hoped to use our cabin as a sort of halfway house before I jumped into the real world. The cabin creeps into my dreams. There are almost no trees in Mali and no water. When they do have rain, everything floods and the crocodiles that have hidden away in the caves come slithering out and swim around."

Talk of the river led them to the landing. In a quick gesture Sheila pulled off her dress and jumped into the water.

"You'll freeze," Anne called and ran for a towel and a robe.

Sheila had worn nothing under the dress.

Wrapped in the robe Sheila said, "In Mali the men consider it indecent for women to wear panties." She stared down at the boulders shouldering up in the river. "Something else they believe, rocks can move around on their own. If rocks can move, we ought to be able to save the cabin. I want to see John."

Anne phoned John. "Come over, I have a surprise for you." John McCraig had a long history with their family. He had helped Anne's grandfather build the cabin. He had taught the Hennert children and grandchildren how to fish and a lot more beside.

After he let Sheila go, John leaned down pretending to tie a lace on his high tops. Sheila was licking her tears; something Anne remembered her doing as a child. With love right there before her, Anne had never missed her husband more.

"John, you aren't going to let them take the cabin."

"Sheila, honey, the bulldozers are just two miles up the river. I can hear them from my place." At the stricken look on Sheila's face, he relented. "Don't worry. It'll be weeks before they get here. Now, let me tell you two what I've been up to."

"I don't want Sheila mixed up in anything foolish."

"Don't worry, Annie. I've finished fighting. I've got a surprise for you. Now that Sheila's here, it makes it all the better."

Dismissing their protests he herded them into his truck. John wasn't an easy driver. He handled his truck with urgent starts and stops as if it were a horse he was breaking in. He sought shortcuts, narrow, rutted two tracks where the grass teased the bucking truck's undercarriage. Anne thought of her adventurous childhood rides with John crowded into the front seat with his son, Sam.

She and Sam would poke each other and giggle. When, as often happened, the tires dug into a sandy trail and spun to a standstill, they would groan and say, "I knew it," and "I told you." Then they would run into the woods and gather branches to go under the wheels.

Sheila asked, "John, do you ever think of our winter rides up to Duluth when I was staying with you, everything snow and the radio playing?"

"And you singing along. There was a song you liked about a bridge over troubled water."

She reached over and hung onto his arm. "I was singing that to you."

Anne remembered the bereft look on John's face when she and Kent left the hospital with Sheila and the baby to go back to Chicago.

"Where are we going?" It was like a kidnapping.

"I found a couple of acres on Lost Creek. You must have been there with Sam, Annie. Your dad and Kent both fished the stream, Mark, too."

John pulled into a clearing. The landscape beside the stream was not as lush as it was along on the big river. It was mostly jack pine and scrub oak, nature's last resort, but along the banks were alder and Juneberries. Browsing deer had neatly sheered off the lower branches of a stand of pine, letting in enough light for ostrich and maidenhair ferns. She heard the sound of the stream insinuating itself among the deadheads and probing the sandy banks. In the clearing Anne saw stakes suggesting the perimeters of a structure.

John was clearly enjoying their surprise. "I'm going to dig the foundation next week. I've already started breaking down my cabin. Nothing wrong with those old logs. I've got someone to truck them over here. Of course a few of them will have to go."

Anne offered, "John, take whatever you want from our cabin."

"Why not? Kent put in double-glazed windows. They're a lot better than mine."

Sheila was marking out rooms with the toe of her sandal.

John said, "What I wanted to talk about is I'd like you to go in with me, Annie. With what we can harvest from my place and yours, I don't see why I wouldn't have enough to build a wing onto the cabin, a sort of guesthouse for you and your family, maybe Sheila here when she gets back from Africa, even Mark if he returns from Canada in some decent way. I've had him out on this stream often enough to know every bend and riffle." New possibilities strengthened his voice. "And those little girls of Laura's. You could all stay in the guest part for now, and then when I'm gone the whole cabin would be yours. I don't have anyone to leave it to, Annie. If I left it to you, you could pass it on. Mark will get married and Sheila, too. There'll be kids."

Anne listened to him create generations; it was biblical in the way they stretched out. "John, it's a lovely idea, but just now I haven't the energy for a project like that. I'm in the process of letting go of responsibilities, not taking them on."

"I'd put up most of the money and I'd keep the place up. I just want your name with mine on the deed. It would bring our two families together."

"Of course we'd love to come up and visit you, John, but I don't see myself taking on that kind of obligation, and I'm not sure about the children. I have no idea when Mark will be back or if he'll even leave Canada, and Laura's husband may take a position with a symphony in another city or some place in Europe, taking Laura and the girls with him."

Sheila had been listening, shuffling her feet in the sandy soil, like an animal getting ready to charge. "What about me?" Sheila asked. "Where will I go when I get back? I don't want to settle down in a city. I've got to have a place where I can think about what I want to do. Please, Mom. Why can't we? It would keep us all together."

Anne knew how a place drew you in, took you over, and made you a part of it, and even when you left it, it stayed with you. "I'm really sorry but I just don't see it. I'd be glad to contribute something, but I don't want to own it."

"Then I don't think I'll go ahead. I can't see myself at my age having the energy to put up a place when I know in a few years strangers are going to be tramping around in it."

"It's not fair to make me responsible for your decision, John. We each have to live our own lives. It makes sense for you to build a place; you've been up here all your life. I have another life and a career and it's not here." Every fall she returned to her college in Chicago to teach Emerson and Thoreau. In their words she explained what she had left behind at the cabin.

John began pulling up the stakes. "If that's how it's going to be, the Robinsons said they'd sell me one of their motel shacks. It's got a little kitchen."

Anne had driven by the one-room houses the Robinsons rented

by the week to tourists. Strung along the main road in town they had a weary, used look. A bright halogen light burned all night to protect against intruders who might be foolish enough to think there was something in those shacks worth stealing. In the winter they weren't even shoveled out. Each house had a tiny porch that faced the road, and Anne had a crushing vision of John sitting on one of the porches, a furious look on his face.

"You're trying to punish me, John, and I won't be intimidated. There's not a reason in the world you can't build a cabin here yourself."

"It takes a lot of heart to start a place from nothing, Annie. You got to imagine how it's going to be, and then when all the complications and disappointments with the building start coming you got to hang on to that vision. If you're not coming in with me, I'm not going to do it. But I understand and I certainly don't blame you. Now I got my trout rod in the back of the truck. It's a nice day, and if you two don't mind sitting for half an hour, I'll get a little fishing done so the drive isn't wasted."

"I don't know what's wrong with you," Sheila accused Anne. "You're acting like it's too late for choices. You might as well be dead and buried." She strode off into the woods; clearly she didn't want to be around Anne.

John pulled on waders postage stamped with rubber patches, got into his vest, and slipped the cord of the landing net over his head. Finally he squashed on a hat, the headband scarified with dry flies. In a minute he was stepping into the stream. Anne thought of Thoreau shedding his trousers and walking down the middle of a river as if it were a highway. Her class on the nature writers was one of the college's most popular, for when was nature writing more attractive than when read in the city?

Anne watched John disappear around a bend, his line, magically missing the overhanging alder bushes as he lashed the stream in impartial punishment, first one side and then the other. She was furious with John and Sheila for making her feel guilty. Everyone wanted something from her. She worried that she was giving up the possibility of returning to this place she loved for a new life, and what if that life wasn't enough?

She was becoming practiced in renunciation. Last month when she opened her condo door, Dan's arms were around her. "I thought I'd surprise you." They had twenty years of casual embraces between them. Like a bird lured into the open by a feast set out for it, her momentary submission alerted her, but she was weakened by the warmth of his body and his restrained strength as he held her. Anne was the first to draw apart, protecting herself, for she felt entitlement in the way he held her, and possession.

Daniel Scott had taken over the family bank. In no time, he had merged the Hennert bank with a smaller one and then a larger one. His aggression would have troubled her grandfather, whose ambitions were always modest, as if success was faintly suspicious. Now Dan was retired and living in Florida. Dan and his wife, Carrie, had been a few years older than Anne and Kent. They had been close friends, comfortably called at the last minute to share a dinner or see a play. Carrie had died two years ago of a sudden heart attack.

Pleased as Anne was to find him there, she was bothered that for several days, while she was unaware of it, Dan had been making plans for a trip to Chicago. It made her uneasy to have been on his mind all that time without her permission.

She said, "Make yourself comfortable," but he was already sitting down, his jacket tossed on a chair, his overnight case at his feet. He was in possession. When the four of them were together, it was Dan who made the decisions. Carrie had once told Anne she wanted for nothing, which had sounded to Anne not so much a measure of happiness as the indication of a meager imagination. Dan's secretary paid all of Carrie's bills. Carrie herself never wrote a check. On the first of each month Dan handed her an envelope of new bills. "I can always ask for more if I need it," she told Anne. She added, "Dan is so generous. I just have to mention something and he gets it for me or something like it only nicer; he has better taste than I do."

Dan's need to take over had a kind side. When Kent was suffering from a breakdown, his parishioners and friends kept away, as if his depression was catching and would rouse their own feelings of melancholy. Dan reached out to Kent, made Kent a project. He would not let him alone. One Saturday afternoon he took him to the Field Museum. Kent returned home with tales of dinosaurs and fossils and the great geological periods, the Cretaceous, the Jurassic, and the Triassic. Dan had shown Kent how to put his problems in perspective.

Before she could issue an invitation, Dan found the drinks tray and the refrigerator. Anne admired the way he measured the liquor by sight and the professional squeeze of the lime. She enjoyed the novelty of having an evening drink made for her. She and Dan had shared years of family crises. They didn't have to dance around each other's politics or faith. Safe territory had been mapped years ago. Anne saw how easy it would be to slip into that life. Now that Kent was gone, she longed for someone to know her so she wouldn't have to keep explaining herself to people.

Dan asked after the children.

"Laura and the girls are fine. Sheila is having an amazing time in Mali."

Dan said, "I don't know what Kent was thinking of letting a daughter sign up for the Peace Corps. Africa's full of diseases. What about Mark? Still hiding out in Canada?"

If she were married to Dan, would he recall Sheila from Africa and order Mark home from Canada? She didn't want him to get his hands on her children. "Mark's not hiding out," Anne said. "He has a job as a fishing guide."

"You don't want him to be a fishing guide for the rest of his life. We have them in Florida. Never make much money and they drink a lot."

"Mark likes what he's doing and he's making enough money to support himself. He never drank much."

"He ought to be here, taking care of you, watching out for your affairs."

"Dan, I've had a responsible job for years. I can take care of myself." That was not completely true. In the summer when she wasn't teaching, silence drove her away from books to television. Each week the characters returned, and if a character ended, there were reruns just as there were in dreams where the dead and the living mingled easily.

Dan said, "I always believed you were too independent for your own good."

"Whatever do you mean?"

"I've always thought you needed a little looking after. I'm volunteering, Anne. There's nothing to keep you in Chicago. You must get tired of the grind of teaching. You'd love Florida. I know it's not easy moving into another woman's home, but you could decorate it just the way you like. I can afford it and I wouldn't interfere."

Would Dan hand her envelopes of money? She tried to imagine herself in Florida. The birds there were disturbing in their boldness, the herons and pelicans in the water right beside you, the sandpipers and egrets following in your footsteps. The osprey, which was properly secretive in the northern woods, nested in Florida on poles put up in the middle of tourist parks. Even the tough Florida grasses fought back when you walked on them. And there was the reluctant sea. Unlike her rivers and the lakes, the ocean refused to let you see its other shore, forcing you to live beside the threat of the unknown.

Was she too quick to abandon this chance? The trick was not to go searching for someone to love, but to learn to love what had been given to you. But what a terrible chance you took when you loved someone. She hadn't been able to keep Kent with her, or, long ago, to protect Sam. She had died with each of them. Dan was older than she was; would she have to live through another loss?

He laid his hand on hers. "We're not too old for a little love, Anne. I've always thought you an enormously attractive woman and I admire your mind. I'd be a sort of classroom of one for you. You could tell me what to read. I've let that part of my brain go."

What woman really likes to be admired for her mind? She saw

herself presenting Dan with a reading list, perhaps quizzing him at the end of each week. Dinnertime discussions on Proust's projection onto Odette of his ambivalent feelings toward his mother? The sensible thing would be to temporize. Sudden decisions were dangerous. She often speculated on what might happen if with a snap of the fingers you could end your life. How many of us would be left? She, herself, would be long gone.

Like an artist confronted with a small canvas, she had created a life that fit the new dimensions of her world. She enjoyed her condo. She liked the smell of the city early in the morning. In spring and fall there were deserted stretches of city beach to walk. It would be a long drive from Florida if she had a sudden yearning to travel north to see where the cabin had been.

He was disappointed and hurt. "You're thinking of Carrie, but I know you're a different woman, Anne. Times have changed. I don't know if it's for the better, but that's how it is. I'd let you have your own life. Independence is a cold pleasure when you're older."

She shivered. She wondered what Kent would have told her to do. But wasn't that the whole idea, that no one should tell her what to do? Wasn't independence something you took, not something that was given?

There was a cool breeze from the stream and she pulled her sweater around her. A jet flew overhead. She tried to read the silent message of the jet's trail. She longed for oracles and entrails. Why couldn't she be like Sheila, grabbing at everything on offer. Hawthorne had written that by stepping aside for a moment, we expose ourselves to the fearful risk of losing our place forever. She looked around her. The last of the lavender florets had opened on the vervain spears. The wintergreen berries and the berries of false Solomon's seal had turned crimson. The hazelnut shrubs were covered with raggedy blooms like yellow spiders. Fall's last blossoms.

Looking down into the water she saw a brown trout fantail away, its movement so quick it barely registered. There were tracks on the sandy bank, paw prints followed by the imprint of a broad train. A beaver. She heard the rusty hinge cry of a blue jay. The jays would stay around all winter, putting up with snow and below-zero weather. Taking their chances.

Laura's two little girls had grown fond of the cabin and blamed her when they learned it would be torn down. She could tell them there would be a cabin after all. If this place were waiting for him, Mark would be more likely to return. Sheila needed it.

After WWI Anne's grandfather had come north. He hired John, and together the two men built the cabin. The grandfather, a returning soldier, had lain awake in his tent night after night thinking of the war and what he had seen. In his journal he wrote: *I finally made my decision and pounded in the stakes for the final time. Tonight I moved the tent inside the vacant perimeter, and what do you know, I slept.*

Anne stepped into what would be the boundary of the cabin she would share with John and her children. Just outside but within easy grasp were all the many things she could not do without.